Content

HOA EMPEROR

THE MOB WAS TOUGH—BUT THE BOARD WAS MURDER!

KERRY LUTZ

HOA EMPEROR

THE MOB WAS TOUGH—BUT THE BOARD WAS MURDER!

Copyright © 2025 by Kerry Lutz

All rights reserved.

No part of this publication may be reproduced, distributed, or transmitted in any form or by any means, including photocopying, recording, or other electronic or mechanical methods, without the prior written permission of the publisher, except as permitted by U.S. copyright law. For permission requests, contact the author or publisher.

The story, all names, characters, and incidents portrayed in this production are fictitious. No identification with actual persons (living or deceased), places, buildings, or products is intended or should be inferred.

Editing, design, and cover by George Verongos

www.LiteraryServices.net

Paperback ISBN: 979-8-9985597-9-2

Hardcover ISBN: 978-1-970521-00-9

Digital ISBN: 978-1-970521-01-6

Library of Congress Control Number: 2025922813

FIRESTARTER
publishers

Chapter 1: Before the Empire

The Boy Who Calculated Pain

Max Vecchio wasn't born—he was abandoned. Found in a Youngstown, Ohio, church dumpster in February 1970, wrapped in a bloody motel towel, three days old and nearly frozen. The nuns at St. Joseph's called it a miracle he survived. His adoptive mother, Rose Antonelli, called it God's plan.

Rose was forty-three when she took him in, a widow whose own son had died in Vietnam. She ran a small religious goods store, selling rosaries and prayer cards to the working-class Catholics of the Rust Belt. Her husband's death had left her comfortable but lonely, and when she saw the newspaper story about the abandoned baby, she felt God calling.

"Some children are born to test us," she would tell her sister. "This one will test me most of all."

The signs were there early. At four, Max organized his toys by size and color with obsessive precision. When another child at daycare disrupted his system, Max calmly walked over and bit through the boy's ear. No crying. No tantrum. Just calculated violence, then back to his blocks.

The psychiatrist said it was trauma from his abandonment. Rose said it was the devil testing her faith.

The Mathematics of Cruelty

By seven, Max's IQ tested at 164. He could multiply three-digit numbers in his head faster than his teachers could write them. He absorbed information like a sponge—but only what interested him. And what interested him was systems. How things worked. How to make them work better. How to break them.

"He doesn't feel things like other children," his second-grade teacher told Rose during a conference. Max had been caught running a lunch money lending operation, charging interest calculated daily, keeping meticulous records in a composition notebook. When confronted, he'd simply asked, "Isn't this how banks work?"

Rose clutched her rosary. "He's learning. He'll find his way to God."

But Max had already found his god: efficiency. The world was full of broken systems and stupid people. Even as a child, he saw it everywhere—the inefficient lunch line, the poorly organized classroom, the wasteful way his mother ran her store. He'd reorganize her inventory at night, maximizing profit margins, until she begged him to stop because her regular customers couldn't find what they needed.

Baptism by Blood

The violence evolved with his intellect. At nine, he discovered that psychological pain was more efficient than physical. Why break someone's toy when you could manipulate three classmates into doing it while you watched? Why fight when you could orchestrate?

But sometimes, efficiency demanded directness.

When Max was eleven, three older boys cornered him after school, demanding to copy his perfect math homework. Max looked at them the way a scientist examines bacteria. Calculated the angles. The biggest boy's knee was vulnerable due to a youth football injury. Max's pencil went through the side of the joint like it was designed for it. The boy would walk with a limp for the rest of his life.

"Violence is just mathematics," Max told the principal, blood splattered on his t-shirt. "Force times velocity equals result."

Rose spent her savings on therapy, lawyers, and prayers. The therapists said "antisocial personality disorder" and "dangerous lack of empathy." The lawyers got him probation. The prayers, Rose hoped, would save his soul.

The Computer Store Revelation

As a teenager, Max developed a noticeable fascination with the school's computer lab. He'd stay late, fingers flying over the keyboard with the same obsessive precision he applied to everything else. The teacher told Rose that he'd mastered programming languages that college students struggled with.

"Maybe this is God's plan," Rose told her sister. "Channel that brilliant mind into something productive."

She'd been saving for months, putting aside every spare dollar from the religious goods store. When Max's fourteenth birthday came, she told him they were going somewhere special—a trip to the Computer City in Akron, twenty miles away.

"I want to get you a computer, Michael," she said, using his baptismal name as she always did. "Something for school. Maybe a nice Apple IIe."

Max nodded politely, but his mind was already calculating. The Apple IIe cost around $1,400. Rose's store brought in maybe $200 profit a week on good weeks. He'd watched her count the register, seen her struggle with the electric bill. She was about to spend nearly several months' profit on him.

The drive to Akron was quiet, with Rose humming hymns and Max staring out the window at the Rust Belt landscape. Factory towns dying slowly, their inefficiencies finally catching up with them. He saw the same pattern everywhere—bad management, outdated systems, people clinging to methods that no longer worked.

The Computer City store was a revelation. Gleaming computers arranged with showroom precision, each one representing exponentially more processing power than the school's ancient terminals. Max moved from machine to machine with the focused intensity of a predator studying prey.

"Which one do you like?" Rose asked, her hand resting on his shoulder.

Max pointed to the basic Apple IIe. "This one's nice, Mom."

The salesperson, a college-aged kid with enthusiasm that bordered on manic, launched into his pitch. "Great choice! This is our entry-level model, perfect for homework and basic programming. With the disk drive and monitor, you're looking at about $1,400."

Rose nodded, opening her worn purse to count bills she'd carefully organized. Max watched her face—the slight tightness around her eyes that meant she was calculating whether they'd have enough for groceries this month.

"Actually," Max said quietly, "I've been saving too."

He reached into his jacket and pulled out a roll of bills that made the salesperson's eyes widen—thirty-three crisp hundred-dollar bills, organized with the same obsessive precision as everything else in Max's life.

"I want that one," Max said, pointing to the top-of-the-line Macintosh system in the corner. "With the expanded memory, external hard drive, and the best monitor you have."

Rose stared at the money in her son's thirteen-year-old hands. "Michael, where did you get this?"

"I've been running some businesses," Max said simply. "Tutoring. Organizing things for people. I'm good with numbers, remember?"

The "businesses" were more complex than tutoring. Max had been fixing the inefficiencies he saw everywhere, charging for his services. He'd reorganized three neighborhood garage sales, tripling their profits and taking a consultant's fee. He'd solved the scheduling problems at two local small businesses, implementing systems that eliminated waste and bottlenecks. He'd even helped the church optimize its bingo nights, increasing revenue by 40% through better game rotation and refreshment pricing.

To Max, it was just applied mathematics. To his clients, it was miraculous problem-solving. To Rose, watching her thirteen-year-old son casually drop nearly $3,300 on a computer system, it was something she couldn't quite process.

"The total comes to $3,247," the salesperson said, trying to hide his excitement at what was probably his biggest sale of the month.

Max counted out the exact amount, leaving the change in Rose's hands. "For gas," he said.

Driving home with Max and the computer equipment carefully secured in the backseat, Rose kept glancing at her son in the rearview mirror. "You earned all that money honestly?"

"I helped people solve problems they couldn't solve themselves," Max replied. "That's honest work."

It was true, technically. Max had identified inefficiencies and optimized systems for paying clients. The fact that some of those optimizations involved information he'd acquired through less legitimate means—school records he'd accessed, competitor data he'd gathered, private information he'd obtained through careful social engineering—was simply part of thorough problem analysis.

Max Meets Macintosh

The computer transformed Max's capabilities exponentially. Within weeks, he'd mastered the operating system, programming languages, and hardware configurations that most adults, after spending months, still couldn't understand. More importantly, he'd discovered networks.

The school district's computer system was pathetically unsecured. Max was inside within hours, not to change grades—his were already perfect—but to understand the architecture of how information flowed, where it was stored, and who had access to what. It was just another system to analyze and optimize.

His first real hack was almost accidental. The high school's scheduling software had a flaw that created conflicts between class assignments and room availability. Students were showing up to classrooms that were double-booked or didn't exist. The administration was blaming student error instead of recognizing the systemic problem.

Max fixed it overnight, rewriting portions of the scheduling algorithm to eliminate conflicts and optimize resource allocation. When students arrived Monday morning, the chaos had been replaced with perfect efficiency. Nobody knew how or why, which was exactly how Max preferred it.

But the real breakthrough came when he discovered the teacher payroll system. Not to steal—that would be inefficient and temporary. Instead, he studied the patterns. Salary distributions, overtime calculations, budget allocations. He began to understand how institutions managed money, where inefficiencies created opportunities, how financial systems could be optimized for maximum extraction.

Rose found him one night at 3 AM, hunched over the keyboard, staring at the glowing screen with the intensity of a monk illuminating manuscripts.

"Michael, you need sleep. School tomorrow."

"I'm learning, Mom. This is important."

She looked at the scrolling code, the financial spreadsheets, and the network diagrams that covered his desk. "What are you learning?"

Max considered how to explain it in terms she'd understand. "How to help people. How to fix broken things. How to make everything work better."

Rose smiled, kissed his forehead, and went back to bed. She never saw the files he was really studying—personnel records, financial data, confidential communications that he'd accessed through patient exploration of the district's network vulnerabilities.

Max wasn't learning to be a hacker in the traditional sense. He was learning to be an optimizer, using digital tools to identify and exploit systemic inefficiencies wherever he found them.

The Evolution of Excellence

Soon, Max had expanded beyond the school district. He'd mapped the computer networks of every major institution in Youngstown—

banks, government offices, small businesses, even the police department. Not to steal or destroy, but to understand how they operated, where they were vulnerable, how they could be improved.

He started offering consulting services to local businesses, using knowledge he'd gained through his network explorations to identify problems and propose solutions. A restaurant with inefficient inventory management. A small manufacturer with scheduling conflicts. A retail store with outdated point-of-sale systems.

Max would analyze their problems, develop optimized solutions, and implement improvements that increased efficiency and profitability. His clients saw him as a teenage genius with an intuitive understanding of business operations. They had no idea their "consultant" had gained his insights by accessing their computer systems and studying their internal data.

"You have such a gift for seeing what others miss," Rose would tell him, watching his growing reputation in the business community.

"I just pay attention," Max would reply. "Most people don't really look at how things work."

The truth was more complex. Max's combination of high intelligence, complete lack of empathy, and sophisticated computer skills allowed him to analyze systems in ways that normal people couldn't. He saw inefficiencies because he felt no emotional attachment to existing methods. He identified solutions because he had no reluctance to exploit vulnerabilities. He succeeded because he operated outside the ethical constraints that limited others.

The Catholic Paradox

Every Sunday, Rose still dragged Max to mass. He'd sit in the pew, analyzing the priest's rhetorical techniques, calculating the collection plate's revenue, studying the stained-glass windows' geometric patterns. The religion itself meant nothing to him, but the system fascinated him. The hierarchy. The rules. The way confession reset the sin counter to zero—a perfect exploit in the moral code.

"You feel nothing in God's house?" Rose would ask, tears in her eyes.

"I feel the same thing you do," Max would lie smoothly. He'd learned to mimic emotions by then, studying faces like mathematical equations. The angle of the eyebrow plus the curve of the mouth equals sadness. Mirror it back. Receive comfort.

But the computer had given him something beyond emotional manipulation—it had given him access to information that made his lies more sophisticated. When Rose worried about the church's declining membership, Max could provide a detailed demographic analysis. When she fretted about the parish's finances, he could suggest optimization strategies that increased donations while reducing costs.

Father McKenna began consulting with Max informally, amazed by the teenager's insights into church administration. Max redesigned their member database, optimized their fundraising campaigns, and implemented financial controls that eliminated waste and fraud.

"That boy has a calling," Father McKenna told Rose. "He sees solutions where others see only problems." Rose nodded hopefully. Maybe this was how God worked—using her son's strange gifts to serve the Church, channeling his cold intelligence toward holy purposes.

She never knew that Max was using his access to church computers to practice more sophisticated hacking techniques, treating the parish network as a training ground for larger operations. The improvements he made were real, but they were byproducts of his education in digital exploitation.

The First Empire

At sixteen, Max built his first criminal enterprise, naturally. The high school's drug trade was pathetically disorganized and dysfunctional: territories unclear, supply chains wasteful, violence random and counterproductive. Max saw a business screaming for optimization.

But now he had digital tools to support his organizational efforts. He mapped dealer territories using demographic software he'd written. He tracked supply and demand using databases he'd created. He monitored law enforcement patterns using access he'd gained to police dispatch systems.

Within three months, he'd consolidated the dealers under a corporate structure. Standardized prices. Established territories based on demographic analysis. Implemented quality control. Effectively reducing violence by 80% through strict enforcement protocols and information superiority that made traditional territorial disputes obsolete.

The operation was managed entirely through encrypted digital communications—messages that routed through proxy servers Max had set up, using infrastructure he'd built through his consulting work with local businesses. He'd learned to hide data streams within legitimate network traffic, making his criminal communications invisible to anyone monitoring internet activity.

Max was never caught, of course. He'd insulated himself through layers of digital and physical delegation, communicated through channels that left no traceable evidence, and maintained operational security that would have impressed intelligence agencies.

When the organization finally fell—betrayed by an emotional lieutenant who'd fallen in love and wanted out of the business—Max had already moved on, lessons learned, profits banked in offshore accounts he'd established using identity information gathered through his hacking activities.

Rose found his money once—the physical cash he kept for emergencies—thirty thousand dollars in neat bundles, hidden in a hollowed-out theology textbook.

"Where did this come from, Michael?" Still calling him by his baptismal name.

"Investments," he said simply. "I'm very good with numbers."

She made him donate it all to the church. He did, then made it back in six weeks through a sophisticated stock manipulation scheme he'd developed using inside information gathered from corporate networks he'd penetrated. This time, he hid it better—in digital accounts that existed in legal gray areas, accessible only through encrypted keys he'd memorized.

The Mother's Faith

Through it all, Rose never stopped believing. When Max was arrested at seventeen—wrong place, wrong time, wrong association with a mob lawyer's son—she mortgaged her house for bail. When he got a full scholarship to college despite his record (the admissions essay about "overcoming adversity" was a masterpiece of manipulative writing, supported by academic records he'd carefully optimized through strategic system access), she cried with joy.

"You see?" she told him. "God has plans for you. You can use that brilliant mind for good."

Max nodded, hugged her, felt nothing. But he'd learned something watching her: true believers were the most useful people in the world. They'd forgive anything, rationalize everything, always offer one more chance. Faith was a system vulnerability he could exploit forever.

Yet something about Rose's faith unsettled him in a way nothing else did. Not her specifically—he'd mapped her psychology perfectly, could predict her responses with algorithmic precision. But the inefficiency of it. Why waste energy believing in redemption for someone who didn't want it? Why persist in hope when the data suggested otherwise?

It was, he realized years later, the only inefficient system he never wanted to optimize. Rose's faith in his redemption was perfect in its imperfection. A glitch in the universe's code that worked in his favor.

The Graduation Gift

The night before he left for college, Rose gave him two things: a rosary that had belonged to her husband, and a letter he wasn't to open until her death.

"Promise me, Michael," she said, clutching his hands. "Promise me you'll try to be good. That you'll use your gifts to help people, not hurt them."

"I promise, Mom," he said, the lie as smooth as silk. He'd learned that promises were just words, contracts written in air. But he kept the rosary. Not out of faith, but as a reminder of the one person whose inefficiency he'd chosen to preserve. Rose Antonelli, who saw a monster and chose to call it son.

Years later, when he'd become Max Vecchio, using his digital skills to revolutionize organized crime financial operations, he still carried it. Through the murders, the extortion, the empire of blood and algorithms, the rosary stayed in his pocket. A reminder that even perfect systems had outliers.

And later still, when he became John Masters in witness protection, building a new empire out of dying Florida communities using everything he'd learned about system optimization and digital manipulation, he'd finger those beads while planning his schemes. Not praying—never praying—but calculating. How to build perfect communities out of broken ones. How to create order from chaos. How to solve problems with spreadsheets, shell companies, and carefully placed bullets.

The Letter

In 2006, Rose died while Max was in federal custody, awaiting his witness protection placement. Heart attack in her sleep, a rosary in her hands. She was seventy-eight and still believed her son would find redemption.

He opened her letter in a federal holding cell:

My Dearest Michael,

If you're reading this, I've gone home to God, still praying for your soul. I know what you are. I've always known. The doctors, the teachers, the police—they all told me. But they didn't understand what I understood. You're not broken, my son. You're not evil. You're unfinished.

God doesn't make mistakes. He made you brilliant and cold for a reason. Someday, you'll find a problem that needs your kind of solving. A place so broken that only someone who feels nothing can fix it without being crushed by the weight of feeling.

When you find that place, remember: redemption isn't about feeling different. It's about choosing different.

I love you. I forgive you. I believe in you still.

Your mother always, Rose

P.S. The rosary I gave you before was my Anthony's. He was a hard man, too, but he built good things. Maybe you will, as well.

Max read it three times, then burned it. Sentiment was inefficiency.

But he always kept the rosary nearby.

And when he found Queens Point—a dying community full of forgotten people, systems so broken they begged for his kind of fixing—he remembered Rose's words. Not about redemption. He was beyond that. But about building.

He'd build an empire out of ruins, using every tool he'd learned—financial manipulation, psychological warfare, digital espionage, and pure organizational brilliance. He'd solve problems with ruthless efficiency. He'd make these decrepit communities into showcases of what brutal competence could achieve.

It's what Rose would have wanted, he told himself. Even monsters could build cathedrals.

Max on Marriage

Max had very strict beliefs about getting married. Marriage, for most men, is a deferred suicide pact. You sign on the dotted line, hand over half your freedom and most of your leverage, and then pray that the other person doesn't change too much—or doesn't realize how much power you've given her.

Women file for 80% of divorces. The other 20% of men had to chew their own legs off to get free.

If you're lucky, you marry someone whose madness aligns with your own. If you're smart, you don't marry at all. In short, marriage was inefficient, and Max hated inefficiency whenever and wherever he found it.

Max? He never had the luxury of luck. But he had clarity. He knew what love was—and what it wasn't. And he knew that if he ever did settle down, it wouldn't be for comfort or companionship... It would be for power.

He wasn't always like this.

There was a time—before the digital empires, the financial manipulations, the quiet killings masked as efficiency—when Max Vecchio was just a child. But even then, something was off. Something cold. Something calculating. The signs were there from the beginning, and anyone paying attention could have seen the shape of the man he would become.

The boy who never cried.

The boy who solved problems with equations—and pain. The boy who was abandoned before he could even speak.

Max never married. Not out of heartbreak, idealism, or even laziness. He avoided marriage for the same reason he avoided timeshares and slot machines—inefficiency.

"Institutional marriage," he once said, "is the original pyramid scheme. One man puts in everything, and a dozen other people— lawyers, therapists, in-laws, florists—profit off the collapse."

He'd done the math. The moment you sign a marriage certificate, you're effectively taking on a silent partner with unlimited veto power and no performance requirements. The return on investment? Diminishing. The liabilities? Practically guaranteed. The system was rigged from the start: sex declines, resentment accumulates, and the state gets final say over what happens to your house, your retirement, and your children.

Max didn't hate love—he just didn't confuse it with contracts.

Marriage, to him, was like buying a used car with no title, no warranty, and a legal obligation to pay for every repair, even after the engine explodes. He preferred freedom, leverage, and never having to explain why he hadn't come home last night.

"I don't dislike women," he once told a stunned dinner guest. "I just prefer not to subsidize their unhappiness."

The Real Max

This is the essential Max Vecchio/John Masters: a man who sees human suffering as an engineering problem, with digital tools that make him exponentially more dangerous. His antisocial personality disorder isn't a bug—it's a feature. Combined with his hacking abilities and systems optimization skills, he can make the hard choices, implement the brutal solutions, and control information flows in ways that others cannot even imagine.

He genuinely transforms these communities. Under his rule, Queens Point goes from a rotting hulk to a gleaming jewel. The crime disappears. The buildings shine. The budgets balance (even as he steals vast sums through digital sleight of hand). He's the ultimate HOA president because he cares nothing for politics or feelings— only results and complete informational control.

But he's also a predator with unprecedented capabilities. The same clarity that lets him see inefficiency lets him see weakness. The same lack of empathy that enables tough decisions enables monstrous ones. The digital skills that help him optimize systems also let him manipulate, monitor, and eliminate threats with surgical precision.

Rose was right: he was unfinished. But not in the way she hoped. He's not moving toward redemption—but evolving into something more dangerous. A criminal who builds. A monster who improves. A problem solver with a laptop, a Glock, and a rosary, turning chaos into profitable order through methods that blend legitimate business optimization with sophisticated digital warfare, and, if necessary, the barrel of a gun.

In the end, Max Vecchio is the dark answer to a dark question: What if the only way to fix broken communities is to be someone broken enough not to care about breaking them further in the process, armed with tools that make such breaking nearly undetectable?

The rosary in his pocket wasn't a reminder of faith. It was a reminder that even God needs killers—especially ones who balance the books and control the networks.

Chapter 2: The Bookkeeper's Betrayal

Cleveland, 2006

The federal courthouse in downtown Cleveland smelled of old wood and fear. Max Vecchio sat in the witness box, his imported suit impeccable, his hands steady as he held a glass of water. Across from him, twelve jurors leaned forward, captivated by the calm precision with which he was dissecting the Torrisi crime family's financial empire.

"Mr. Vecchio," the prosecutor said, holding up a ledger marked as Exhibit 47-B. "Can you explain what these entries represent?"

Max allowed himself a small smile. The same smile he'd worn twenty years earlier when he'd first discovered his gift for turning chaos into profit.

Ohio State University, 1985

The gambling and crime operation at Ohio State had been pathetically amateur when Max arrived as a freshman. Football bets scribbled on napkins, drug deals conducted in dorm hallways with all the subtlety of a brass band, territories undefined and constantly disputed. It offended him on a fundamental level.

By sophomore year, he'd consolidated it all.

"You're thinking too small," he told Robert Breslin, the senior who thought he ran campus vice. They sat in a booth at a campus diner, Max's notebooks spread between them like battle plans. "You've got three different crews selling the same product to the same customers at different prices. It's inefficient."

Bobby, thick-necked and slow, had tried to intimidate him. "You think you can just walk in here—"

"I think I already have," Max interrupted, sliding a piece of paper across the table. "That's what you grossed last semester. This is what you could have made with proper organization. The difference is $147,000."

Bobby stared at the numbers. "How do you know what I made?"

"Because your bagman can't do math and your dealers skim exactly 18% on average. It's all patterns, Bobby. Predictable, wasteful patterns."

Within six months, Max had restructured the entire campus underground economy. Gambling ran through a central book with satellite collectors. Drugs moved through a hub-and-spoke distribution system that minimized exposure. Territories were assigned based on demographic analysis of student populations. Violence dropped to near zero because violence was bad for business, and Max had made everyone too much money to risk the operation over petty disputes.

But more importantly, he'd learned how to control the rich kids.

The Puppeteers' Strings

Bradley Whitmore III had everything—legacy admission, trust fund, cocaine habit, and a father who sat on the boards of three Fortune 500 companies. He also had a gambling problem that Max exploited with surgical precision.

"I can't cover this," Bradley whimpered in Max's off-campus apartment, staring at a debt sheet showing $82,000 in losses. "My father will kill me."

Max leaned back in his chair, fingers steepled. He'd been expecting this moment, had engineered it over months of calculated credit extensions and sure-thing tips that weren't.

"Your father never has to know," Max said smoothly. "But I'll need some favors."

The favors started small. Introductions to other wealthy students. Inside information about their families' businesses. Access to parties where deals were discussed over champagne and cocaine. Max never used drugs himself—he'd seen the wreaked inefficiency in users around the world—but he understood their value as tools.

By senior year, he had a network of compromised rich kids who owed him everything. When Bradley's father mentioned problems with union organizers at one of his factories, Max saw an opportunity.

"I know some people who handle that sort of thing," he said casually at a country club lunch Bradley had arranged. "Discrete. Effective."

That introduction led to another, which led to another, until Max found himself in a downtown Cleveland restaurant, sitting across from Vincent "Vinny" Torrisi himself.

The Cleveland Connection

"College boy," Vinny said, cutting into a veal chop with the same casual precision he used to order murders. "My associate Frankie B. says you're smart. Says you run numbers."

"I run systems," Max corrected. "Numbers are just the language."

Vinny laughed, a sound like gravel in a cement mixer. "You got balls, correcting me. I like that. You know who I am?"

"Vincent Torrisi. Born 1943, Collinwood neighborhood. Took over the family from your uncle in '88 after his heart attack. Currently running gambling, protection, and construction throughout Northeast Ohio. Annual gross approximately forty million, though your bookkeeper is skimming at least two."

Vinny's fork stopped halfway to his mouth. "What?"

Max pulled out a single sheet of paper. "I had dinner at Maximo's last Tuesday. Your bookkeeper, Sal Innucci, was three tables over with a woman who wasn't his wife, wearing a watch that cost way more than his stated salary. He paid cash. Serial numbers in sequence, which means he's pulling directly from collections."

Vinny set down his fork, his eyes going cold. "You been watching my people?"

"I've been solving puzzles," Max said. "It's what I do. Your organization is inefficient. I could fix that."

Two days later, Sal Innucci disappeared. A week after that, Max Vecchio became the Torrisi family's new strategic financial advisor and CFO.

The Rise

For fifteen years, Max revolutionized organized crime in Cleveland. He turned a loose confederation of neighborhood crews into a corporate structure that would have made Fortune 500 CEOs envious. Every dollar was tracked, every operation optimized, every potential problem identified before it became actual.

"You're like a fucking computer," Vinny told him once, watching Max work through ledgers that would have taken normal accountants weeks to decipher. "No emotion, just numbers."

"Emotion is inefficiency," Max replied, not looking up from his calculations.

He knew where every body was buried because he'd calculated the optimal disposal sites. He knew every bribe, every kickback, every skeleton in every closet because information was just another system to be organized. The FBI would later call his records "the most comprehensive documentation of organized crime ever assembled."

But Max had made one miscalculation. He'd assumed the Torrisi family operated as rationally as he did.

The Betrayal

It started with a juke joint in Hough, a money-losing operation that Vinny insisted on keeping open for "sentimental reasons." Max had shown him the numbers—they were bleeding $30,000 a month on a bar that served watered-down drinks to old men playing dominoes.

"Shut it down," Max advised. "The building's worth more as condos."

"That was my father's place," Vinny growled. "It stays open."

"Sentiment is expensive," Max said.

"Everything's about money with you," Vinny's son, Little Vinny, interjected. A coked-up moron who'd been promoted far beyond his competence because of blood. "Some things matter more than profit."

Max looked at him with the same dispassion he'd shown that bleeding student thirty years ago. "Name one."

The meeting ended badly. Over the following months, Max noticed changes to and in the pattern of his relationship with the "family." He was excluded from certain meetings. His access to some accounts was restricted. Little Vinny was making decisions that cost the family money—lots of money.

Max did what he always did: he analyzed the pattern. And the pattern said he was disposable and being positioned as a scapegoat for the family's declining fortunes.

So, he made a calculation.

The Deal

"Two hundred and thirty-seven indictments," the federal prosecutor said, spreading photos across the table like tarot cards. Each one a Torrisi family member or associate. "Including seventeen murders. You can document all of this?"

Max nodded. "Every transaction. Every order. Every body. I have copies of everything."

"And you'll testify?"

"I'll do more than that," Max said. "I'll explain their entire operation so clearly a child could understand it. I'll give you convictions."

The prosecutor leaned back. "Why? Why turn on them now?"

Max straightened his tie, a gesture he'd perfected to seem human. "They became inefficient. Bad for business."

It was partly true. But the real reason was simpler: survival. Max had seen the writing on the wall, calculated the odds, and made the only logical choice. Sentiment was inefficiency, and loyalty was just sentiment by another name.

The Trial

For six days, Max Vecchio testified with the same calm precision he'd once used to organize campus gambling. He explained money laundering schemes as if he were teaching accounting. He detailed murder conspiracies with the emotional investment of someone reading a grocery list.

"Mr. Vecchio," Vinny's defense attorney asked during cross-examination, "do you feel any remorse for betraying men who trusted you?"

Max considered the question with the same analytical approach he applied to everything. "Remorse requires emotional investment. I invested in efficiency. They chose inefficiency. The outcome was predictable."

The jury convicted on all counts.

Witness Protection

"You'll be John Masters," U.S. Marshal Clint Moore explained, handing over a new driver's license. "Insurance adjuster, recently divorced, moving to Florida for a fresh start."

"Insurance," Max mused. "Analyzing risk, calculating probabilities. Appropriate."

"Keep your head down," Clint warned. "The Torrisi family has long memories and longer reach."

But Max wasn't worried about the past. He was already analyzing his future. Florida was full of retirees, HOAs, condo boards—all systems begging for optimization. All problems waiting for solutions.

As the plane descended toward Fort Lauderdale, Max fingered the rosary in his pocket—the one his adoptive mother had given him, the one reminder of his past he'd kept. Rose had believed he could be redeemed, that he could use his gifts to help people. Looking down at the sprawling communities below, each one a pocket of inefficiency waiting to be fixed, Max smiled. He was about to help people. He was going to solve their problems, organize their chaos, and make their communities run like clockwork.

The fact that he'd also rob them blind was just...optimization. After all, every system had waste. And waste was meant to be collected by someone smart enough to see it. In Cleveland, he'd been a bookkeeper who knew where the bodies were buried. In Florida, he'd be a problem solver who disposed of his problems accordingly. Same skills. Better climate.

Chapter 3: Let Bylaws be Bygones

The Opportunity Hunter

Max Vecchio—John Masters to anyone who asked—had been circling South Florida's over-fifty-five communities like a shark smelling blood in the water. Three months of reconnaissance had revealed what he'd suspected: the entire system was broken, run by drunk managers and corrupt boards bleeding money from residents who were too old or too trusting to fight back.

The classified ads section of the Sun-Sentinel had become his hunting ground. Estate sales that had been running for months. Properties that couldn't sell. Communities so dysfunctional that even desperate retirees wouldn't move in. It was exactly the kind of systemic failure that made Max's pulse quicken.

That's when he found Queens Point, a massive over-fifty-five community with 1500 units. It was in a pronounced state of disrepair, the victim of decades of deferred maintenance and crooked boards. Precisely the type of broken system that John Masters thrived on. He clearly saw the potential for optimization.

The estate sale ad had been running for six months: *"Lakefront 2BR/2BA, Queens Point, estate must sell, all offers considered."* Six months meant desperation. In South Florida's hot real estate market, decent properties often moved in days. Something that sat for half a year was damaged goods.

Max drove through Queens Point on a Tuesday morning, cataloguing the decay with professional interest. Cracked sidewalks. Faded paint. The pool equipment looked like it hadn't been serviced since the Carter administration. The kind of 1970s retirement community that had been built fast and maintained poorly, now sliding into not-so-genteel collapse.

Perfect.

The estate sale was being held in Unit 247, a ground-floor lakefront that should have been premium real estate. Instead, it looked like a time capsule from 1973—avocado green appliances, burnt orange shag carpet, wood paneling that had gone from trendy to tragic to potentially valuable again if you had the vision to see it.

Max found the personal representative, a harried-looking lawyer named Dennis Kraftman, who clearly wanted this headache off his books.

"How long has this been on the market?" Max asked, examining the ancient Frigidaire refrigerator that was the same color as split pea soup.

"Six months," Kraftman admitted. "The market's been...difficult."

"Difficult" was lawyer-speak for "this place is unsellable." Max had done his homework. The asking price had dropped from $89,000 to $67,000 to $52,000. The estate that Kraftman oversaw was bleeding carrying costs on a property nobody wanted in a community the world was happy to forget.

"I can close in cash," Max said. "This week."

Kraftman's eyes lit up. "The current asking price is—"

"Forty-two five," Max interrupted. "Take it or leave it."

It wasn't a negotiation. It was conquest disguised as real estate. Kraftman tried to maintain dignity—talked about market conditions and comparable sales—but they both knew the estate was drowning and Max was throwing it a concrete life preserver.

"I'll need to consult with the family—"

"You have until tomorrow morning," Max said, handing him a business card. "After that, I'm looking at Cypress Woods."

Kraftman called that evening. Max owned Queens Point Unit 247 by Friday.

The System Mapping

Moving into Queens Point was like conducting an autopsy on the American Dream. Everything was original equipment, even the rotary phone in the kitchen that was probably installed when Nixon was president. But Max wasn't interested in aesthetic improvements. He was interested in understanding the organizational structure that had allowed this place to rot.

The HOA office was his first stop. A converted storage closet with water-stained ceiling tiles and filing cabinets that looked like they'd been salvaged from a government surplus auction. The woman behind the desk was typing hunt-and-peck style on a computer that belonged in a museum.

"Hi," Max said, projecting the friendly concern of a new resident. "I'm John Masters, just moved into 247. Wondered if you could tell me about the community association management?"

"Oh, that's United Community Management of South Florida, or UCM as we refer to it," the woman said without looking up. "Veronica Santiago handles us. She's here Tuesdays and Fridays, nine to noon."

United Community Management of South Florida. Max made a note. The fact that the manager was only on-site six hours a week explained a lot about Queens Point's condition.

"And the board?"

"President's Roger Bleir in 156. Been president since...oh, forever. Sweet man, but he's getting up there, you know?" She finally looked up, her expression sympathetic. "Are you having a problem already?"

"Just trying to understand how things work," Max said. "Former business owner, old habits."

"Well, board meetings are the third Thursday of the month, 7 PM in the clubhouse. Not much excitement, if you ask me."

Max thanked her and left, already planning his approach. Roger Bleir, elderly president, probably overwhelmed and ready to delegate. A part-time manager who couldn't possibly provide adequate oversight. And a community full of retirees who'd stopped paying attention years ago.

It was a criminal's paradise.

The Professional

Max timed his first encounter with Veronica Santiago perfectly. Tuesday morning, 9:15 AM, catching her as she was setting up in the makeshift HOA office. He'd done his research—University of Miami MBA, fifteen years in community association management, CAM license in good standing. Overqualified for managing dying retirement communities, which meant she was either hiding something or stuck.

She looked up when he knocked on the door frame. Mid-forties, attractive in a washed-out Florida kind of way that suggested intelligence being slowly ground down by bureaucratic stupidity. Blonde hair pulled back efficiently, clothes professional but tired. The kind of woman who'd started with big plans and ended up managing pool maintenance schedules for people who complained about everything but paid for nothing.

"Ms. Santiago? I'm John Masters, new resident in 247. Wondered if I could ask you a few questions about community finances."

Veronica's expression shifted from polite interest to guarded wariness. In her experience, residents who asked about finances were either troublemakers or auditors—neither made her job easier.

"What kind of questions?"

"The kind that might require privacy," Max said, glancing meaningfully at the open office space. "Maybe we could continue this over coffee?"

She studied him—clearly not another retiree, too focused to be a time-waster, but asking the kind of questions that usually led to problems. "I have about twenty minutes before my next appointment. There's a Starbucks on Federal Highway."

"The latte is on me," he replied.

The Seduction

The Starbucks was generic corporate sterile, which made it perfect for the kind of conversation Max had in mind. Over lattes—oat milk for her, breve for him—he laid out what he'd observed about Queens Point with the precision of someone who understood financial dysfunction.

"I've been reviewing the publicly available documents," he began, pulling out a folder of printouts. "Reserve fund study hasn't been updated in five years. Assessment increases averaging 12% annually for the last three years, but no visible improvement in amenities or maintenance."

Veronica's coffee cup paused halfway to her lips. "You've been here less than a week."

"Former business owner," Max said smoothly. "I have a background in financial analysis. Old habits." He leaned forward slightly. "What I'm seeing suggests systematic problems that go beyond deferred maintenance."

"Such as?"

Max opened his folder and pulled out a spreadsheet he'd created based on public financial reports. "Seventeen thousand, four hundred and thirty-two dollars missing from the reserve fund between Q3 and Q4 last year. Emergency repairs that cost 40% more than comparable work in neighboring communities. Maintenance contracts with companies that don't appear to exist."

Veronica set down her coffee cup and looked at him with new interest. "You're not a typical retiree, are you?"

"And you're not a typical community manager," Max replied. "MBA from the University of Miami, fifteen years in the business, managing communities that should be beneath your skill level. What's the story there, Veronica?"

She laughed, but there was no humor in it. "The story is that community association management in South Florida is run by alcoholics and idiots, and the residents are too old or too scared to care. I make fifty-four thousand a year dealing with boards that think Robert's Rules of Order is a suggestion and residents who call me every time their garbage disposal makes noise."

"And United Community Management?"

"Is run by Earl Morrison, who should have retired ten years ago but can't afford to because he spent his pension on bourbon and bad investments. He manages thirty-seven communities with all the competence of a brain-damaged orangutan."

Max smiled. "Tell me how you really feel."

Veronica studied him over her coffee. "What's your angle, Mr. Masters? Nobody moves to Queens Point and immediately starts analyzing financial statements. Not unless they have a reason."

Max made a calculated decision to show part of his hand. "I spent several decades fixing broken systems. Identifying inefficiencies. Eliminating waste. I'm supposedly retired now, but I look at this place and I see..."

"A disaster?"

"Opportunity." He leaned back, watching her reaction. "What would it take to fix Queens Point? Really fix it?"

"New board. New management. Actual financial controls. Competitive bidding for contracts." Her voice carried the frustration of someone who'd been thinking about solutions for years. "It's not complicated. It's just impossible with the current power structure."

"What if it wasn't impossible?"

She laughed again, this time with genuine amusement. "Unless you're planning a hostile takeover, Roger and his cronies aren't going anywhere. They've been running this place like their personal kingdom for fifteen years."

John smiled. "Hostile takeovers are my specialty."

The Alliance

Their meetings became regular. Always public at first—coffee at the clubhouse, lunch at the mediocre deli on Glades Road, perfectly appropriate for a new resident seeking guidance from the community manager. Max listened to her ideas with the intense focus of someone who actually valued her intelligence, asked questions that showed he understood not just the numbers but the strategy behind them.

"You're wasted in this position," he told her after reviewing her proposed budget reforms. "This is CEO-level thinking."

"Yeah, well, CEOs don't usually end up managing retirement communities," she said, but he caught the pleased flush in her cheeks.

The transition from professional to personal was gradual, calculated on Max's part, but surprisingly genuine in its execution. He found himself actually enjoying her company—her sharp mind, her dark humor about the community management industry, the way she attacked problems with elegant solutions that no one ever implemented.

"You're not what I expected," she told him over dinner at Blue Moon Fish Company, an upscale restaurant in Fort Lauderdale. Their fourth dinner together, but the first that felt like a date.

"What did you expect?"

"Another bored retiree playing Napoleon. We get them every few years—someone who thinks they'll sweep in and change everything. They usually last one board meeting before reality crushes them."

"I don't crush easily," Max said.

"No," she agreed, her eyes holding his across the candlelit table. "I'm starting to see that."

Later, in her Coral Springs condo, as they sat on her balcony overlooking a pool that actually worked, she asked the question he'd been waiting for.

"What do you really want, John?"

He could have lied, played the civic-minded retiree concerned about property values. Instead, he gave her a piece of truth wrapped in plausible motivation.

"I want to build something perfect. A community that actually works. Where the buildings are maintained, the finances are transparent, and the systems function like they're supposed to." He paused, looking at her intently. "And I want to work with someone who understands what that takes."

"Someone like me?"

"Someone exactly like you."

She kissed him first, but he was the one who turned it into something more—a claiming, a binding, a promise of what they could accomplish together if they stopped accepting other people's incompetence.

The Revelation

In bed afterward, as she traced patterns on his chest with the languid satisfaction of a woman who'd been sexually and professionally frustrated for too long, Veronica laid out the scope of Queens Point's corruption with post-coital clarity.

"It's not just seventeen thousand," she said. "That's just what's obvious from the public documents. Roger's been skimming for years—fake maintenance contracts, inflated repair costs, kickbacks from vendors. I estimate at least two hundred thousand over the past five years."

"You documented this?"

"I tried. When I first took over the account three years ago, I thought I could clean it up. Implement proper controls, demand competitive bidding, audit the vendor relationships." She laughed bitterly. "Roger and Harold—he's the vice president—they made it clear that my job depended on not asking uncomfortable questions."

"So you stopped asking."

"I stopped asking. Fifty-four thousand a year isn't much, but it's what I have. Community management jobs aren't exactly growing on trees, and Earl Morrison made it clear that one word from Roger would end my career."

Max pulled her closer, calculating rapidly. She had access to all the financial records. She understood the systems. She was already frustrated with the corruption but felt powerless to stop it. And now she was emotionally invested in him.

"What if I told you we could fix this? All of it. The corruption, the incompetence, the waste."

"I'd say you're dreaming."

"What if I told you we could do it in a way that benefits us both? Professionally and personally."

She propped herself up on an elbow, studying his face in the dim light from the bedside lamp. "How?"

"We take over Queens Point. Remove the corrupt board, implement your reforms, turn it into a showcase community. You get the professional recognition you deserve. I get to build something worthwhile. And we get to work together."

"John, it's not that simple. Roger has been president for fifteen years. Harold owns multiple units. The residents are mostly elderly and don't want conflict—"

"The residents want their community to work," Max interrupted. "They want their assessments spent properly, their buildings maintained, their property values protected. They just need someone to show them how badly they're being robbed."

Veronica was quiet for a long moment, her business mind working through the possibilities. "Even if we could expose the corruption, getting elected to the board would require—"

"Would require demonstrating competence, showing results, and giving residents something better than what they have now." Max smiled in the darkness. "Trust me, I know how to run a campaign."

"This is insane," she said finally.

"This is opportunity," he corrected. "The question is whether you're ready to take it."

She looked at him—really looked at him—seeing past the surface charm to something harder underneath. A man who didn't just identify problems but eliminated them. Who didn't just plan takeovers but executed them. And she sensed an attraction deeper than she had ever experienced. It was the combination of danger, attraction and purpose, whose aphrodisiac powers were inescapable.

"What aren't you telling me?" she asked.

"Nothing you need to know right now," Max said honestly. "But everything you'll want to know eventually."

She kissed him again, slower this time, tasting possibility and danger in equal measure. "Okay," she said against his lips. "Let's take over Queens Point."

The Campaign Begins

They started with intelligence gathering. Veronica had access to three years of financial records through her management company. Max had techniques for extracting information that went beyond official documents. Together, they built a comprehensive picture of Queens Point's dysfunction that was both detailed and damning.

"Harold Weinstock is the key," Veronica explained, scrolling through property ownership records on her laptop. "He owns eight units through various LLCs, gives him disproportionate voting power. But here's the interesting part—he's been using association funds to pay for improvements to his rental units."

"That's embezzlement."

"That's Tuesday at Queens Point. But it's also documentable." She clicked through bank records. "Forty-three thousand in 'emergency repairs' last year, thirty-one thousand of which went to units Harold owns."

Max studied the data, his mind already working through the implications. "What about Roger?"

"Roger's more sophisticated. Kickbacks from contractors, inflated invoices, phantom emergency repairs. Classic skimming operation, but spread across multiple vendors and disguised as legitimate maintenance expenses."

"How much total?"

"Conservative estimate? Three hundred thousand over five years. Maybe more if we dig deeper."

John leaned back in his chair, genuinely impressed. "And Earl Morrison knows about this?"

"Earl Morrison enables it. Happy boards mean steady management fees. He doesn't ask questions as long as the checks clear."

"Which means when we expose this, we're not just taking on the board. We're threatening Morrison's entire business model."

Veronica nodded grimly. "This isn't just about Queens Point. If we succeed here, it threatens the way he operates all thirty-seven communities. He'll fight back."

John smiled. "Good. I prefer opponents who fight back. Makes the victory more satisfying."

The Opening Gambit

The Queens Point HOA meeting room smelled of stale coffee and years of wax buildup. John Masters sat in the back row; his legal pad filled with notes that would have terrified anyone who could decipher his shorthand. Six weeks of observation had mapped every weakness in the board's structure, every personality conflict. Every procedural vulnerability.

The board president, Roger Bleir, was struggling through the agenda with all the authority of wet cardboard. Seventy-eight years old, half-deaf, and fully overwhelmed. The other board members were equally ineffective—a collection of retirees who'd volunteered for the illusion of purpose, not the reality of responsibility.

"Motion to approve last month's minutes?" Roger wheezed.

Silence. Half the audience was asleep. John smiled. It was like watching a Commodore 64 try to run modern software. The system wasn't just broken—it was begging to be replaced.

Veronica sat in the designated manager's chair, taking notes with sharp, angry movements, occasionally shaking her head at Roger's fumbling. Even in this dysfunctional setting, she maintained professional composure, but Max could see the frustration bleeding through her practiced neutrality.

He'd found his entry point weeks ago. Now it was time to use it.

The Public Challenge

After the meeting dissolved into its usual chaos—an argument about whether the pool should close at 9 or 10 PM that somehow lasted forty minutes—Max approached the board table where Roger was gathering his papers with shaking hands.

"Mr. Bleir? John Masters, unit 247. I was hoping you could help me understand something."

Roger looked up, ready to dismiss another retiree with a complaint about lawn maintenance. But John wasn't what he expected—contained energy that suggested purpose rather than retirement.

"If it's about the pool hours—"

"It's about the $17,000 missing from the reserve fund."

The room, which had been emptying, suddenly went quiet. Veronica's head snapped up from her notes. Harold Weinstock, the vice president, stopped mid-conversation with his usual sycophants.

John pulled out a printed spreadsheet. "I've been reviewing the public financial statements. There's a discrepancy between the Q3 reserves and Q4 opening balance. Seventeen thousand, four hundred and thirty-two dollars, to be exact."

Roger's face went pale. "I'm sure there's an explanation—"

"I'm sure there is," John agreed pleasantly. "Which is why I'm asking. As a concerned resident who just invested his retirement savings in this community."

Harold stepped forward, his face flushed with the indignation of someone who'd been caught but refused to admit it. "Who are you to come in here making accusations?"

"I'm not making accusations," John replied calmly. "I'm asking questions about publicly available financial data. Unless you consider basic financial literacy to be accusatory?"

A murmur went through the remaining residents. Mrs. Maxwell, who'd been arguing about pool hours, suddenly looked very interested in the conversation. Bob Patterson pulled out his own copy of the financial statements, squinting at numbers he'd never bothered to examine before.

"The board reviews all financial matters in executive session," Harold blustered. "Residents don't need to concern themselves—"

"Residents absolutely need to concern themselves with how their assessment money is spent," John interrupted, his voice carrying the authority of someone who understood exactly how money moved through organizations. "It's our money, Mr. Weinstock. Our community. Your fiduciary responsibility to all of us."

Veronica watched the exchange with professional fascination. In three minutes, this new resident had accomplished what she'd been unable to do in three years—force the board to publicly address their financial irregularities. The residents were paying attention now, asking questions, demanding answers.

Roger fumbled through his papers. "The...the reserve study will be updated...we're getting quotes..."

"The reserve study is five years out of date," Max said, consulting his notes. "Florida statute requires updates every three years. The association is in violation of state law."

"Now see here—" Harold began.

"I'm not trying to cause trouble," Max said, his tone reasonable but implacable. "I just want to understand how this community operates financially. Perhaps Ms. Santiago could provide some clarity?"

All eyes turned to Veronica. She was trapped between her professional obligations to the board and her growing respect for someone who was finally asking the right questions.

"The financial statements are accurate as reported," she said carefully. "Any questions about specific line items should be directed to the board for clarification."

It was a masterful non-answer that technically supported her employers while subtly confirming John's concerns. Harold relaxed slightly, thinking she was on his side. But John caught the careful phrasing, the professional way she'd avoided actually defending the board's financial management.

"I'll be requesting copies of all vendor contracts and payment records for the past three years," John announced to the room. "As a resident, I have the right to inspect association records."

"That's...that's a lot of paperwork," Roger stammered.

"I have time," John said simply.

The Resistance

Ed Torrance saw through them immediately.

Seventy years old, twenty-five years in Naval Intelligence, the kind of man who noticed when patterns changed. He'd watched John work the room, saw how he coordinated with Veronica without seeming to, recognized the tactical precision of their campaign.

"You're being played," he told a group of old-timers at the pool the next morning. "This guy shows up out of nowhere, suddenly he's trying to overthrow everything? Ask yourself why."

"Because Roger's stealing from us," Martha Maxwell replied, clutching her copy of the financial statements. "Did you see those numbers? Seventeen thousand dollars just...gone."

"Maybe. But what makes you think this Masters character is any better? Nobody moves to Queens Point and immediately starts conducting financial audits. Not unless they have an agenda."

Ed started his own investigation. He discovered John's background didn't quite add up—the insurance company he'd supposedly worked for had no record of him. The business address on his previous tax returns led to a mail drop. Even his references were questionable when pressed for details.

He confronted John at the community pool on a Tuesday morning, choosing a public venue where retreat would be difficult.

"Mr. Masters," Ed said, approaching with military bearing. "Funny thing about that insurance company you mentioned— Midwest Mutual has never heard of you."

John looked up from his newspaper, projecting calm authority. "I said I was an independent adjuster. I worked as a contractor for various firms over the years. Midwest Mutual was one client among many." He folded his paper carefully. "I'd be happy to provide references, though I'm curious why my employment history is more interesting than the missing reserve funds."

"Because people who ask a lot of questions usually have something to hide."

"Do they?" John stood slowly, his smile never wavering. "Or maybe people who deflect questions about missing money are the ones with something to hide."

Ed felt the conversation slipping away from him. Around the pool, other residents were listening, and John's reasonable tone was making Ed look paranoid and defensive.

"I know what you are," Ed said quietly.

"What am I, Mr. Torrance?"

"Trouble."

John's smile widened. "For whom?"

The Fire

Three nights later, Ed Torrance's garage went up in flames.

The Palm Beach County Fire Department blamed faulty wiring—Ed's unit was one of the original builds, forty years of deferred electrical maintenance finally catching up. The investigation was perfunctory; accidental fires in aging buildings were common enough that arson wasn't even considered.

Ed himself barely escaped, stumbling out in his pajamas as flames consumed his 1987 Buick LeSabre and forty years of accumulated possessions. The heat was so intense it cracked the windows of neighboring units and left a smell of melted plastic that lingered for weeks.

John was the first neighbor to arrive with a fire extinguisher, playing the concerned resident perfectly. He helped Ed to safety, offered his guest room, projected nothing but genuine worry for an elderly neighbor's welfare.

"Thank God you're okay," John said, wrapping a blanket around Ed's shoulders as fire trucks arrived. "Do you need me to call anyone? Family?"

Ed looked at him through the smoke and chaos, seeing past the performance to something much darker underneath. But what could he say? That the newest resident had somehow committed arson with perfect timing? That forty-year-old wiring had conveniently chosen to fail just as Ed was becoming a problem?

"My daughter in Boca," Ed said finally. "I'll...I'll stay with her for a while."

"Smart," John replied. "Take all the time you need to recover."

Veronica arrived minutes later, equally concerned, equally helpful. Together, they were the picture of good neighbors responding to tragedy. Only Ed saw the predator's satisfaction in John's eyes, recognized the relief in Veronica's expression that a threat had been neutralized.

The message was clear to anyone intelligent enough to receive it: resistance had consequences.

Ed moved out the following week, officially for recovery but really because he understood that some battles couldn't be won by elderly Navy veterans armed only with suspicion and integrity.

The Coalition

With Ed's departure, the path forward became clear. John began recruiting allies systematically, identifying residents whose frustrations with the current board could be channeled into political support.

Martha Maxwell, whose assessment had mysteriously doubled the previous year while her neighbor's stayed flat. Bob Patterson, whose repeated requests for hallway lighting repairs had been ignored for eight months. Sarah Williams, who'd been trying to get proper financial audits for three years.

One by one, John listened to their complaints, documented their concerns, and gradually built a coalition of the frustrated and forgotten.

"The problem isn't that the board is evil," John explained to a small group gathered in Sarah Williams' living room. "The problem is that they're incompetent. Roger means well, but he's overwhelmed. Harold owns multiple units, which creates a conflict of interest. And without proper financial controls, mistakes become systematic problems."

"What can we do about it?" Martha asked. "They've been in charge forever."

"We elect better leadership," John said simply. "People who understand fiduciary responsibility and aren't afraid to implement proper oversight."

"Like who?" Bob demanded.

John smiled. "Like us."

The Evidence

Veronica provided the documentation that made their case undeniable. Three years of financial records that revealed a pattern of systematic theft disguised as maintenance expenses. Vendor contracts that violated state bidding requirements. Emergency repairs that cost three times market rate and somehow always benefited Harold's rental properties.

"This isn't just seventeen thousand," she explained to the growing coalition, her laptop displaying spreadsheets that told a story of institutional corruption. "This is over three hundred thousand in questionable expenses over five years."

The numbers were devastating when presented clearly. Emergency pool repairs that cost $15,000 for work that should have been $5,000. Landscaping contracts with companies owned by Roger's son-in-law. Assessment increases that went into Harold's pocket instead of community improvements.

"How did this happen?" Sarah asked, her voice shaking with anger.

"It happened because nobody was watching," John replied. "Because residents trusted the board to act in their best interests, and the board interpreted that trust as permission to treat association funds as their personal piggy bank."

"What do we do?"

"We file a formal complaint with the state licensing board. We demand a forensic audit. And we run candidates in the next election who will implement proper financial controls."

Martha looked around the room. "Who's going to run?"

"I will," John said.

The Campaign

John's campaign for HOA board president was a masterclass in suburban politics. He didn't attack Roger personally—the old man was clearly overwhelmed rather than malicious. Instead, he focused on systems, processes, and the need for professional management of community resources.

His campaign literature was simple and devastating: "Your assessments have increased 47% over five years. Your property values have declined 12%. Your reserve funds are depleted. Isn't it time for change?"

He held coffee hours where residents could review the financial evidence Veronica had compiled. He organized information sessions about state HOA law and residents' rights. Most importantly, he listened to every complaint, documented every concern, and promised specific solutions rather than vague improvements.

Harold tried to fight back, organizing his own coalition of residents who feared change. But his defense of the status quo rang hollow when confronted with documented evidence of financial mismanagement.

"Mr. Masters doesn't understand how we do things here," Harold argued at a community meeting that drew the largest crowd in Queens Point's history.

"I understand exactly how you do things here," John replied calmly. "The question is whether residents want to continue paying for your mistakes."

The room erupted in applause. Harold's support crumbled as residents realized they'd been subsidizing his lifestyle for years.

The Election

The special election was called after a formal petition signed by 60% of Queens Point residents. Harold's illegal voting structure was challenged and overturned by the state licensing board. Roger, overwhelmed and exhausted, resigned rather than face a public audit of his administration.

John ran unopposed for president. Sarah Williams, backed by his coalition, ran for treasurer—her accounting background and reform proposals made her the obvious choice for financial oversight. Bob Patterson took the secretary position, and Martha Maxwell became the new vice president.

"Are you sure about this?" Veronica asked him the night before the election, as they reviewed their plans for Queens Point's transformation. "Working together this closely—people might notice our relationship."

John pulled her closer on the couch of his still-avocado-appliance kingdom. "You're the community manager. I'll be the board president. It's a professional relationship that happens to benefit from personal compatibility."

"And Earl Morrison?"

"He will have to accept that his days of enabling corruption are over, at least at Queens Point. Your management contract gives you significant discretion in how you handle day-to-day operations."

"Until he decides I'm more trouble than I'm worth."

"By the time he figures out what we're really doing, it'll be too late to stop us."

The election was a landslide. John won with 87% of the vote. The new board was entirely composed of reform candidates who'd pledged to work with Veronica to implement proper financial controls and transparency measures.

Roger Bleir was outraged. He had run Queens Point as his own personal fiefdom for years. The thought of this sketchy newcomer showing up and taking over made him apoplectic with rage. He vowed that he would get even with Masters if it was the last thing he ever did. His fair skin had turned purple with anger. And then a funny thing happened. No one saw Roger for days. Finally, his daughter from New York called the Palm Beach County Sheriff's Office for a wellness check as her father had stopped calling. The deputy broke into Roger's house and found him dead on the floor. No signs of struggle, the coroner ruled it a heart attack. And so ended the opposition to John Masters' new regime. Lessons learned in Cleveland, applied in Florida.

The Transformation

Their first board meeting was a masterclass in efficient governance, with Veronica providing professional guidance that subtly steered every decision toward their shared vision. Forensic audit approved unanimously—with Veronica recommending the auditing firm. New maintenance contracts put out for competitive bidding—with Veronica managing the process. Financial reporting systems overhauled—with Veronica designing the new procedures.

"Ms. Santiago has been invaluable in helping us understand proper HOA management," John announced at their first public meeting as the new board. "We're fortunate to have such professional guidance during this transition."

Veronica nodded modestly from her position at the manager's table. "The board's commitment to transparency and accountability makes my job much easier. It's refreshing to work with leadership that prioritizes residents' interests."

To the audience, it looked like perfect cooperation between a reform-minded board and a competent manager. Behind the scenes, it was a carefully orchestrated takeover that gave them control over every aspect of Queens Point's operations.

"I have to admit," Martha Maxwell said after their third monthly financial report showed actual surplus funds, "it's amazing what proper management can accomplish."

Queens Point began to transform visibly. The pools were cleaned and repaired properly—by contractors Veronica selected through her "competitive bidding process." The buildings got long-overdue maintenance that had been deferred for years—work managed by vendors who understood the new efficiency standards. The landscaping went from embarrassing to enviable—maintained by a company that appreciated consistent oversight.

Property values, stagnant for a decade, began to rise. Nobody questioned the remarkable turnaround or wondered why the new board president and the community manager seemed to anticipate each other's needs so perfectly.

The Empire Begins

Six months later, John and Veronica stood on the patio of Unit 247— their unofficial command center, though they maintained complete professional discretion in public. Queens Point spread below them, gleaming in the sunset. Clean, organized, efficient.

"Phase one complete," Veronica said, raising her wine glass.

"You sound like we're conquering territory," John replied, amused.

"Aren't we?" She gestured at the transformed community. "I control the day-to-day operations through my management authority. You control the policy decisions through the board. Every contract, every expenditure, every major decision flows through us."

"And Earl Morrison hasn't noticed?"

"Earl Morrison is too drunk and too lazy to notice anything beyond his monthly management fees. As long as Queens Point keeps paying UCM and doesn't generate complaints, he doesn't care how I run it."

Masters smiled. "And the board?"

"The board thinks they're implementing reform. They have no idea they're just rubber-stamping our agenda." She turned to him, her eyes bright with the satisfaction of competence finally unleashed. "Sarah Williams actually thanked me yesterday for 'helping her understand treasurer responsibilities.'"

"What about rumors of my background—"

"Doesn't matter," she interrupted. "What matters is that we built something that works. That we're good at this."

John pulled her closer, looking beyond Queens Point to the neighboring communities visible in the distance. Millennial Village was in even worse shape—gang problems, deferred maintenance, a board that met in secret and published no financial reports. Harbor Gardens was hemorrhaging money through vendor kickbacks that made Harold's scheme look amateur. Cypress Woods was fighting a losing battle against drug dealers who'd moved into vacant units.

All of them were managed by United Community Management, which meant all of them were ripe for the same kind of intervention they'd just completed at Queens Point.

"So, what's phase two?" Veronica asked.

John reached into his briefcase and pulled out a thick manila folder, setting it on the coffee table between them. "We're going to take over United Community Management."

Veronica's wine glass froze halfway to her lips. "What?"

"Earl Morrison isn't just an incompetent drunk," Max said, opening the folder to reveal bank statements, wire transfer records, and financial documents that made her eyes widen. "He's been personally benefiting from these communities' decline for years. Look at this."

The papers showed a complex web of financial transactions—millions in misallocated funds finding their way into Earl's secret offshore accounts in the Cayman Islands and Switzerland. Maintenance contracts that were inflated by 200%, with the excess routed through shell companies back to Morrison's personal holdings. Emergency repair funds that had been systematically drained for everything from his yacht payments to his daughter's private school tuition.

Veronica gasped, her professional mind quickly processing the scope of the theft. "John, where did you get this?"

"Don't worry about that," he said smoothly. "I have financial contacts all over the world who provide information when properly incentivized. The important thing is what we do with it."

She flipped through page after page of documented corruption. "This is...this is millions of dollars. He's been stealing from every community he manages."

"Exactly. Which means he's vulnerable. And vulnerabilities create opportunities." John/Max leaned forward, his voice carrying the quiet intensity of someone laying out a battle plan. "The next step is we take over United Community Management—secretly. You become the CEO, but still hands-on CAM at the thirty-seven different declining communities. We rebrand the company with a pledge of new management, new direction, new life for our communities. And I work behind the scenes as your silent partner."

"How do we—"

"We show Earl that we have the goods on him, and he can do it the hard way or the easy way. Clean, simple, surgical. He takes his stolen millions and disappears to whatever tropical paradise corrupt managers dream about. You take over operations with a mandate to reform the entire system."

Veronica was quiet for a long moment, studying the evidence spread across the table. "But we have a problem," she said finally.

"What's that?"

"We can't have United's CEO making fifty-four thousand a year. The board of directors would never believe I could attract quality management talent at that salary level."

Max smiled. "Are you open to a three-year contract at, say, two hundred and seventy-five thousand per year, plus a high-end car, expense reimbursement, performance bonuses, and profit sharing, along with a lucrative deferred compensation program?"

Veronica almost fainted. The wine glass slipped from her fingers, fortunately empty, and clattered onto the coffee table. "Are you kidding me?"

"Not kidding. You'll be running a company that manages thousands of depressed properties with values that could be worth several times their present value under the right management. Your compensation should reflect that responsibility." He gathered the financial documents back into the folder. "Plus, we'll need to make this look completely legitimate. High-end executive compensation, proper corporate governance, the whole package."

"But what if Earl refuses to leave?"

John's smile turned predatory. "I think if he wants to stay out of federal prison—or even worse consequences—he'll be happy for the opportunity of a quiet exit to a very comfortable retirement. The kind he's already stolen for himself."

Veronica looked at him with a mixture of admiration and fear. "You're talking about taking over an entire management company. Thirty-seven communities. Thousands of residents. And major problems due to corruption and incompetence fueled by alcohol."

"I'm talking about building an empire," Max corrected. "Queens Point was just the proof of concept. Now we scale up."

She stood and walked to the balcony railing, looking out at the community they'd transformed in just six months. Under their management, Queens Point had gone from a rotting embarrassment to a showcase property. Property values had increased over 25%. Units were now in heavy demand as news of the turnaround spread. Other management companies were trying to poach their proven reform model.

"This could actually work," she said slowly.

"It will work. We have the evidence to remove Earl. We have the expertise to run the operations. We have the track record to prove our competence. And we have thirty-seven, correction now thirty-six broken communities full of residents who are desperate for competent management."

Veronica turned back to face him. "When do we make our move on Earl?"

"Monday morning. I've arranged a meeting at his office—just you, me, and him. We present the evidence, offer him the choice between cooperation and federal prosecution, and by Tuesday, you're the new CEO of United Community Management."

"And you?"

"I'll be your primary investor and strategic consultant. Officially, I'm a retired business executive who saw the potential in your management philosophy and decided to back your acquisition of the company. Unofficially..." He stood and joined her at the railing. "Unofficially, I'm your partner in building the most successful community management empire South Florida has ever seen."

Veronica looked down at Queens Point one more time—their first conquest, their proof of concept, their launch pad for something much larger. "You know this is completely insane."

"The best opportunities usually are."

She kissed him then, tasting ambition and possibility and the intoxicating flavor of power that was finally within reach. "Okay," she whispered against his lips. "Let's steal a company."

Max smiled in the darkness, feeling the familiar rush of a plan coming together perfectly. Queens Point had been the opening move. United Community Management would be the foundation of their empire.

And Earl Morrison, drunk and corrupt and utterly unprepared for what was coming, would be the first major casualty.

The games were about to get much more interesting.

Chapter 4: The Sunshine Takedown

The Earl Morrison Reckoning

Monday morning arrived with the precision of a Swiss watch, and Max Vecchio—playing John Masters to the world—had never been more prepared for a meeting. The United Community Management offices sat in a strip mall between a nail salon and a tax prep service, which told you everything you needed to know about Earl Morrison's ambitions.

The office itself was a monument to community decline—numerous broken ceiling tiles, fluorescent lighting that hummed with electrical problems, and furniture that looked like it had been salvaged from a government surplus auction. Earl Morrison sat behind a desk that was somehow both too large and too small for the space, his face carrying the broken capillaries of a man who'd been drinking his lunch for decades.

"Veronica," Earl said, not bothering to stand. "And Mr. Masters, right? The new guy at Queens Point. Heard you've been stirring things up."

John smiled his most disarming smile. "Just helping neighbors understand their rights and responsibilities. Nothing more."

"Right." Earl's bloodshot eyes narrowed. "So what's this about? John, you said it was urgent."

Veronica placed the manila folder on Earl's desk with the ceremonial gravity of someone serving divorce papers. "We need to discuss the future of United Community Management."

Earl opened the folder, and his face went through a remarkable transformation—from bored irritation to concern to genuine fear in the space of thirty seconds. Bank statements showing his accounts in the Cayman Islands. Wire transfer records linking maintenance funds to his personal yacht payments. Invoices for his daughter's private school that had somehow been categorized as "community relations expenses."

"Where did you get this?" Earl's voice had lost its casual authority.

"Does it matter?" Masters asked, settling back in his chair. "The question is what happens next. You have two choices, Earl. Choice one: This becomes a federal investigation. Embezzlement, wire fraud, racketeering under RICO statutes. You'll spend your golden years in a federal penitentiary, assuming you survive the stress."

Earl was sweating now, despite the over-aggressive air conditioning. "What's choice two?"

"Choice two," Veronica said smoothly, "is you retire. Effective immediately. Health reasons, stress, whatever story makes you comfortable. You transfer all United Community Management assets, contracts, and client relationships to my new company as your designated successor. Clean transition, no questions asked."

"You?" Earl laughed, but there was hysteria in it. "You're a $54,000-a-year employee. You can't run a management company."

"Actually," John said, pulling out another folder, "Veronica will be running it as CEO, and she'll finally be putting her MBA to good use. I'll be serving as primary investor and strategic consultant, having recognized the tremendous potential in reforming South Florida's community management industry."

Earl stared at the papers John spread across his desk. Corporate restructuring documents. Bank loan approvals. A business plan that projected United's gross profits growing into the many millions within a few years.

"This is insane," Earl muttered. "These properties are worth hundreds of millions—"

"Hundreds of millions in depressed property values that could be worth several billion under the right management," John corrected. "You've been content to skim cream from communities, speeding up their death spiral. We're talking about resurrection. Total transformation. Making these places into showcase properties that triple in value."

Veronica leaned forward. "Earl, you've stolen approximately $3.7 million over the past eight years. Not bad for a drunk with minimal business skills. But you've reached your ceiling. Keep going, and you'll get caught. Federal prison, asset forfeiture, criminal restitution. Or..." She gestured to the contract. "Take the golden parachute. Retire quietly to whatever tropical paradise you've been planning."

Earl read through the contract with the desperate attention of a drowning man studying a life preserver. The terms were generous—he kept his stolen millions, got a consulting fee for the transition, and walked away clean. All he had to do was sign over his life's work to a woman he'd been paying peanuts for years.

"How do I know you won't come after me later?"

"Because we need you gone, not destroyed," John said. "Prosecution would be messy, time-consuming, and generate the kind of attention that interferes with business. This way, everyone wins. You disappear with your money. We take over operations. The communities get competent management. Efficiency."

Earl stared at the documents for another five minutes, occasionally glancing at the evidence of his crimes. Finally, with the resignation of a man who'd always known this day would come, he signed.

"Effective immediately?" he asked.

"Effective immediately," Veronica confirmed. "I'll handle the transition announcements to the boards and residents. You're taking an extended vacation for health reasons, and I'm stepping up as interim CEO. By the time you return from your 'recovery,' you'll have decided the stress isn't worth it, and I'll be permanently installed."

Earl Morrison gathered a few personal items—a coffee mug, a photo of his yacht, a bottle of bourbon from his desk drawer, and walked out of United Community Management for the last time. He didn't say goodbye.

The Transformation

When they got hold of United's bank accounts and money market funds, they received another pleasant surprise. Earl hadn't raked off the recent skim yet, and there was over $1.5 million waiting for them. Within twenty-four hours, Veronica Santiago had transformed from a $54,000-a-year community manager to the CEO of a company managing thirty-seven communities with thousands of units and hundreds of millions in property assets. The change was more than financial—it was revolutionary.

The first order of business was moving United's headquarters from the run-down strip mall to a proper corporate office in downtown Boca Raton. Twentieth floor, ocean and Intracoastal views, the kind of space that announced serious business to clients and competitors alike. Veronica's new office was a monument to executive authority—mahogany desk, leather furniture, and a conference table that could seat twelve.

"This is more like it," she said, standing at her floor-to-ceiling windows overlooking the Intracoastal Waterway. "Earl was thinking like a small-time operator. We're building an empire."

John smiled from her new executive chair. "The physical space matters. Clients need to believe they're dealing with a premium operation. First impressions create lasting expectations."

The salary increase was equally transformative. $275,000 plus bonuses and perks represented more than money—it was freedom, security, and the ability to live like the successful executive she'd always been capable of becoming. The signing bonus, compliments of Earl, covered the down payment on a waterfront condo in Highland Beach. The company car was a mid-sized Audi sedan that announced success without ostentation. Even her wardrobe evolved—designer suits that projected authority rather than competence.

But the real change was psychological. For years, Veronica had been implementing other people's decisions, managing other people's visions, constrained by budgets and bureaucracy that prevented her from achieving what she knew was possible. Now, every decision flowed through her. Every contract was hers to negotiate. Every strategic direction was hers to set.

"Thirty-seven communities," she said, reviewing the portfolio spread across her new conference table. "Most of them disasters. Deferred maintenance, corrupt boards, residents who've given up hope of improvement."

"Which makes them perfect for what we're planning," John replied. "People are grateful for competence when they've been living with incompetence. They'll support changes that would be controversial in well-run communities."

The business model was elegant in its simplicity. Identify dysfunctional communities with corrupt or incompetent boards, of which they already had thirty-six, since Queens Point had already been "rescued." To bring their existing residents on board, all they had to do was document the financial mismanagement and deferred maintenance. They then put forth their plan, consisting of professional management services that would "restore fiscal responsibility and community pride." They would install reform-minded board members who understood the need for decisive leadership. Then they would transform the properties through aggressive improvement programs that dramatically increased values while generating substantial profits through vendor "relationships" and management fees.

"It's not exactly fraud," Veronica mused, studying financial projections that showed United's revenue potentially increasing by 500% over three years. "We really are improving these communities."

"That's what makes it perfect," Max agreed. "The best operations provide genuine value while extracting maximum profit. Residents get better communities. We get wealthy. Everyone wins."

"Everyone who matters, anyway."

The Expansion Doctrine

The conference room at the Boca Raton Library wasn't meant for empire building, but John Masters had learned that the best conspiracies happened in plain sight. He stood before a projector screen showing a map of United's South Florida HOAs, each one color-coded by dysfunction level. Green meant the community was functioning relatively well. Yellow meant the community was down but not out. Red meant catastrophic. There was a lot of red and yellow, but not much green.

"Ladies and gentlemen," John said to the twelve carefully selected residents, "we're here because we share a common problem. Our communities are failing because management and the boards have failed. But Ms. Santiago and I have proven that once reform is implemented, the improvements happen almost immediately, leading to higher property values and happier residents."

Veronica sat to his right, professional in her new navy Armani suit, taking notes that were actually tactical observations. She'd handpicked this group—frustrated board members, sidelined treasurers, anyone with influence and grievance. Seeds for the garden they were about to plant.

"Queens Point was once like your communities," John continued, clicking to before-and-after photos. Crumbling facades versus pristine buildings. Empty pools versus aqua paradise. "Six months ago, we implemented resident-driven reform. Today, our property values are up over 25% and still rising."

Martha Maxwell, now a true believer, stood up. "It's true. John and Veronica saved our community. They can save yours, too."

The "Sunshine State Resident Empowerment Coalition" was born that afternoon. Later, it would also offer free advisory services to non-United declining HOAs—community advocacy— transparency initiatives. All the right buzzwords to hide what it truly was: a hostile takeover disguised as a helping hand. For right now, their intent was to bring all of UCM's HOAs on board.

"We're not here to run your boards," John lied smoothly. "We're here to empower *you* to run them better."

"United Community Management has committed to immediately taking all necessary steps to bring your communities up to the highest standards and improving your quality of life," Veronica added, her new executive authority lending weight to every word. "We believe that professional management combined with engaged resident leadership creates the optimal environment for community success."

Afterwards, in the parking lot, Veronica lit a cigarette—a habit she'd quit years ago but recently restarted under the stress of rapid expansion. "That was quite a performance."

"It's not a performance if you believe it," John replied, studying the list of target communities. "We are empowering them. We're giving them what they need—competent leadership."

"Your leadership."

"Eventually." He smiled. "But they have to want it first."

The Millennial Village Play

Millennial Village was perfect for the next phase—eleven hundred units of architectural depression, filled with young families who'd bought in before realizing "affordable" meant "abandoned by management." The pools had gone green years ago, hosting all types of algae. The playground was a tetanus farm. The roads had potholes that could swallow a Prius.

The board president, Levi Grant, was everything wrong with his generation condensed into human form. Twenty-eight, man-bun, more interested in his TikTok following than fiduciary duty. He'd won the election on promises of "disrupting traditional HOA culture" but had mostly disrupted basic maintenance.

John met him at a coffee shop that served $8 lattes and had exposed brick walls—Levi's natural habitat.

"I love what you're doing," John said, and Levi preened. "Using social media to engage residents. Building community through transparency. It's exactly what HOAs need."

"Right?" Levi leaned forward, eager. "The old guard doesn't understand. Everything's changing. We need to think outside the box."

"Absolutely. Though I imagine the practical challenges are significant. Budget constraints, vendor relationships, legal compliance..."

Levi's enthusiasm dimmed slightly. "Yeah, that stuff's been...challenging. The previous board left things pretty messy."

John nodded sympathetically. "I've been through the same thing at Queens Point. Actually..." He paused, as if the idea just occurred to him. "Would you be interested in some informal mentoring? No charge, just one president to another."

Levi's eyes lit up. "That would be amazing! I could really use someone who gets it, you know?"

Over the next month, John became Levi's guru. Weekly coffee meetings where John fed him just enough good advice to seem invaluable while subtly undermining his confidence. He'd praise Levi's "vision" while pointing out all the ways he was failing to execute it.

"Your social media engagement is fantastic," John would say. "Two thousand followers! Though I noticed the playground still hasn't been fixed. How are you handling the liability issue?"

"Liability?" Levi would respond, panic creeping into his voice.

"Oh, you haven't done a safety audit? With all those exposed bolts and rusty edges? That's...brave."

John documented everything. Every deferred maintenance issue. Every missed deadline. Every violation of Florida HOA statutes that Levi didn't even know existed. He shared these "concerns" with Veronica, who shared them with her carefully cultivated network of Millennial Village residents.

The playground accident was inevitable. Six-year-old Sophia Mondell fell from rusted monkey bars that had been flagged for repair eighteen months earlier. Broken arm, screaming mother, and suddenly Levi's TikTok followers meant nothing compared to a seven-figure liability claim.

The emergency board meeting was standing room only. Parents with pitchforks, metaphorically speaking. Levi tried to deflect, talking about "systematic failures" and "inherited problems," but John had prepared the residents too well.

"Mr. Grant," said Patricia Williams, a pediatric nurse John had been cultivating, "you've been president for over a year. You've posted 347 TikToks about 'revolutionizing HOA culture.' How many of those addressed playground safety?"

Levi sputtered. John sat in the back, taking notes, occasionally offering supportive nods that somehow made Levi look worse.

By the end of the night, Levi had resigned. The board vice president, overwhelmed by the prospect of taking over, asked if anyone had experience with crisis management.

John raised his hand reluctantly, as if the weight of civic duty compelled him. "I'd be willing to serve as interim advisor. Just until you find proper leadership."

The vote was unanimous.

"Additionally," John continued, "I suggest keeping the new reorganized United Community Management that led the Queens Point turnaround. Their CEO, Veronica Santiago, has personally assured me that she can do for Millennial what she did for my community, Queens Point. I would urge all of you here to come over and see what she has accomplished. We had the same issues as you, and it seemed completely hopeless, and yet look at it today. And it happened so fast."

Within a week, Millennial Village had overwhelmingly voted to have the new United work their magic and restore their once-beautiful community.

United We Fall

While John orchestrated Levi's downfall, Veronica executed her own operation against their competitors. She knew every management company in South Florida—their contracts, their methods, their sins. More importantly, she now had the resources and authority to compete against them effectively.

The first target was Atlantic Association Management, which handled twelve communities in Broward County through a combination of kickbacks and willful negligence. Their CEO, Richard Plevin, was a cocaine-functional executive who thought embezzlement was a perk of the position.

Veronica arranged lunch at the Ritz-Carlton, arriving in her new Audi and designer suit—the visual representation of serious competition. Richard arrived twenty minutes late, pupils dilated, talking too fast about his new boat.

"Veronica! Looking gorgeous as always. Still slumming it with the communities? Oh, wait, I heard you got Earl's job. Congrats, sweetheart."

"Thank you," she said, sliding a folder across the table. "I'm reaching out to discuss transition opportunities. Several of your clients have expressed interest in United's services."

Richard's smile faltered as he opened the folder. Falsified maintenance invoices. Kickback documentation. A particularly damning email thread about "creative accounting" on reserve funds.

"This is... Where did you get this?"

"Does it matter?" Veronica sipped her wine. "The question is what happens next. Option one: This becomes a class-action lawsuit. Criminal charges. A Florida Attorney General investigation, perhaps the Feds will get involved as well, looks like a strong case of mail fraud. Ugly."

Richard's face had gone from cocaine flush to corpse pale. "What's option two?"

"Atlantic transitions management of Harbor Gardens, Cypress Woods, Palm Aire, and the nine other HOAs to United Community Management. Smooth handover. Your reputation intact. Your freedom intact."

"That's extortion."

"That's business." Veronica stood, leaving a business card on the table. "United Community Management. Premium service for premium communities. You have forty-eight hours."

She left him there, sweating through his $3,000 suit. By the time she reached her car, she had a text from John: "Levi's out. Your timing remains impeccable."

They were becoming a machine. Efficient. Ruthless. Perfect.

Kingdom Building

Within six weeks, United Community Management had grown from thirty-seven communities to fifty-two, comprising over 10,000 units with thousands of residents. John installed hand-picked boards, all grateful for his "guidance" and deferential to his expertise. Veronica handled the newly formed vendors' corporate structure, creating layers of LLCs that would make ownership nearly impossible to trace while maximizing profit extraction.

The transformation was genuine—that was the beautiful irony. Properties were repaired. Budgets balanced. Crime decreased. Property values rose. John's obsession with efficiency meant these communities dramatically improved under their control. He was a benevolent dictator, as long as you defined benevolent as "orderly" rather than "kind."

"Our annual management 'fees' have doubled," Veronica reported one evening, reviewing their portfolio in John's Queens Point condo. "Plus, the service contracts, vendor "relationships," and special assessments. We're looking at another 50% total revenue growth by year-end."

"The money's secondary," John said, studying architectural plans for Harbor Gardens' renovation. "It's about building something that works."

Veronica laughed. "The money's secondary? Who are you and what did you do with John Masters?"

He looked up, and for a moment she saw past his calculated exterior to something deeper—the obsessive need to create order from chaos that drove everything he did. "Rose always said I could build good things," he muttered, then caught himself. "The money matters. But it's a tool, not the goal."

"Rose?"

"No one, just someone from Cleveland." He returned to the plans. "Harbor Gardens needs a complete infrastructure overhaul. New plumbing, electrical, foundation work. Fifteen million minimum."

Veronica recognized the deflection but filed the name away. Rose. Someone from his past who still mattered to him. Even sociopaths had ghosts, apparently.

Her new lifestyle reflected their success. The waterfront condo with harbor views. The German sedan. The designer wardrobe. The exclusive gym membership. The executive assistant who managed her calendar and screened her calls. All the trappings of legitimate corporate success, earned through methods that, while questionably legitimate, were undoubtedly effective.

"I never imagined it would scale this quickly," she said, reviewing their expansion plans. "Fifty-two communities in nine months. At this rate, we'll control every major HOA in South Florida within three years."

"Scalability was always the goal," John replied. "Individual communities are small-time. Regional dominance creates real power."

The Rollins Problem

Janice Rollins had served as United Community Management's in-house counsel for eight years—long enough to know where every body was buried. Literally. One maintenance worker had "fallen" down an elevator shaft after threatening to blow the whistle on Earl's financial shenanigans. Janice never said a word. She cashed her checks, kept her secrets, and planned for early retirement.

But then everything changed. Earl Morrison disappeared, Veronica Santiago took over the CEO seat, and John Masters stormed in like a corporate hitman. Overnight, United Community transformed from a backwater operation into the hottest name in HOA management.

Janice was too smart not to see the writing on the wall. The day Earl caved to Veronica's demands, she quietly began photocopying files. Not to save United—that ship had already hit the iceberg—but to figure out who had steered it into the ice. The speed and precision of United's so-called "turnaround" was too clean to be random. Someone was pulling strings behind the scenes, and Janice wanted insurance before they decided she knew too much.

The paperwork led to more paperwork, which led to John Masters. And John Masters led nowhere. His background was too perfect. Insurance adjuster, recently divorced, early retirement—it read like a witness protection cover story because that's exactly what it was. Janice had dealt with enough criminals during her career to recognize the pattern. But witness protection meant federal, which meant serious crimes, which meant leverage.

She started with public records. John Masters had existed for exactly eighteen months before appearing in Queens Point. Before that, nothing. But there were echoes—behavioral patterns that reminded her of something. The methodical takeover of territories. The systematic elimination of opposition. The obsession with organizational efficiency.

Then she found it, buried in an old DOJ press release about organized crime convictions in Cleveland. A passing reference to testimony from "a former associate identified only as M.V.," who had provided "extensive documentation of the Torrisi crime family's financial operations."

M.V. Max Vecchio.

The timeline fit. The skill set fit. And when she found an old photo from a Cleveland newspaper—grainy, distant, but showing Vinny Torrisi with his "financial advisor"—the face fit too.

John Masters was Max Vecchio, even after the extensive plastic surgery. The eyes never lied, and looking back at her were two of the most soulless, cold portals she'd ever seen. Which meant Veronica Santiago was sleeping with a former mob underboss who'd sent dozens of men to federal prison.

Janice waited three days, tracking Veronica's routine. Thursday evenings: a quiet wine bar on Las Olas before heading home—alone, usually. John rarely appeared in public with her unless it was strictly HOA business. Smart. Distance protected them both.

The garage was poorly lit, half empty. Janice stepped out from behind a concrete pillar just as Veronica reached for her Audi's door handle.

"Ms. Santiago."

Veronica's hand went to her purse—mace, gun, maybe both. "Ms. Rollins. Earl's old lawyer. Here for a severance check?"

"We need to talk."

"I doubt that." Veronica's voice stayed calm, but her eyes flicked to the stairwell, the exit ramp—calculating options.

"Max Vecchio."

Veronica's expression stayed neutral, but her pupils flared. Fight or flight. "Never heard of him."

"No, but you're sleeping with him. Building an empire with him. Probably half in love with him—though God knows why. The man's a sociopath."

"You mean John Masters. You're delusional."

Janice held up a slim folder. "Cleveland, financial adviser to the Torrisi family. Flipped witness when they set him up. Starred in Ohio's biggest RICO case. Vanished into witness protection. Resurfaced in Queens Point as John Masters, insurance adjuster turned community savior." She smiled thinly. "Your boyfriend has more blood on his hands than the entire United board combined."

Veronica took the folder but didn't bother to open it. "Assuming your bedtime story checks out, what do you want?"

"I want you to grasp what you're tied to. The feds will shelter him—until they don't. The moment he's a liability, or someone like me makes too much noise, he'll disappear. And you'll be left behind. Or buried with him."

"Is that a threat?"

"It's a warning. You're sharp, Veronica. Maybe the sharpest player in this mess. Get out while you still can."

Veronica stepped closer, and Janice instinctively stepped back. What she saw in Veronica's eyes wasn't fear or rage—it was recognition.

"You think I don't know?" Veronica said, voice low but cutting. "You think I'm some naïve woman swept off her feet by a dangerous man? I knew. Second day. The way he read people. How he solved problems. The precision of his violence."

"Then why—"

"Because he's building something worth it. These communities were rotting—bled dry by incompetents like Earl, protected by lawyers like you. Now they work. People live better lives. And you want to burn it down over old bodies? Old crimes?"

"He's using you."

Veronica's smile was a blade. "We're using each other. And we're winning. So take your folder, your righteous warnings, and your moral high ground—and fuck off. Cross us again, and you'll learn John's not the only one who finds permanent solutions to minor problems."

She slid into her Audi, engine roaring to life, and vanished up the ramp—leaving Janice standing alone in the stale concrete hush, folder in hand, wondering if she'd just been threatened by a mob wife or a true believer.

Both were deadly.

Together, they were untouchable. And Veronica Santiago—once a lowly CAM scraping by on fifty-four grand a year—was now the cover story in Community Management Executive Magazine.

"Community Management Executive of the Year," she said, holding up the issue with her photo on it. "Not bad for a girl who handled resident abuse and management neglect just a short while ago."

John Masters smiled from the executive couch in her new high-rise office. The view from the twentieth floor stretched over the Intracoastal and the sprawl of condos and subdivisions they now quietly controlled.

"You earned it. Regional dominance this fast is unheard of in this business."

"We earned it," she corrected. "It was always a partnership."

Her success wasn't just cosmetic. The condo, the car, the designer wardrobe, the corporate jet access—all were perks of real operational power. But the true triumph was structural: United didn't just manage neighborhoods—it ran them. Every vendor, every contract, every capital project funneled through United's oversight. Residents saw better amenities and rising home values. HOA boards saw headaches vanish. Nobody questioned the system producing such tangible results.

"Five years from now," Veronica mused, scanning the expansion map, "we'll control the entire Southeast. A monopoly hidden behind free-market competition."

"Think bigger," John said. "HOAs coast to coast. Once they rely on us for security, capital improvements, and compliance, we're untouchable. And property values give us political clout without needing a single vote."

She leaned down and kissed him—ambition and seduction mixing as one.

"To the empire."

"To the empire," he echoed. "Long may it reign."

Outside, South Florida's subdivisions hummed under United's new rule: peaceful streets, pristine common areas, efficient dispute resolution—and invisible control from the twentieth floor.

Residents slept easy, grateful for the order. They didn't realize they were no longer homeowners but subjects. In John Masters' world, that was a fair trade for perfection.

Their quiet hostile takeover of suburbia advanced daily: one HOA at a time, one capital project at a time, one subtle loyalty test at a time. And anyone who resisted found out what Earl Morrison, Levi Grant, and Richard Plevin had learned the hard way:

In Florida, John Masters and Veronica Santiago cast the longest shadows. And shadows, properly managed, can swallow entire worlds.

Weeks later, standing on the balcony of a private oceanfront resort overlooking the Atlantic, Veronica raised her champagne glass. "To the empire."

"To the empire," John agreed. "And to the people who trust us to build it."

Fifty-two communities, thousands of units, and skyrocketing property values. It was a success by any measure, built through competence, maintained through loyalty, and financed by the kind of systematic profit extraction that would have impressed his old Cleveland associates. John and Veronica had transformed Sarah Winters from a struggling lifestyle blogger to the editor-in-chief of their media empire that shaped opinion across their communities. United Living Magazine—a glossy publication that arrived monthly in thousands of resident mailboxes. Unsurprisingly, it focused on the transformation happening throughout their properties. The ministry of perception was making things look pretty good. And it was all paid for by advertising sponsored by United's contractor network, paying tribute to the company that was underwriting their Bentleys.

The Turnaround Formula

United Community's turnaround formula was deceptively simple but executed with military precision. The moment John Masters' team took control of a failing community, the checklist came out—and nothing was left to chance.

Step one: Light everything up. Every dark corner, parking lot, alley, and side yard got high-efficiency LED floodlights. United's engineers made sure residents could walk a dog at midnight and feel like they were strolling at high noon. Safety first—and nothing made people feel safer than bright lights that pushed shadows out of hiding.

Step two: Landscaping the John Masters way. His trusted landscaper, Emilio Sanchez, made it an art form. Emilio and his crew would slip deep into the Everglades, uproot the healthiest palms and tropicals they could find, then truck them back under cover of night. Queens Point had been the first test case: in a single weekend, dull, dying hedges were replaced with lush foliage that looked like a five-star resort.

Step three: Total security overhaul. State-of-the-art cameras blanketed every entrance, parking lot, hallway, and blind spot—all piped live to United's new monitoring center. Residents got mandatory Ring doorbell cameras on every unit—funded, installed, and remotely monitored by United's security team. If something moved where it shouldn't, Masters' people saw it before the local cops did.

Step four: Fix the perimeter. Broken fences, rotting gates, and crumbling walls were rebuilt or replaced entirely. Every crack sealed, every vulnerability closed. Nothing said "safe community" like a fortress you didn't realize you were living inside.

Step five: Upgrade the lifestyle. Pools resurfaced, rec centers renovated, new high-end playgrounds that looked like they were lifted from a theme park (and some of them were). Fresh paint, structural repairs, and hurricane-proof windows, shutters, and doors that could shrug off a Category 5 storm. Owners felt protected—because they were.

Step six: The final reveal—the clubhouse. Always the last piece. While the rest of the neighborhood transformed visibly week by week, the clubhouse stayed boarded up behind temporary fences. Residents whispered about what was happening inside—until opening day, when they discovered a designer interior worthy of a boutique hotel, complete with a staffed lounge, event space, and on-site concierge. It became the crown jewel of the turnaround, a subtle reminder that United delivered what it promised.

Step Seven: The quiet real estate grab. Behind the security upgrades and luxury amenities, John Masters ran an invisible play:

picking up abandoned, fire-damaged, or squatter-filled units for pennies on the dollar. Sometimes they "found" the previous owners; sometimes they didn't. The shell LLCs that filed the deeds were untraceable to United. Once the community was cleaned up and reimagined, those same units were renovated and sold off at many times their "purchase" price—tidy profits that never showed up on United's books but always funded the next acquisition.

All of this wasn't free—but it didn't feel crushing either. United used a calculated mix: tapping unused reserve funds, levying special assessments where needed, upping monthly fees, and, when the math required it, acquiring low-rate interest-only bank loans secured by the communities that were back-end loaded, when the balloon kicked in five years later. Insurance companies jumped into the fray, competing with banks for preferred lender status. Monthly dues mostly stayed stable, after the big initial increase and then creeping up only slightly—usually less than local inflation—while property values shot through the roof.

Queens Point: the first proof

The test case at Queens Point stunned everyone—owners, realtors, and the local press. In under a year, what had been a sagging, half-vacant complex riddled with crime became one of Palm Beach County's most sought-after addresses. Units that had sat unsold for years were now commanding premiums. Realtors who once told buyers to "skip Queens Point" were now chasing listings door to door.

Most powerful of all? The residents themselves became United's fiercest defenders. Happy homeowners made the best marketing team money couldn't buy—because they didn't have to be paid to spread the gospel.

The Capital Improvement and Security Revolution

The turnaround at Millennial Village was United Community Management's proof that Queens Point was no accident. John

Masters' blueprint wasn't just theory but a systematic formula that could revive even the most neglected neighborhoods.

When United began implementing the plan, Millennial Village was a cautionary tale: gang graffiti on playground slides, swing sets rusted into scrap metal, potholes deep enough to total a car, and families fleeing in droves. Home values were in free fall, and the few residents left behind lived with deadbolts and crossed fingers.

At the first community meeting, John faced a packed clubhouse and delivered the new gospel.

"We're not here to patch holes and repaint swing sets. We're here to make sure the same problems never come back. This is comprehensive transformation—not a band-aid."

Then came the presentation: dazzling renderings of a reimagined Millennial Village. Disney-grade playgrounds. Smooth roads that looked borrowed from an airport runway. Security so advanced it would make a gated celebrity compound look sloppy.

Veronica laid out the math.

"The total investment is twelve point seven million dollars—funded through reserve funds, special assessments, borrowing facilities, and partnerships with vendors who share our vision."

What she didn't say was that every dollar moved through United's machine: management fees, construction markups, vendor rebates, and strategic "consulting" routed through layers of shell companies—a tidy side stream that funneled 30% of the project cost straight back to the empire they were building.

One resident, Patricia Williams—a nurse and the HOA's biggest cheerleader—asked the question on everyone's mind:

"How do we pay for this without bankrupting the neighborhood?"

John didn't miss a beat.

"Every dollar you put in today generates three dollars in increased property value tomorrow. It's not an expense—it's your best investment. Just look at Queens Point. Before the transition, the place was half empty, and you couldn't give it away. Once the board was replaced and management committed to the turnaround, units are in tight supply, and prices have gone through the roof. "

It wasn't a lie. Properly renovated communities in South Florida routinely saw resale values jump so high that the cost felt trivial in hindsight. And once residents saw new roofs, fresh paint, and sparkling pools, they stopped asking uncomfortable questions about invoices and balance sheets.

The Security Solution

But all the cosmetic upgrades in the world wouldn't matter if crime kept families locked behind deadbolts. That's where David Krauss came in.

Krauss, a former Army Ranger with a specialty in urban warfare, had been studying the gang problem at Harbor Gardens, United's other flagship project. His conclusion: it wasn't rocket science—just neglected basic security, emboldened street thugs, and zero real deterrent.

"Three core members," Krauss explained, pointing to grainy surveillance images taped to the conference room wall. "A dozen fringe kids. Operating out of vacant units, Earl's people never bothered to secure. Classic territorial intimidation."

"Earl avoided problems," Veronica said. "We solve them."

"Permanently," John agreed.

Krauss' fix was threefold.

Phase one: Eyes everywhere. New high-def cameras with facial recognition and motion sensors, all streaming to United's new security nerve center in downtown Boca Raton. Carefully placed informants inside the community.

Phase two: Legal squeeze—trespassing arrests, code violations, coordination with local cops who suddenly found budget for extra patrols.

Phase three: For the stubborn holdouts? Well…Krauss handled that personally.

Meanwhile, every resident's front door got a Ring camera—mandatory, installed and monitored by United's team. Fences were repaired, gates reinforced, entry points locked down tighter than a luxury condo tower.

Within six weeks, the gang had evaporated. A few ringleaders were picked up on old warrants, thanks to anonymous tips. Others moved on, persuaded by late-night conversations with Krauss about career development opportunities in other zip codes. Harbor Gardens went from "avoid after dark" to "safest block in the zip code" almost overnight.

"Problem solved," Krauss said, submitting his final report. "Permanently."

The Model: Fast, Visible, Unquestionable

Between the rapid-fire capital improvements and the ironclad security matrix, United's transformation recipe became legend in South Florida HOA circles. What had once been dying communities were now thriving showpieces—and nobody cared to look too closely at the margins or the methods.

One broken neighborhood at a time, John Masters and Veronica Santiago rewrote the rules of suburban living—making safety, beauty, and order look like prosperity and progress. And once a community signed on, there was no going back.

From Millennial Village to Harbor Gardens, the message was clear: If you want perfection—you pay United. And if you cross them—you pay another way.

The Communications Empire

Sarah Winters, their editor-in-chief of United Living, shaped opinions across their fifty-two communities, with more non-United communities on the way, showcasing the transformation happening throughout their properties.

"It's not propaganda if it's true," Sarah said, reviewing the latest issue. "Every success story we publish actually happened. Every improvement we highlight really exists. The truth always speaks for itself."

The magazine was beautifully produced—professional photography, compelling human-interest stories, detailed financial reporting that made United's fees seem like bargains compared to the value they delivered. Each issue reinforced the same message: United Community Management gets results that other companies can't match.

But the real influence came through digital channels. Facebook groups for every community, NextDoor presence, Instagram accounts that showcased daily improvements, even TikTok content that made HOA management seem aspirational rather than bureaucratic.

"We're not managing perception," John explained to his team. "We're creating reality through coordinated communication. Residents see improvements happening because improvements *are* happening. They share success stories because they're experiencing success."

Recently hired master hacker and digital support chief Tommy Rodriguez's analytics showed the impact. Resident satisfaction scores had increased by 73% across their communities. Property listing times had decreased by 45%. Most importantly, opposition voices had been marginalized not through suppression but through overwhelming positive content.

The Financial Innovation

The transformation of United's financial systems had been Veronica's personal obsession. Earl Morrison's approach to community finance had been primitive—collect assessments, pay bills, hope for the best, and always remember, you have the right to remain silent. United's new approach treated every community like a sophisticated investment portfolio that was expected to yield a highly positive rate of return, the more positive, the better—by whatever means necessary.

"We're not just managing properties and money," Veronica explained to the United board of directors—a carefully chosen group of business leaders who provided legitimacy without asking uncomfortable questions. "We're optimizing financial performance through strategic planning and professional execution."

The numbers were impressive. Under Earl's management, the average community in their portfolio had seen property values decline by 12% over five years while assessments increased by 30%. Under United's management, those same communities were seeing property values increase by 50–100% the first year and 15% annually thereafter, while assessment increases were held to inflation rates after the initial increase required to fund the improvements.

"How is this possible?" asked board member Nelly Foster, a retired bank executive who understood financial statements.

"Efficiency and scale," Veronica replied. "Instead of each community negotiating separately with vendors, we leverage our combined purchasing power. Instead of deferring maintenance until problems become emergencies, we implement preventive programs that cost less over time. Instead of accepting substandard service, we demand excellence and get it."

What she didn't mention was the sophisticated profit extraction happening through vendor "relationships." United's "preferred vendors" were often subsidiaries of shell companies that John and Veronica controlled. The communities got excellent service at competitive rates, but substantial profits flowed back to them through management fees and strategic partnerships. They proved that successful communities provide many more opportunities for side deals and profit extraction than failing ones.

"The result," Veronica continued, "is communities that improve continuously while generating sustainable profits for United. Everyone wins."

The Garland Problem

Eunice Garland had been watching United's expansion with growing alarm. Her new blog, "HOA Empire Watch," documented every acquisition, every transformation, every suspicious pattern she could identify. But she was sandboxed by Tommy. Her readership dropped to basically zero. He managed to get her blacklisted on Google and most major search engines. When everyone else is posting about new amenities and property value increases, her complaints about assessment structures sound petty."

Her twelve subscribers were mostly conspiracy theorists and cranks who made her legitimate concerns seem hysterical. Their outrageous user comments made Eunice look like a complete flake with zero credibility.

The breakthrough came when she connected United's vendor relationships to a network of shell companies registered in Delaware. The paperwork was complex but clear; money was flowing from community assessments through United to companies that existed only on paper, then disappearing into offshore accounts.

"It's brilliant," she admitted to herself, studying the financial flows on her laptop. "Completely legal, technically legitimate, but designed to extract maximum profit from every transaction."

Her latest blog post, "The United Empire: How One Company is Monopolizing South Florida HOAs," included detailed financial analysis and corporate structure diagrams. It was thorough, accurate, and ignored by everyone who mattered.

Until Agent Dale Harrison called.

"Ms. Garland, this is Agent Harrison with the FBI's Financial Crimes Unit. I understand you've been investigating United Community Management."

Eunice's hands trembled slightly. "I have."

"We've been monitoring some of the same activities. Would you be available for a meeting? There are aspects of this situation that go beyond HOA management. Federal aspects."

“When?”

“Tomorrow. Aventura Mall, parking garage, third level outside Macy’s. Noon. And Ms. Garland? Come alone. For your own safety.”

The Federal Interest

Agent Harrison was younger than Eunice had expected—early forties, with the careful eyes of someone who’d seen too many financial crimes. They met in his car, parked between a soccer mom’s SUV and a teenager’s Honda, the perfect cover for a conversation that could destroy United’s empire.

“What do you know about Max Vecchio?” Harrison asked without preamble.

Eunice felt her breath catch. “I know he became John Masters. I know he’s been building a criminal enterprise disguised as community management.”

“Do you know why he was in witness protection?”

“Cleveland mob. Financial crimes. He testified against organized crime figures.”

Harrison nodded. “Forty-seven convictions. Over two hundred million in asset forfeitures. The biggest RICO case in Ohio history. Max Vecchio was our star witness because he understood how modern organized crime actually worked—not through violence and intimidation, but through legitimate businesses and financial manipulation.”

“And now he’s using those skills to steal from retirees.”

“Now he’s using those skills to build something much more ambitious. We think United Community Management is the foundation for a new kind of criminal enterprise. Regional monopoly disguised as business success. Political influence through property values. The kind of operation that could corrupt local government, influence elections, and generate hundreds of millions in untraceable profits.”

Eunice felt the weight of what Harrison was describing. "What do you need from me?"

"Keep watching. Keep documenting. But be careful—Max Vecchio eliminated problems permanently in Cleveland. John Masters might do the same thing here."

"Are you going to arrest him?"

Harrison was quiet for a long moment. "That's complicated. Witness protection creates legal challenges. But if United's operations threaten federal interests, we have options."

As Eunice drove home, she understood that she was no longer just a concerned citizen exposing HOA corruption. She was an FBI informant investigating a criminal enterprise that reached from suburban Florida to federal courtrooms in Washington.

The empire John and Veronica had built was more dangerous than even she had realized.

The Celebration

The United Community Management annual meeting was held at the Marriott Harbor Beach Resort, with over 300 residents from their managed communities in attendance. It was part corporate presentation, part political rally, and part revival meeting—a celebration of transformation that reinforced every message they'd been broadcasting.

John took the stage to thunderous applause, wearing the navy suit that projected authority without arrogance. Behind him, a massive screen displayed before-and-after photos of their communities— visual proof of the miracles they'd accomplished.

"All to recently, many of you lived in communities that were failing," he began, his voice carrying easily through the ballroom. "Deferred maintenance, crumbling infrastructure, financial mismanagement, declining property values, security concerns that made you afraid in your own homes."

Nods throughout the audience. These people remembered the bad times.

"Today, you live in showcase communities that other HOAs try to emulate. Property values that have increased by an average of 28%, many even higher. Amenities that rival luxury resorts. Security that makes you feel safe, whether you're walking your dog at dawn or entertaining grandchildren at sunset."

The applause was genuine, sustained, grateful. These weren't paid supporters—they were residents who'd experienced dramatic improvements in their quality of life.

Veronica followed with a financial presentation that was both transparent and reassuring—total investments of $127 million across their communities. Property value increases that generated over $400 million in additional homeowner equity. Once renovated, assessment increases held to an average of 3.2% annually while neighboring communities struggled with double-digit increases.

"This is what professional management achieves," she concluded. "Not just maintaining communities but transforming them. Not just collecting fees but creating value."

The evening ended with testimonials from residents—unscripted, heartfelt expressions of gratitude that no marketing budget could purchase. Martha Maxwell talked about feeling safe for the first time in years. Bob Patterson described bringing his grandchildren to visit without embarrassment. Patricia Williams spoke about the pride she felt, showing friends her transformed community.

As residents mingled during the reception, John and Veronica worked the room like the political figures they'd become. Every handshake was remembered, every concern noted, every compliment filed away for future use.

"You've built something remarkable," said Nelly Foster, the retired bank executive on United's board. "This isn't just business success—it's social transformation."

"Thank you," John replied. "We're just giving communities what they deserve—competent management and genuine care."

Later, as they went to their suite overlooking the Atlantic, Veronica raised her champagne glass. "To the empire."

"To the empire," John agreed. "And to the people who trust us to build it."

United stood at fifty-two communities (with more on the way) — over 15,000 units. Property values were at all-time highs, and annual revenues were through the roof. It was success by any measure, built through competence, maintained through loyalty, and financed by the kind of systematic profit extraction that would have impressed Max's old Cleveland associates.

The only question was how much larger it could grow before someone with real power decided to stop them.

But tonight, overlooking the ocean that had brought him to this new life, Masters felt untouchable. The ministry of perception was working perfectly.

And perception, properly managed, could indeed become reality.

Chapter 5: The Tech Revolution

The Upgrade

When Earl Morrison reluctantly invested in technology, it failed spectacularly and threatened his ability to collect management fees. His approach to innovation was reactive at best, catastrophic at worst. The man who'd run United Community Management for three decades had embraced exactly three technological advances: fax machines in 1994, basic websites in 2003, and smartphones only after his flip phone literally fell apart in 2018.

"Look at this disaster," John Masters said, surveying United's IT infrastructure during his first week as strategic consultant. The computers were Windows XP machines that belonged in a museum. The phone system required actual cables and couldn't handle conference calls. The database was a collection of Excel spreadsheets stored on individual hard drives with no backup system.

"The only thing missing is a rotary phone," Veronica added, poking at a CRT monitor that was older than some of their employees.

John had been passionate about technology ever since Rose took him to that computer store in Ohio when he was a teen. He'd always stayed ahead of the curve—latest iPhone, iPad Pro, Mac Studio, whatever cutting-edge equipment could give him an advantage. His personal setup was worth more than Earl's entire IT budget for the past five years.

"This ends now," John had announced. "We're implementing a complete technology overhaul. State-of-the-art everything."

The transformation was immediate and comprehensive. Voice over IP phone systems that could handle hundreds of simultaneous calls. High-end PCs with 30-inch monitors that made staff productivity soar. Cloud-based databases that could be accessed from anywhere with triple authentication and military-grade security. Wi-Fi networks throughout all community facilities with enterprise-level bandwidth.

The staff was elated. Workers who'd been struggling with dial-up internet speeds suddenly had access to broadband connections that actually made their jobs enjoyable. The 30-inch monitors alone increased efficiency by 40%—employees could see entire spreadsheets, review multiple documents simultaneously, and read financial reports without squinting.

"This is incredible," said Patricia Valdez, United's senior administrative coordinator. "I can actually do my job now instead of fighting with equipment that predates my college graduation."

But the technology upgrade was just the foundation for John's real innovation: total information awareness disguised as community convenience.

The Digital Revolution

The conference room at United Community Management's newly expanded headquarters smelled of fresh paint and ambition. Twenty floors above downtown Boca Raton, floor-to-ceiling windows overlooked a kingdom that John Masters and Veronica Santiago were systematically conquering, one broken HOA at a time.

"Earl Morrison ran this company like it was still 1995," Veronica said, gesturing at the wall of state-of-the-art monitors Tommy Rodriguez was installing. "Paper files, Excel spreadsheets, a phone system that belonged in a museum. He had money in forgotten accounts that could have been put to good and profitable use. No wonder these communities were falling apart."

John studied the command center taking shape around them. Each screen would eventually display real-time data from their 52 communities: maintenance requests, financial flows, security camera feeds, even social media sentiment analysis. It was a level of technological sophistication that would have impressed Pentagon strategists.

"Earl's incompetence was our opportunity," John replied. "But competence without control is just expensive consulting. We're building something more powerful than management—we're building influence."

The team Veronica had assembled reflected their new ambitions. Glenn Sawyer, the failed political consultant, understood messaging and narrative control. Sarah Winters, the lifestyle blogger, had access to the social media networks that shaped suburban opinion. Tommy Rodriguez brought hacking skills that made government spook networks look amateur. And David Krauss, their new head of security, had twenty years of military experience that would prove invaluable in cleaning up the gang problems plaguing several communities.

"Perception is reality," John said, addressing his newly assembled communications team. "And reality is what we tell them it is."

He clicked to the first slide of his presentation—a map of South Florida showing their communities color-coded by transformation status. Green meant fully optimized. Yellow indicated work in progress. Red marked problem areas that required special attention. Since their last review, there were noticeably more green communities and fewer yellow and red ones.

"Every story has multiple angles," John continued. "We simply ensure residents see the right one. But more importantly, we ensure they participate in creating that story."

The Technology Infrastructure

Tommy Rodriguez had been working eighteen-hour days upgrading United's entire digital infrastructure. Earl Morrison's "system" had been a disaster—outdated software, unsecured networks, and data management that violated basic professional standards.

"Look at this," Tommy said, pulling up Earl's old resident database. "Names spelled wrong, missing contact information, financial records stored in random folders. How did anyone manage anything?"

"They didn't," Veronica replied. "They just collected fees and hoped nothing exploded. That's why these communities were dying."

The new system was a masterpiece of integration. Every resident had a comprehensive profile—not just contact information and payment history, but maintenance requests, compliance issues, family members, employment status, even social media activity. The financial modules tracked every dollar flowing through every community with real-time reporting that would satisfy the most demanding auditors.

But the real innovation was the project management system. Earl had handled capital improvements through handshake agreements and bar napkin contracts. United's new approach treated every project like a military operation—detailed planning, resource allocation, progress tracking, and quality control that guaranteed results.

"Harbor Gardens needs fourteen million in infrastructure work," John said, reviewing the engineering reports they'd commissioned. "New plumbing, electrical systems, road repairs, security upgrades. Under Earl's system, that would take five years and cost twenty million while half the money disappeared into vendor kickbacks."

"Under our system?" Veronica asked.

"Eighteen months, fourteen million total cost, and every dollar accounted for." John smiled. "Plus a 'reasonable' profit margin for United's management and oversight."

The profit margin was more than reasonable—it was substantial. But residents would get exactly what they paid for: dramatically improved communities that functioned like luxury resorts instead of subsidized housing for the elderly.

The Big Brother App

Tommy Rodriguez had never stopped working eighteen-hour days, even after fully updating United's computer systems. At 3 AM one morning, inspiration struck. The young hacker knew the truth better than anyone: the most powerful surveillance systems are the ones people install themselves—and a smartphone app was the ultimate Trojan horse for voluntary data collection.

"We need to talk," Tommy said, appearing in John's office with the manic energy of someone who'd been living on caffeine and stimulants and stumbled onto a world-altering idea. "I have something that changes everything."

John looked up from vendor contracts on his new Mac Studio.

"What kind of idea?"

"United Community needs an app. But not just any app—the most sophisticated community management and resident engagement platform ever built."

Tommy flipped open his laptop, revealing polished mockups he'd been developing in secret. The interface was flawless: clean, intuitive, easy enough for a retiree to navigate but powerful enough to run an entire neighborhood from a pocket.

"Residents pay dues, receive late payment notices, submit maintenance requests, check facility schedules, get hurricane alerts, talk to neighbors, access HOA docs—everything they need in one place. And we can even allow advertising which will help it pay for itself in the first month alone!"

John studied the screens—and instantly saw the real prize: absolute control disguised as convenience. "What else does it do?"

Tommy's smile turned predatory. "Everything."

"But what's the cost?" asked John.

"I can get a team on it tomorrow. You're looking at $495,000 complete with monthly upgrades and around $175,000 per year for updates and system maintenance, said Tommy, calming down from the caffeine induced euphoria.

John said, "Let's do it now and there's a $100,000 bonus if its completed within 30 days for you. We will be billing every HOA, $4.99 per resident, per month in licensing fees. This will bring in 7 figures per year and that's before the inflation adjustments. And

Tommy, you are now officially Vice President of Digital Infrastructure. Now get back to work."

The Surveillance Architecture

Behind the friendly icons and pastel color scheme, Tommy had embedded a data-harvesting system that would make the NSA envious. The app requested permissions that seemed harmless: contacts for a resident directory, location for facility check-ins, camera and microphone access for voice commands and maintenance photos.

Once installed, it quietly became an all-seeing sentinel.

"It tracks every website visited, every call made, every text sent," Tommy demonstrated on the admin dashboard. "Cookies integrate with social media—we map Facebook groups, political leanings, shopping habits, even dating app behavior."

Geolocation took it further: not just where residents went, but who they met, how long they stayed, and whether their routines matched their claims. Combined with United's expanding network of facial recognition cameras, it painted a live, precise portrait of every resident's day.

"And the real genius," Tommy continued, eyes gleaming," is the environmental monitoring. With permissions, we can activate microphones and cameras remotely—officially for emergencies, fall detection, medical crises."

John raised an eyebrow. "Unofficially?"

"Unofficially, we can listen in, watch, and gather intel no normal surveillance could touch."

John grasped the scale instantly. This wasn't just community management—this was total information dominance.

The Legal Cloak

Veronica, standing by the door, asked the obvious question: "Privacy laws? Consent? Lawsuits?"

"We're bulletproof," Tommy said. "It's all buried in the terms of service (TOS). 'Community safety and service optimization.' They tap 'I agree'—that's consent. It's all legal, all disclosed. Nobody reads forty-seven pages of fine print."

Features Residents Would Beg For

To the average resident, the app was a miracle. Instant alerts for storms and break-ins. Doorbell cam notifications, emergency contact info, and disaster preparation. A clean calendar for rec center bookings and HOA events. The new 911 shortcut linked emergencies directly to United's security hub, cutting response times by more than half.

"Mrs. Patterson had her heart attack," David Krauss reported after the first rollout, "and we had paramedics at her door in four minutes instead of twelve. The system saves lives."

Beta testing proved the fall detection worked: accelerometers and AI flagged medical crises before family members even knew. In the board's eyes, it was a marvel. For Tommy, it was the perfect cover for unprecedented data mining and harvesting.

The Behavioral Engine

The app's secret core, known only to Tommy, John, and Veronica, was its behavioral analysis engine—an AI that built psychological profiles for every resident. It tracked chats, payments, social posts, and even the tone of voice during calls, then scored each user based on their loyalty to United's management.

Tommy pulled up a sample on the dashboard: "Martha Kowalski: Highly Loyal, 94% certainty. Attends events, posts positively, never complains—she's a Community Champion."

One click later: "Eunice Garland: Potential Disruptor, 87% probability. Less social, private messages with other skeptics, negative sentiment in posts. We watch her."

Veronica scrolled through the flags, both impressed and unnerved: "We can see trouble before it even starts."

"And fix it before it does," John added. "Redirect, neutralize, convert—clean and quiet."

The Political Engine

It didn't stop at the HOA's doorstep. The app's political reach extended into real-world influence: voting histories, donations, party leanings, city council interactions—all mapped, predicted, and leveraged.

"We know how every resident votes," Tommy bragged, pulling up color-coded precincts. "Harbor Gardens is 78% likely to back the tax hike. Millennial Village is 82% against. For any issue important to United, we can target messages accordingly and embed them into the advertising engine."

It was a data mining paradise—disguised as a neighborhood app.

The Privacy Paradox

The most disturbing part? Residents loved it.

They raved about app features at meetings. They pushed reluctant neighbors to install it. They even demanded upgrades: sleep tracking, wellness monitoring, daily health scores.

"We're giving them exactly what they crave," John said. "Safety, connection, status. At the expense of all their data. The residents are the product."

The Compliance Engine

When the app heard a dog bark, it cross-checked the pet registry. Parking GPS flagged violations before the neighbor could snitch. Noise sensors detected parties during quiet hours and auto-sent polite reminders.

No more angry fines—just a friendly nudge. Compliance soared. Complaints vanished. Residents thanked United for protecting community harmony.

The Citizen Score

Tommy's final masterstroke was the Citizenship Evaluation System or CES.

Each resident got a live score. Good behavior moved them from Bronze to Silver to the coveted Gold—unlocking perks like event invites, early facility booking, and glossy features in United Living Magazine.

Martha Kowalski hit 97. She became a living PR machine, praising United at meetings, social feeds, and parties.

Patricia Williams, a Silver-tier climber, cut her complaints and doubled her positive posts. Bronze residents got polite recognition to keep them quiet—no push to do more, just enough to feel seen.

"It's high school all over again," muttered Dorothy Kim, demoted after questioning a vendor contract. "Except your GPA is loyalty to United."

The Empire's Social Contract

The old Max Vecchio would have been envious. No more broken knees, no blackmail—just brilliant psychological hooks that made people crave constant surveillance.

"We built a panopticon (a prison with cells arranged in a circle, so that the people in them can be seen at all times from the center)," John told Veronica one night, watching usage stats hit record highs. "A prison where the inmates beg for more cameras, not fewer."

And the residents lined up to thank him for the privilege.

Orwell warned that Big Brother would always be watching. United proved Big Brother doesn't just watch—he guides you, shapes you, and trains you to be the perfect citizen.

And you love him and thank him for it.

Chapter 6: The Pickleball Empire

The Discovery

John Masters first encountered pickleball on a Tuesday morning at Harbor Gardens, where three elderly residents had improvised a court using badminton nets and what appeared to be ping-pong paddles the size of dinner plates. The sight should have been amusing—septuagenarians darting around a tennis court, swinging oversized paddles at a plastic ball that sounded like a maraca when hit.

Instead, John felt the familiar flutter of opportunity recognizing itself.

"What exactly are you playing?" he asked Martha Kowalski, who was taking a water break after what she claimed was her "morning warm-up."

"Pickleball," she said, her face flushed with exertion and enthusiasm. "It's like tennis, but better. Easier on the joints, more strategy, way more fun. My daughter taught me when I visited her in Arizona."

John watched the other players continue their game. They were moving constantly, clearly engaged, displaying more energy than he'd seen from residents during any other community activity. More importantly, they were paying for the privilege—Martha mentioned her new paddle had cost $89, and she was considering upgrading to a $150 model.

"How often do you play?" John asked.

"Every day," Martha replied. "Sometimes twice a day. There's a whole group of us now—twelve people who've gotten obsessed. We're trying to talk the board into converting one of the tennis courts, but you know how that goes."

John did know. The tennis courts at every United Community Management property were monuments to inefficiency—expensive to maintain, rarely used, taking up premium real estate that could be generating revenue instead of consuming it. At Harbor Gardens, the four tennis courts saw maybe six hours of actual play per week while consuming thousands of dollars annually in maintenance, resurfacing, and liability insurance.

But if residents were willing to play pickleball every day, multiple times per day, and pay premium prices for equipment...

"Tell me more about this game," John said.

The Research Phase

Within 48 hours, John had compiled a comprehensive analysis of the pickleball phenomenon that was sweeping Florida and the nation. What he discovered was both amusing and alarming: the fastest-growing sport in America was sending elderly players to emergency rooms at unprecedented rates.

"Look at these statistics," Veronica said, reviewing his research in United's conference room. "Pickleball-related injuries increased 400% last year. Torn Achilles tendons, broken hips, shoulder dislocations. It's like a geriatric gladiator arena."

"And they love it," John replied, scrolling through social media posts from pickleball enthusiasts. "They're getting injured and going right back to play. It's addictive."

The medical data painted a clear picture: elderly people in questionable physical condition were convinced that a sport involving quick lateral movements, sudden stops, and aggressive reaching was somehow "easy on the joints." Emergency rooms across South Florida were treating pickleball injuries that ranged from minor sprains to major orthopedic surgeries.

"It makes no sense," Veronica continued. "Why would someone with arthritis and balance issues think rapid direction changes are a good idea?"

"Because they're having fun," John said. "And people will risk anything for fun, especially when they're isolated, bored, and trying to feel young again." John had a brief flashback to his Cleveland days. The mob was known as the caterers of life, providing their customers with prostitution, strippers, gambling, and drugs, all in the name of pleasure.

But John didn't care about the medical implications. What interested him was the economic potential. Pickleball equipment was expensive, courts required specialized surfaces, and players were willing to pay for instruction, league fees, tournament entry costs, and premium facility access. The sport was generating revenue streams that traditional tennis never achieved.

More importantly, it solved his tennis court problem efficiently. The underutilized courts that consumed maintenance budgets could be converted to pickleball facilities that generated income while increasing resident satisfaction.

"This is our next major initiative," John announced. "We're going to become the premier pickleball destination in South Florida."

The Business Model

John's financial genius had always operated through systematic analysis of opportunity and methodical exploitation of market inefficiencies. Pickleball represented both—a growing market with minimal professional infrastructure and customers willing to pay premium prices for quality experiences.

He spent the weekend designing what would become Pickleball of South Florida, a comprehensive business model that would transform United's tennis courts from cost centers into profit generators. Tommy created a dedicated Pickleball of South Florida app. It collected fees, reserved courts, scheduled lessons and clinics, and monitored residents' play so that injuries could be detected and impending health risks could be calculated. Understanding that most residents wouldn't have their phones on the courts, he created a smartwatch app that handled all the tracking for them. United started giving out the watches as a premium for memberships and lesson packages. Pretty soon, virtually all the pickleball players had smartwatches.

"We're not just adding pickleball courts," he explained to Veronica as they reviewed his business plan. "We're creating a complete ecosystem. Courts, instruction, leagues, tournaments, equipment sales, private lessons, clinics, even corporate events, and, of course, comprehensive monitoring."

The financial projections were staggering. Converting existing tennis courts would cost approximately $15,000 per court—minimal compared to the revenue potential. Court rental fees, lesson charges, league registrations, and tournament entry costs could generate $5,000–$7500 annually per court, while equipment sales and pro shop operations added additional revenue streams.

"Multiply that across fifty-two communities," John continued, "and we're looking at over two million annually in direct revenue, plus indirect benefits from increased property values and resident satisfaction."

But the real genius was in the structure. Pickleball of South Florida would be nominally independent and of course a nonprofit entity—that contracted with United's communities for facility management and programming. This created distance between United and the revenue extraction while maintaining control over operations.

"We need someone to run it," Veronica said. "Someone with credibility in racquet sports but flexible enough to follow directions."

John smiled. "I know exactly the person."

The Tennis Pro

Ken Burdick had been pestering John about pickleball for months, but until now he had been ignored. The former tennis professional had never quite achieved tour-level success, but his forty years in racquet sports had taught him to recognize trends. He'd been teaching pickleball lessons at Queens Point on an informal basis, using the tennis courts during off-peak hours and splitting fees with the community.

"John, this sport is exploding," Ken said during their meeting at the Queens Point clubhouse. "I've got a waiting list of thirty people who want lessons. Martha Kowalski plays four hours a day, and she's talking about entering tournaments. These people are obsessed."

Ken was perfect for John's purposes—enthusiastic about the sport, desperate for steady income, and naive about business operations. His tennis credentials provided legitimacy, while his financial situation guaranteed compliance with whatever structure John implemented.

"I want to offer you something bigger than lessons," John said. "How would you like to be the founder and president of Pickleball of South Florida?"

Ken's eyes widened. "You're serious?"

"Completely serious. We're going to build the premier pickleball operation in the state. Professional courts, certified instruction, league play, tournaments that draw players from across the Southeast. You'd be the face of the operation, the name on the door, the expert everyone comes to for pickleball excellence."

John outlined the opportunity: Ken would receive a base salary of $75,000 annually, plus percentages of revenue from lessons, leagues, and tournaments. He'd have a company car, expense account, and the kind of professional recognition that had eluded him during his tennis career.

"What's the catch?" Ken asked, because forty years in the sports industry had taught him that offers this good always came with conditions.

"No catch," John replied. "You run the day-to-day operations, manage the instructors, coordinate with communities. I handle the business side—finances, expansion, strategic planning. You do what you love, I do what I'm good at."

Ken agreed immediately, not understanding that he was signing up to be the public face of an operation designed to extract maximum profit from elderly people's recreational obsessions. But he didn't need to understand the business model—he just needed to execute it.

The Merchandise Opportunity

The next challenge was equipment procurement. Pickleball required specialized paddles, balls, nets, court surfaces, and accessories that were expensive when purchased through traditional retail channels. But John's Cleveland background had taught him that every legitimate business could benefit from creative supply chain management.

That's when Manny Gonzales came to his attention.

The small-time gangster had pulled off what authorities called the "Port Everglades Great Pickleball Heist"—an unsophisticated theft that netted hundreds of thousands of dollars' worth of nets, rackets, balls, clothing, and accessories from a shipping container that had been sitting unguarded for three days. Manny had inside information about the shipment and timing but lacked the business connections to move the merchandise efficiently.

"He's sitting on inventory with a retail value of four hundred thousand," Tommy Rodriguez reported during their weekly briefing. "But he's trying to sell it through pawn shops and flea markets. Getting maybe thirty cents on the dollar."

John saw opportunity where others saw crime. Manny had solved United's supply chain problem while creating his own distribution challenge. A simple transaction could benefit everyone involved while providing Pickleball of South Florida with a substantial competitive advantage.

The meeting was arranged at a Denny's in Pompano Beach— neutral territory where a legitimate businessman could theoretically encounter a struggling entrepreneur without raising suspicions. Manny was younger than John had expected, mid-thirties with the nervous energy of someone who'd made a big score but didn't know how to cash out safely.

"I understand you have inventory that might interest me," John said, ordering coffee and projecting the calm authority of someone who'd negotiated deals in much more dangerous circumstances.

"Depends what you're looking for," Manny replied, studying John's business attire and wondering if he was talking to a cop, a customer, or a competitor.

"Pickleball equipment. Large quantities, competitive pricing, no questions about provenance."

Manny relaxed slightly. "I got paddles, balls, nets, clothing, shoes—everything you need to stock a pro shop. High-end stuff, retail value maybe four hundred K."

"What are you looking for?"

"Cash deal, quick transaction, clean exit." Manny leaned forward. "I got heat, you know? Need to relocate, start fresh somewhere else."

John had expected this. Manny's theft had been effective, but he left tracks—security cameras, witnesses, and physical evidence would eventually lead to arrest warrants. The smart move was converting merchandise to cash and disappearing before law enforcement connected the dots.

"Ten thousand cash," John offered. "Plus, a one-way ticket to Santo Domingo and documentation that gets you through airport security without complications."

It was a fraction of the merchandise value, but Manny was getting more than money—he was purchasing freedom from prosecution and a chance to start over in a country without extradition treaties.

"That's less than 10% of retail," Manny protested.

"Retail assumes legitimate sales channels and customer access," John replied. "You're wholesaling stolen merchandise to someone who's taking all the risk for moving it. Ten thousand buys you a clean exit and lets you sleep without worrying about federal agents."

Manny considered his options. Prison versus poverty in the Dominican Republic wasn't a difficult choice.

"Deal," he said.

The Implementation

Within three months, United's communities had been transformed into pickleball destinations that would have impressed country club developers. Professional courts with regulation surfaces, premium nets, and lighting systems that allowed evening play. Pro shops stocked with high-end equipment that Manny had provided at below wholesale prices. Instruction programs led by Ken Burdick and a team of certified professionals who understood both the sport and customer service.

"This is incredible," Martha Kowalski said, testing her new paddle on the freshly surfaced courts at Harbor Gardens. "It's like having a private club in our own community."

The transformation was comprehensive. Each community received 4–6 pickleball courts, depending on available space and resident interest. Leagues were organized by skill level and age group, ensuring that beginners weren't intimidated while competitive players had appropriate challenges. Tournaments attracted participants from neighboring communities, generating revenue while building United's reputation as the premier pickleball destination in South Florida.

But the real success was in the revenue generation. Court rental fees, lesson charges, league registrations, tournament entries, equipment sales, and pro shop profits created multiple income streams that flowed through Pickleball of South Florida to United Community Management.

"We're generating over \$140,000 monthly across all properties," Veronica reported during their quarterly review. "Annual projections show we'll hit two million in direct revenue, plus indirect benefits from increased property values and reduced maintenance costs."

The maintenance savings were substantial. Tennis courts required expensive resurfacing, net replacement, and specialized cleaning that pickleball courts didn't need. The increased usage meant residents were actively maintaining facilities through their participation rather than United bearing full responsibility for upkeep.

"Plus," John added, "resident satisfaction scores have increased by 40% in communities with pickleball facilities. People are happier, more active, more engaged with community life."

It was another example of John's business philosophy: the best operations provided genuine value while generating maximum profit. Residents got world-class recreational facilities and programming. United got substantial revenue and reduced costs. Even Ken Burdick was earning more money than he'd ever made in tennis instruction.

The Expansion

The success at United's communities attracted attention from other HOAs throughout South Florida. Property managers were calling daily, requesting information about pickleball facility development and programming services. Ken Burdick was being invited to speak at industry conferences about recreational facility optimization.

"We're getting requests from communities in Palm Beach, Miami-Dade, even as far north as Jacksonville," Ken reported during their monthly planning meeting. "Everyone wants what we've built."

John saw opportunity in the external demand. Pickleball of South Florida could expand beyond United's properties, contracting with other communities for facility development and program management. This would generate even more revenue while establishing United as the industry leader in recreational facility innovation.

"But we maintain exclusivity within our communities," John insisted. "Our residents get premium access, preferred scheduling, member pricing. External communities get standard service at market rates."

The expansion model was elegant. Pickleball of South Florida would design and install courts for other communities, then provide ongoing management services including instruction, leagues, tournaments, and equipment sales. United's residents would receive benefits that reinforced their decision to live in professionally managed communities.

"It's a competitive advantage," Veronica explained to United's board of directors. "Residents choose our communities partly because of amenities that other HOAs can't provide. Pickleball is becoming our signature offering."

The financial impact was even more significant than projected. Pickleball operations were soon generating over $2.5 million annually in direct revenue, with kickbacks and skimmed profits flowing through shell companies back to United's operations. Equipment sales alone were producing six-figure profits through Manny's discounted inventory and premium retail pricing.

The Unintended Consequences

The only downside was the injury rate, which continued climbing as elderly residents pushed themselves beyond reasonable physical limits in pursuit of pickleball excellence. Emergency rooms throughout South Florida were treating increasing numbers of pickleball-related injuries, from minor sprains to major orthopedic emergencies.

"Martha Kowalski tore her ACL last week," Ken reported with obvious concern. "She's seventy-four and was playing four hours a day. Her doctor said the injury was consistent with aggressive athletic activity by someone half her age."

"Is she okay?" John asked, though his concern was more about liability than Martha's welfare.

"She'll recover, but she'll need surgery and months of physical therapy. The scary part is she's already talking about getting back on the court as soon as possible."

John understood the psychology. Pickleball provided elderly residents with something they'd lost—competitive engagement, social interaction, and physical challenges that made them feel vital and young. The fact that their bodies couldn't handle the demands was irrelevant compared to the psychological benefits.

"We need comprehensive liability waivers," John decided. "Medical clearances for anyone over sixty. Insurance coverage that protects United and Pickleball of South Florida from injury claims."

"What about limiting playing time or requiring rest periods?" Ken suggested.

"What about personal responsibility?" John replied. "These are adults making informed decisions about their recreational activities. We provide safe facilities and professional instruction. What they do with those resources is their choice."

It was a cold calculation, but John had learned in Cleveland that business success required separating emotional considerations from financial realities. Pickleball was generating substantial profits while providing genuine recreational value. The fact that some participants were injuring themselves was unfortunate but not actionable.

The liability waivers were comprehensive, requiring medical clearances and explicit acknowledgment of injury risks. Insurance coverage was expanded to protect United and its subsidiaries from potential claims. Legal counsel confirmed that properly documented recreational programs created minimal exposure as long as facilities were maintained, instruction was professional, and the liability waivers were airtight.

The Empire Expands

By year-end, Pickleball of South Florida had become the largest recreational sports operation in the region. All fifty-two United communities featured world-class pickleball facilities. External contracts with twenty-two additional HOAs provided design, installation, and management services. Ken Burdick had been featured in industry publications as an innovator in community recreation programming.

"This is bigger than I ever imagined," Ken said during their annual planning meeting. "We're not just providing recreation—we're creating community. People are making friendships, staying active, finding purpose in retirement."

John nodded, reviewing financial reports that showed Pickleball of South Florida generating over two million annually, while providing cover for additional profit extraction through vendor "relationships" and management fees. It was his most successful legitimate business operation, proving that suburban residents would pay premium prices for quality recreational programming.

"What's next?" Veronica asked. "Tennis? Golf? Swimming?"

"Pickleball was unique because it solved multiple problems simultaneously," John replied. "Underutilized facilities, inactive residents, revenue generation, competitive differentiation. We need to find the next opportunity that provides the same comprehensive benefits."

But for now, pickleball was enough. The operation had transformed United's communities into destinations that attracted active retirees willing to pay premium assessments for premium amenities. Property values had increased across all facilities, wait lists had developed for available units, and resident satisfaction scores far exceeded industry benchmarks.

The residents were thrilled with their world-class recreational facilities. Ken Burdick was earning more money than he'd ever dreamed possible. United was generating substantial profits while providing legitimate value.

And John Masters had proven once again that the most successful criminal enterprises were the ones that didn't look criminal at all. The pickleball empire was complete, profitable, and perfectly legal. Just the way Max Vecchio had always preferred his operations—efficient, profitable, and impossible to prosecute.

Even when someone inevitably got hurt.

Chapter 7: The Benevolent Fixer

The Mathematics of Mercy

Mrs. Dorothy Anderson's foreclosure notice arrived on a Tuesday, the same day her wheelchair ramp finally gave out. John Masters found her crying on her front steps, unable to get into her own home, the pink legal notice crumpled in her arthritic hands.

"Mrs. Anderson," John said, approaching with calculated concern. Max Senior, the retired military Belgium Malinois, strained at his leash, sensing distress with the engineered empathy John himself lacked. "What's wrong?"

Dorothy looked up, tears cutting channels through her makeup. Seventy-three years old, widowed, living on social security and her husband's meager pension. She'd been a music teacher once, before arthritis stole her piano and poverty stole her dignity.

"I'm going to lose my home," she whispered, holding up the notice. "Six months behind. They're starting proceedings. And now I can't even get inside."

John studied the ramp—rotted wood, rusted bolts, a lawsuit waiting to happen. Then he looked at the notice—$3,847 in back assessments, late fees, attorney charges. Compound interest turning misfortune into catastrophe. The inefficiency of it offended him more than the cruelty.

"Let me help you inside first," he said, lifting her with surprising gentleness. She weighed nothing, bird bones and resignation. He settled her in her recliner, noting the expired medications, the stack of past-due bills, the photographs of a life that had been larger.

"I'll make some calls," he said.

"I can't pay," Dorothy protested. "I can barely afford food."

"I didn't ask for payment."

Within two hours, John had restructured Dorothy's entire life. The back assessments were transferred to a payment plan with zero interest—he'd eat the cost personally rather than let the inefficiency persist. A contractor arrived to install a new ramp, aluminum and concrete, built to last longer than Dorothy would. Her medications were refilled through a program Veronica had found, legitimate but underutilized.

"Why?" Dorothy asked as John reviewed the paperwork with her. "Why help me?"

John looked at her, running calculations. The truth—that her suffering was a systemic inefficiency that offended his need for order—wouldn't translate. So he offered a different truth, one she could digest.

"Because strong communities take care of their most vulnerable members," he said. "And because you'll remember this. When others ask about United Community, about the changes we're making, you'll tell them the truth. Won't you?"

Dorothy nodded eagerly, already composing testimonials in her head. "Of course. Anything. You saved my life."

No, John thought, watching gratitude transform her face. *I optimized it.*

That evening, he made a note in Dorothy's file: "Investment: $4,347. Return: Vocal advocate, intelligence source, living propaganda. ROI: Infinite."

Compassion was just lubrication for the gears of control.

The Uber Equation

Bruce Gordon's Honda CRX died at 247,000 miles, expiring in the Millennial Village parking lot with a grinding mechanical scream that sounded almost human. John found him kicking the tire, a gesture as futile as it was understandable.

"Fucking piece of shit!" Bruce shouted, then noticed John. "Sorry, Mr. Masters. Bad morning."

John recognized Bruce from the resident files—forty-four, divorced, two kids he saw on weekends, working three jobs to make child support. Uber driver, DoorDash delivery, weekend security guard. The kind of man ground down by systematic inefficiency, bleeding productivity through exhaustion.

"Car trouble?" John asked, though the answer was obvious.

"Car death," Bruce corrected. "Transmission finally went. That's...that's all my income. Gone." He laughed bitterly. "Guess I'll be the one walking next month when I can't make rent on this condo."

John walked around the Honda, noting the bald tires, the rust cancer, the duct tape holding the bumper. Transportation poverty—a perfect example of how being poor was expensive. Bruce probably spent more maintaining this wreck than on lease payments for something reliable.

"You drive Uber full-time?"

"Forty, fifty hours a week. More during season." Bruce slumped against the dead car. "Made enough to survive. Without it..."

John did quick math. Bruce's Uber income, minus gas and maintenance. His child support obligations. His rent at Millennial Village. The cascade failure of losing transportation. One broken transmission destroying an entire life architecture.

"Come with me," John said.

At the used car lot, Bruce stood frozen as John negotiated with the dealer. Not for charity—John didn't do charity. But Bruce was a resident, and resident instability was community instability. A desperate man might steal. A homeless man definitely would. Better to invest in prevention.

"2018 Toyota RAV4," the dealer said. "One owner, 37,500 original miles, full service history. Perfect for ride-share."

"I can't afford—" Bruce started.

"You'll pay me back," John interrupted. "Hundred a month, no interest. Skip payments when things are tight. The car stays in my name until it's paid off."

It was predatory lending dressed as kindness. Bruce would pay forever, grateful for the chain. But he'd also have income, stability, and the ability to function. And he'd tell everyone about John Masters, the HOA president who saved him when banks wouldn't.

"Why?" Bruce asked, signing papers with shaking hands.

"Because you're a good father," John lied smoothly. The truth—that a stable resident was a predictable resident, and predictability was control—wouldn't inspire the loyalty he needed. "And good fathers deserve a chance."

Bruce broke down crying. John patted his shoulder, feeling nothing but satisfaction at a problem solved. Another gear in his machine, oiled and functional.

That night, John updated Bruce's file: "Car loan: $8,500. Terms: Indefinite. Return: Permanent loyalty, community intelligence, mobile advertisement. Status: Owned."

Every kindness was an investment. Every investment paid dividends.

The Golden Retriever Gambit

Jose Suarez hadn't smiled in three weeks, not since Pepper died. The ancient chihuahua had been his only family, his reason to get up, his excuse to walk the grounds of Harbor Gardens every morning. Without the dog, Jose was just another lonely widower counting pills and waiting for the end.

John noticed the change in routine. Jose's morning walks had been predictable—7:15 AM, counterclockwise around the complex, thirty-two minutes exactly. Their absence created a gap in John's surveillance patterns, but more importantly, it signaled resident deterioration. Depression was contagious. One visibly declining resident could spiral into community-wide malaise.

He found Jose on his porch, staring at nothing. Seventy-eight years old, veteran, no children, just a pension and loneliness.

"Morning, Jose."

Jose looked up, surprised. People had stopped greeting him since Pepper died. "Mr. Masters. Sorry, I haven't been walking. I know you like us to keep active."

"I heard about Pepper. I'm sorry."

Jose's eyes welled. "Sixteen years. She was all I had left."

John sat on the porch step, a calculated gesture of equality. He thought of Rose, his adoptive mother, and her endless faith as he felt for her rosary beads in his pocket. She would have hugged Jose, offered prayers, genuine comfort. John could only offer solutions.

"Have you thought about another dog?"

"Can't afford it: adoption fees, vet bills, food. Pepper ate my scraps. A new dog..." Jose shrugged. "Fixed income."

John made a decision. Not from empathy—he felt Jose's pain the way a mechanic feels engine knock, as a problem requiring repair. But problems unsolved were inefficiencies, and inefficiencies were intolerable.

The next morning, John knocked on Jose's door, holding a leash attached to a golden retriever puppy. Eight weeks old, all paws and enthusiasm, a $2,000 bundle of therapeutic energy.

"His name's Max Jr.," John said. "After my dog. He needs a home."

Jose stared. "I can't—"

"First year's vet care is covered. Food too. Call it a community wellness initiative." John handed over the leash. "He needs walking. Every morning. Seven-fifteen."

The puppy launched itself at Jose, all tongue and love, and the old man's defensive walls crumbled. He dropped to his knees, gathering the dog like a life preserver, sobbing into golden fur.

"Why?" Jose asked between tears. "Why do this?"

John watched the bonding with clinical satisfaction. "Because happy residents make happy communities. And because you'll train him well. When people ask about him, you'll tell them where he came from. Won't you?"

"Everyone," Jose promised. "Everyone will know what you did."

What I did, John thought, *was eliminate a failure point in my system.*

Within a week, Jose was back on his morning walks, now stopping every few yards as neighbors cooed over the puppy. Each interaction spread the story: John Masters, who cared enough to notice a lonely old man, who spent his own money to heal a broken heart.

John's file on Jose was updated: "Dog investment: $2,000 plus $150/month maintenance. Return: Restored routine, community morale boost, living testimonial, enhanced surveillance coverage. Status: Optimized."

Love was inefficient. But its appearance was invaluable.

The Collection Always Comes

Three months later, John called in his markers.

Dorothy Anderson sat in the Cypress Woods community center, addressing a packed room of residents concerned about a proposed assessment increase. She'd been prepped by Veronica but spoke from genuine conviction.

"I hear your concerns," she said, steady in her wheelchair. "Nobody wants to pay more. But let me tell you what John Masters did for me."

She told the story—the foreclosure, the ramp, the saved home. By the time she finished, half the room was wiping eyes. The assessment passed unanimously.

Bruce Gordon became John's mobile intelligence network. Driving residents to appointments, airports, shopping, he heard everything. Who was unhappy. Who was organizing. Who was asking questions.

"That Eunice lady," Bruce reported during one of his "loan payment" meetings. "She's been talking to some lawyer. Shows her papers sometimes, makes calls after."

"Interesting," John said, making notes. "Keep listening. And Bruce? That payment's waived this month. You're doing good work."

Bruce beamed like a child praised by a strict father. "Anything you need, Mr. Masters. Anything."

Jose Suarez walked Max Jr. past every building, every day, a living reminder of John's benevolence. The dog wore a collar with a tag: "Gift from John Masters." Subtle as a sledgehammer, effective as one too.

When a group of residents began organizing against the new security cameras, Jose attended their meeting.

"You're worried about privacy?" he said, Max Jr. at his feet. "Let me tell you about safety. About community. About a man who sees what we need before we know we need it."

The opposition crumbled. Who could argue with a man whose life had been saved by kindness?

The Interior Architecture

Veronica found John in his home office, updating resident files with new intelligence. Each act of kindness meticulously documented, its returns carefully tracked.

"You're building an army," she observed, reviewing his notes.

"I'm building a community," John corrected. "The fact that it's loyal is secondary to the fact that it functions."

"Do you believe that?"

John looked up from his files. "I believe that disorder is waste. Suffering is inefficiency. What I did for Dorothy, Bruce, Jose—it eliminated waste. That it also created loyalty is...synergy."

"You feel nothing for them."

"I feel satisfaction. A problem solved is inherently satisfying."

Veronica studied him, this man who could calculate kindness like compound interest. "What about Rose? Did you feel nothing for her?"

John's hands stilled on the keyboard. "Rose was different."

"How?"

He was quiet for a long moment, stroking the rosary beads and processing. "She was inefficient. Faith is inefficient. Hope in the face of contrary evidence is inefficient. But she persisted. That persistence was... noteworthy."

"You loved her."

"I appreciated her. The way you appreciate a beautiful algorithm or an elegant solution. She believed I could be redeemed. That belief was mathematically improbable but internally consistent. I respected the consistency."

"And these people? Dorothy, Bruce, Jose?"

"They're components. Maintained components function better than neglected ones. It's not complex."

But Veronica heard something else in his voice. Not emotion— John was incapable of genuine emotion as most understood it. But something adjacent. Pride, perhaps. The satisfaction of a system running smoothly, of problems solved, and solutions implemented.

"You're helping them," she said.

"I'm optimizing them. If that appears helpful, it's because optimization often does."

"And when they can't be optimized anymore? When Dorothy's too sick to advocate, Bruce too broken to drive, Jose too old to walk?"

John returned to his files. "Then they'll be replaced by components that function. But until then, they serve their purpose. And serving a purpose is its own kindness."

It was the closest he could come to compassion—seeing utility in everyone, maintaining them like equipment, ensuring they ran until they couldn't. In John's world, being useful was being valued. And being valued, even as a component, was better than being discarded.

The Reputation Engine

Word spread through the United's communities like a benevolent virus. John Masters notices. John Masters helps. John Masters solves problems others ignore.

Maria Gonzalez's grandson needed school supplies—they appeared on her doorstep. Tom Patterson's truck needed tires—a "community safety grant" covered them. Sarah Kim's daughter got into nursing school but couldn't afford scrubs—an "education encouragement envelope" arrived.

Each kindness cost less than a thousand dollars. Each generated returns exponentially greater. A hundred small investments creating ten thousand testimonials and social proof, building a mythology that no investigator could penetrate.

"He's like a mob boss," Eunice Garland told Janice Rollins during one of their clandestine meetings. "But instead of breaking legs, he fixes wheelchairs. How do you fight that?"

"You document the money," Eunice insisted. "Every kindness has a cost. He's buying loyalty with stolen funds."

"Prove it. Prove any of it. All anyone sees is a man who helps. A man who cares."

It was the perfect crime. Stealing with one hand while healing with the other. Building an empire on the foundation of solved problems and salvaged lives.

Late at night, John would review his charity spreadsheet, calculating returns on kindness like stock portfolios. Dorothy Anderson: 847% ROI. Bruce Gordon: 1,240% ROI. Jose Suarez: Infinite return, still calculating.

"Compassion is just lubrication for the gears of control," he would tell Veronica.

But sometimes, walking the communities, seeing Dorothy wave from her new ramp, watching Bruce drive residents in his reliable RAV4, greeting Jose and Max Jr. on their punctual rounds, John felt something adjacent to what others called satisfaction.

Not happiness. He was incapable of happiness as humans understood it. But the pleasure of a balanced equation. The contentment of efficient systems. The peace of problems solved.

Rose had believed he could help people. In his twisted, calculated way, he was. The fact that every kindness was a collar, every gift a chain, didn't change the reality: lives were improved, suffering was reduced, order was optimized.

The Benevolent Fixer had built his reputation one $500 favor at a time. And every debt, financial or emotional, would be collected with interest.

In John Masters' world, kindness was just another currency. And he was very good with money.

And then it hit him, he could set up a non-profit to help residents in need and to help himself to millions in the process.

Chapter 8: The United Community Foundation

The Philanthropy Facade

John Masters understood that true power required more than surveillance and financial control—it demanded the appearance of virtue. He'd learned this from watching the old Cleveland bosses who built churches while burning competitors, who sponsored Little League teams while running numbers operations, who donated turkeys at Thanksgiving while breaking legs for unpaid debts.

The most untouchable criminals were those who wrapped their operations in charity and community service. And in South Florida's retirement communities, nothing generated goodwill faster than helping elderly residents navigate the financial challenges of fixed-income living.

"We need a foundation," John announced during United's monthly strategy meeting. "Something that makes us indispensable to residents' wellbeing while creating additional revenue streams and tax advantages."

Veronica looked up from her tablet, immediately understanding the implications. "Charitable giving that flows through our management structure. Perfect PR cover plus financial optimization."

"Exactly. Every dollar residents donate comes with gratitude toward United. Every resident we help becomes a permanent ally. Every act of charity becomes armor against criticism."

Tommy Rodriguez, their digital operations specialist, was already seeing the technological possibilities. "The app can integrate donation features, volunteer coordination, even automated charitable giving from resident accounts. We can make charity as convenient as paying HOA dues."

"And just as profitable," John added with a smile that would have made his Cleveland associates proud.

The Board Presentation

Veronica pitched the concept to United's board of directors with the perfect blend of altruism and business pragmatism. The conference room overlooked downtown Boca Raton, where morning sun cast everything in golden light that made even the most cynical proposals seem wholesome.

"Ladies and gentlemen," she began, addressing the carefully chosen collection of retired executives who provided legitimacy without asking uncomfortable questions. "We have an opportunity to address a growing challenge in our communities while strengthening United's market position."

She clicked to her first slide: demographic data showing the financial vulnerability of elderly residents across their fifty-two communities. Fixed incomes. Rising healthcare costs. Property tax increases. The mathematics of retirement have left many residents struggling despite outward appearances of prosperity.

"Last month alone, we had six residents fall behind on assessments due to medical emergencies," Veronica continued. "Three more requested payment plans because of prescription cost increases. These are good people facing temporary hardships, not deadbeats trying to avoid their obligations."

Board member and retired bank executive Nelly Foster, nodded sympathetically. "What's our current policy for residents in financial distress?"

"Standard collection procedures," Veronica replied. "Late fees, payment plans, ultimately liens and foreclosures if necessary. It's efficient, but it's also destroying community morale and generating negative publicity."

John stood up, projecting the quiet authority that had made him indispensable to the board's decision-making. "We propose creating the United Community Foundation—a charitable organization that allows communities to help neighbors while providing tax advantages and positive publicity for all involved."

The concept was elegant in its simplicity. Each HOA would contribute a small percentage of its annual surplus to the foundation. Residents could make additional voluntary donations. Corporate sponsors would provide funding in exchange for promotional opportunities. The foundation would then assist residents facing genuine financial hardships while generating goodwill that protected United from criticism.

"Imagine the optics," John continued. "Instead of United Community Management foreclosing on a cancer patient's home, the United Community Foundation pays her assessment while she recovers. Instead of bad publicity, we get local news coverage about corporate social responsibility."

Nelly Foster was taking notes. "What about legal structure? Tax implications? Oversight requirements?"

"501(c)(3) nonprofit organization," Veronica answered smoothly. "Full tax-exempt status, professional board of directors, transparent financial reporting. We'll operate with the same standards as major charitable foundations while maintaining operational efficiency."

"And United's role?"

"Administrative services only," John replied. "We'll provide management, accounting, and coordination services at cost. The foundation will be technically independent while benefiting from our professional expertise."

At cost meant whatever they determined was reasonable compensation for foundation management. Still, the board didn't need to understand the profit extraction mechanisms that would make charitable giving surprisingly lucrative for United's operations.

The Voluntary Contribution System

Within sixty days, every HOA in United's portfolio had received a carefully crafted proposal for foundation participation. The language was designed to make refusal seem selfish while making participation appear inevitable.

"The United Community Foundation represents our commitment to the principle that neighbors help neighbors," the letter began. "By contributing just two percent of annual operating surplus, your community joins a network of caring residents who ensure that temporary hardships don't become permanent tragedies."

The psychology was perfect. Two percent sounded minimal—most communities had larger budget variances from accounting rounding errors. The contribution was positioned as insurance against future problems rather than additional expense. And the social pressure from other participating communities made holdouts seem callous and antisocial.

Most boards approved the contributions unanimously during routine budget meetings. The few that resisted found themselves facing opposition candidates during the next election cycle—candidates who happened to be endorsed by residents' groups that Tommy's digital intelligence network had identified as politically active.

"It's fascinating how quickly board composition changes when residents feel their leadership lacks community spirit," John observed, reviewing election results that had replaced resistant board members with foundation supporters.

Harbor Gardens had been the most stubborn holdout, with board president Dorothy Kim arguing that charitable giving should be voluntary rather than quasi-mandatory. Her replacement, elected with 73% of the vote, made foundation participation his first official act.

"Democracy in action," Veronica noted with satisfaction. "Residents want leadership that cares about community welfare."

The Fundraising Machine

Tommy Rodriguez approached foundation fundraising with the same systematic precision he'd applied to digital surveillance. The United Community App became a charitable giving platform that made donations as convenient as online shopping while collecting data about residents' financial capacity and charitable preferences.

"Watch this," Tommy demonstrated, pulling up the app's fundraising interface. "Mrs. Patterson wants to contribute to the foundation but doesn't want to write checks. She can set up automatic monthly donations directly from her bank account. The system tracks her giving history, sends thank-you messages, and even provides tax documentation."

But the real innovation was in event organization. Tommy had identified the peculiar enthusiasm elderly residents showed for activities that combined social interaction with charitable giving. Bake sales, craft fairs, charity auctions, holiday markets—events that generated revenue while creating community engagement.

"The Millennial Village 'Fleece Market' raised $8,000 last month," Tommy reported with obvious pride in his wordplay. "Residents donated items they no longer needed, bought different items from their neighbors' donations, and United collected administrative fees for organizing the whole thing."

The fleece market concept was genius in its simplicity. Residents felt good about decluttering their homes for charity. They felt good about finding useful items at reasonable prices. They felt good about supporting a worthy cause. And United generated revenue from vendor fees, transaction processing, and "event coordination services."

"Plus," Tommy added, "we now have a detailed inventory of residents' possessions, spending patterns, and disposal habits. The data is invaluable for predicting everything from health declines to financial stress."

For those communities with golf courses, the charity golf tournaments were even more profitable. Corporate sponsors paid premium fees for logo placement and networking access to affluent retirees. Equipment vendors provided products at cost in exchange for promotional opportunities. Even the country clubs reduced their rates to support community charitable activities.

"Last quarter's tournaments netted seventy-three thousand in donations," Veronica reported. "But the indirect benefits were worth twice that—corporate relationships, political connections, media coverage that money can't buy."

The Assistance Program

To maintain credibility, the foundation needed to provide genuine assistance to residents facing real hardships. John insisted that the help be both meaningful and strategically useful, creating grateful allies while generating positive publicity.

The first major case was Eleanor Randall, an eighty-seven-year-old widow whose husband's medical bills had drained their savings before his death. She was three months behind on HOA assessments and facing eviction from the home she'd lived in for fifteen years.

"This is perfect," John said, reviewing Eleanor's situation. "Long-time resident, genuine hardship, sympathetic circumstances. We pay her assessment arrearage, arrange payment plans for future obligations, and generate enough positive publicity to justify the foundation's existence."

The intervention was beautifully orchestrated. A small ceremony in Eleanor's honor, with local news coverage and photographs of grateful residents. Testimonials about United's compassion and community spirit. Social media posts that went viral throughout South Florida's retirement communities.

"Mrs. Randall's case proves that United Community Management isn't just about managing properties," John told the Channel 7 news crew. "We're about managing communities—caring for residents, supporting neighbors, ensuring that temporary setbacks don't become permanent tragedies."

Eleanor Randall became the foundation's poster child, appearing at fundraising events and board meetings to describe how United had saved her home and her dignity. Her gratitude was genuine, her advocacy was enthusiastic, and her influence within the community was substantial.

"She's worth more than any marketing campaign," Veronica observed, watching Eleanor convince skeptical residents to support United's latest assessment increase. "Grateful beneficiaries are the most powerful advocates."

The Strings Attached

Every foundation recipient signed agreements that were positioned as gratitude acknowledgments but functioned as behavioral contracts. The language was carefully crafted to seem appreciative rather than controlling, but the obligations were clear to anyone who read the fine print.

Recipients agreed to "community volunteerism when health and circumstances permit." They committed to "positive representation of United Community Management's charitable mission." Most importantly, they consented to "ongoing communication about foundation programs and community initiatives."

"We're not controlling their behavior," John explained to critics who questioned the language of the agreement. "We're ensuring that charitable recipients understand their role in promoting the foundation's mission and encouraging other residents to participate in community support programs."

The practical effect was that foundation beneficiaries became United's most vocal supporters during board meetings, community discussions, and resident surveys. They defended assessment increases, praised management decisions, and criticized anyone who questioned United's policies or methods.

"Eleanor Randall spoke for twenty minutes about United's excellence during the budget meeting," David Krauss reported. "She shut down three different complaint attempts and personally vouched for the new security contracts."

The foundation recipients formed an informal network of grateful advocates who amplified United's messaging while marginalizing opposition voices. They attended community events, participated in social media discussions, and provided testimonials that criticized United, which seemed heartless and ungrateful.

The Tax Optimization Strategy

Veronica had structured the foundation to provide maximum tax advantages for all participants while generating substantial revenue for United's operations. The charitable contributions were tax-deductible for community associations. Corporate sponsorships qualified as business expenses for vendors. Even individual donations provided residents with tax benefits while funding operations that ultimately served United's interests.

"We're operating three distinct revenue streams," Veronica explained to United's accounting team. "Direct donations from communities and residents. Corporate sponsorships from vendors seeking access to our demographic. And administrative fees for foundation management services."

The administrative fees were the most profitable component. United charged the foundation for accounting services, legal counsel, event coordination, digital platform management, ad strategic planning. These fees were calculated as percentages of foundation revenue, ensuring that United's compensation increased along with charitable giving.

"Last quarter, we generated two hundred thirty thousand in foundation management fees," Veronica reported. "Plus indirect benefits from vendor relationships, political connections, and promotional value that enhance our market position."

The vendor sponsorships were particularly lucrative. Companies desperate for access to affluent elderly consumers paid premium rates for foundation partnership opportunities. Pharmaceutical companies sponsored health screening events. Financial services firms funded investment education seminars. Even luxury travel companies supported foundation activities in exchange for marketing access.

"Longevity Pharmaceuticals paid fifty thousand to sponsor our health and wellness fair," Tommy noted. "They got direct access to eight hundred residents over age sixty-five, plus detailed health questionnaires that provide insights into medication usage patterns."

The Political Protection Network

The foundation's most valuable function was political protection. Local politicians who might otherwise scrutinize United's operations became supporters once they were invited to foundation events and asked to speak about community service and corporate responsibility.

County Commissioner Marta Ramirez had been asking uncomfortable questions about HOA assessment practices until she was invited to present the foundation's annual community service award. The photo opportunity—her shaking hands with Eleanor Randall while United executives applauded—effectively ended her criticism of community management practices.

"Politicians love being associated with charity," John observed, reviewing media coverage from the awards ceremony. "It's much harder to investigate a company that's regularly feeding hungry families and paying medical bills for cancer patients."

The foundation's board of directors included carefully chosen community leaders who provided political credibility while maintaining operational independence. A retired judge, a former city manager, a prominent physician, and a respected business owner—all lending their reputations to United's charitable mission while having minimal involvement in actual foundation operations.

"We've achieved perfect political insulation," Veronica noted during their quarterly strategy review. "Any criticism of United now sounds like criticism of charitable giving and community support. We're literally untouchable."

The Empire's Moral Foundation

By year-end, the United Community Foundation had become another crown jewel of John and Veronica's empire. Annual donations exceeded $800,000. Corporate sponsorships provided additional revenue and political connections. Media coverage consistently portrayed United as a caring, community-focused management company that went beyond contractual obligations to support residents' welfare.

"We've solved the fundamental problem of criminal enterprise," John said, reviewing foundation reports in his office. "Traditional operations generate opposition because they're purely extractive. We've created a system where residents thank us for taking their money and generously giving a little back under certain circumstances."

The foundation recipients formed a protective network of grateful advocates who defended United against any criticism. The charitable giving provided tax advantages and positive publicity that enhanced United's market position. The corporate sponsorships generated revenue while building relationships with vendors and political figures.

Most importantly, the foundation made opposition to United's policies seem morally questionable. How could residents complain about assessment increases when those increases funded charitable programs that helped their neighbors? How could they criticize management fees when those fees supported a foundation that paid medical bills and prevented foreclosures?

"Max Vecchio used violence and intimidation to control territory," John reflected. "John Masters uses charity and community service. Same result, better public relations."

Veronica smiled, reviewing the latest foundation newsletter, which featured photographs of smiling residents at community events, grateful beneficiaries receiving assistance, and United executives presenting oversized checks to local charities.

"The residents love us," she said. "The politicians support us. The media celebrates us. And we're more profitable than ever."

"Because," John concluded, "nothing protects a criminal enterprise better than genuine good works funded by systematic profit extraction. We're not stealing from these communities—we're helping them become more generous."

The United Community Foundation had achieved something unprecedented in criminal history: a protection racket where the victims volunteered to pay tribute and thanked their extractors for the privilege of supporting worthy causes.

It was the perfect crime disguised as perfect charity, and everyone involved felt grateful for the opportunity to participate.

Chapter 9: The Whisper Network

The Canary Falls

Ellen Marquez had been a Gold Tier resident for three months—the second resident to achieve this status after Dorothy Anderson. A retired elementary school teacher, sixty-eight years old, beloved by three generations of Queens Point children who still called her Mrs. M. She volunteered for every committee, attended every meeting, and baked cookies for new residents. Her reputation score was a perfect 1000 until the morning it wasn't.

"System error," Tommy Rodriguez said, frowning at his monitors in the command center. "Ellen Marquez just dropped to Yellow. No, wait... Red. That can't be right."

John Masters looked up from his morning reports. "Show me."

The screens filled with Ellen's data. Her payment history: perfect. Meeting attendance: perfect. Social media presence: positive and community-focused. But there, buried in the algorithmic calculations, was the poison pill—a single flagged association.

"She visited her nephew last week," Tommy explained, pulling up the data. "Mario Restrepo. He's on our watch list—attended three meetings of the Harbor Gardens Accountability Group. They're the ones questioning the assessment increases."

"And the system dinged her for visiting family?"

"The algorithm doesn't distinguish. Association with flagged individuals impacts score. It's...working as designed."

John studied the data, his mind calculating consequences. Ellen Marquez wasn't just any resident—she was a pillar, a load-bearing wall in the community's social structure. Her fall would be noticed. Questioned.

"Override it," Veronica suggested from her workstation. "Manual adjustment. No one needs to know."

"No," John said slowly. "Let it stand. But watch the reaction. This is data, too."

The reaction came faster than expected. Within hours, Ellen's phone was ringing. Friends confused by her suddenly delayed maintenance request. The parking enforcement officer—who'd always given her a wave—writing a ticket for being two inches over the line. The community newsletter, which always featured her volunteer work, omitting her from the monthly recognition.

By evening, a small group had gathered in Ellen's living room. Six residents, all in the unofficial Yellow or Red Tier, all sensing something fundamentally wrong with the golden teacher's sudden fall from grace.

"It's not right," Ellen said, serving tea with shaking hands. "Thirty years in this community. I've never missed a payment, never caused trouble. My nephew visits for lunch and suddenly I'm... what did they call it? A 'community risk'?"

"The same thing happened to me," said Martin Glück, a retired accountant who'd questioned the budget at a board meeting. "One question about vendor selection, and my score tanked. Now I wait two weeks for a plumber while Gold Tier residents get same-day service."

"We need to be careful," whispered Janet Kim, glancing at Ellen's smart doorbell. "They're watching. Always watching."

Ellen stood up, unplugged the doorbell, and pulled the batteries from her smoke detector for good measure. "Then let them watch this: I'm done being afraid in my own home."

It was the first crack in the facade—not from a malcontent or troublemaker, but from the heart of the community itself. And like all cracks, it would either be repaired or spread.

The Journalist's Instinct

Maya Trent hadn't wanted to be a substitute teacher. For fifteen years, she'd been an investigative reporter for the Miami Herald, breaking stories on corruption, fraud, and abuse of power. But journalism was dying, newspapers were bleeding staff, and at forty-five, she found herself teaching seventh-grade social studies to pay the bills.

She was helping Timothy Weil with his tablet after class when she noticed it—a routing anomaly in the school's network traffic. Data packets being mirrored to an external server. Her reporter's instinct, dormant but not dead, perked up.

"Timothy, where did you get this tablet?"

"It's the school's. From the donation program. Some company gave them to all the students." He showed her the label: Donated by United Community Foundation.

Maya's blood chilled. She knew that name—the property management company that had taken over her apartment complex last year. The one that had installed new security systems and smart locks that somehow always knew when she was home.

That night, in her cramped apartment, Maya did what she did best: dig. United Community Foundation was a web of LLCs and shell companies, but at the center was John Masters. Public records showed his meteoric rise from newcomer to HOA emperor. But his past? That was a black hole that started eighteen months ago.

She pulled out her old reporter's notebook and began connecting dots. The donated tablets weren't just educational tools—they were surveillance devices, routing student data through United Community Foundation's servers. But why would an HOA management company want to monitor middle schoolers?

The answer came when she cross-referenced student addresses with HOA properties. Seventy percent overlap. They weren't watching the kids—they were watching the families through the kids.

Maya felt the old thrill, the electric sensation of a story coming together. But she also felt fear. Real journalists had editors, lawyers, and institutions backing them. She was just a substitute teacher with a laptop and too much curiosity.

She opened an encrypted messaging app and typed: "Anyone else notice their HOA knows too much?"

Within minutes, responses flooded in. She'd touched a nerve, found others who felt the invisible chains. The whisper network had found its voice.

The Garage Conspiracy

They met in Martin Glück's garage at 10 PM on a Thursday. Phones went into an old microwave—Martin's idea, he'd read about it online. Eight people in folding chairs, looking like a sad book club rather than a resistance cell.

Ellen Marquez was there, her Gold Tier pin still attached to her cardigan out of habit. Martin had spreadsheets showing assessment irregularities. Janet Kim brought screenshots of her reputation score dropping after she'd liked a Facebook post about HOA overreach. And Maya Trent brought journalism—the ability to turn grievances into narrative.

"We need to be smart about this," Maya said, standing before a whiteboard she'd brought. "They have all the power, all the data, all the systems. But they have one weakness—they need us to comply. Their whole system is built on voluntary submission."

"Voluntary?" scoffed Robert Paulson, a new addition whose red-tier status came from noise complaints about his jazz practice. "They made my life hell until I stopped playing. That's not voluntary."

"But you stopped," Maya pointed out. "You could have kept playing, taken the fines, fought it. But the cost was too high. That's the genius of it—they make resistance more expensive than compliance, but it's still a choice."

Ellen raised her hand, a lifetime of teaching habits. "So what do we do? I can't afford to stay in the red tier. My medications alone..."

"We document everything," Maya said, writing on the whiteboard. "Every delayed service, every score change, every suspicious pattern. We build a case that even the comfortable Green Tiers can't ignore."

"And then?" Martin asked.

"Then we publish. Not through official channels—they own those. Through whisper networks, social media, guerrilla tactics. Death by a thousand posts."

What none of them noticed was the thin wire running under the garage door, connected to a device the size of a matchbox. Every word was being transmitted, analyzed, and tagged by PRISM (Personal Responsibility & Incentive Shaping Model). The resistance was cataloged before it could even resist.

The Digital Counterstrike

John Masters read the transcript of the garage meeting with the same detachment he'd once used for FBI wiretaps of mob meetings. Amateurs playing at revolution, unaware they were already caught.

"Shall we move on them?" Tommy asked, fingers poised over his keyboard. "Drop them all to Black Tier? That's the new classification you approved—essentially digital exile."

"No," John said, surprising both Tommy and Veronica. "Let them think they're hidden. But begin countermeasures. Subtle ones."

"Subtle how?" Veronica asked.

John pulled up Maya Trent's file. "Miss Trent is our catalyst. Former journalist, trained to find patterns and connections. She's teaching our children while investigating us. That's...inefficient."

He began typing. Within minutes, Maya's digital life began to shift. Emails delayed just long enough to miss deadlines. GPS apps routing her through traffic. Streaming services buffering at crucial moments. Not enough to prove manipulation, but enough to fray nerves, increase stress, and create doubt.

"Gaslighting," Veronica observed.

"Optimization," John corrected. "A stressed mind makes poor decisions. Poor decisions discredit movements."

But that was just the beginning. John launched Project Harmony—a wellness initiative offering free mental health resources to residents. Counselors, support groups, stress management workshops. All staffed by professionals who happened to report unusual statements or concerning behaviors back to the United Community Foundation.

"We're not just watching them," John explained to his inner circle. "We're inside their heads. Every fear, every doubt, every crack in their resolve gets documented and leveraged."

Glenn Sawyer, the political operative, raised concerns. "This is beyond surveillance. This is psychological warfare. If it ever comes out..."

"It won't," John said with finality. "Because the people who might expose it will be too busy dealing with their mysteriously complicated lives to organize effectively."

The TikTok Bomb

It started as a joke. Brittany Weil, Timothy's older sister, made a TikTok video titled "My HOA Knows When I Pee" about the smart water meters that tracked usage patterns. She meant it as comedy—complete with jump cuts, meme music, and exaggerated reactions.

But the comments weren't laughing.

"OMG, mine does this too! I got a letter about 'unusual water usage' when I had food poisoning!"

"My HOA sent me a 'wellness check' because my sleep pattern changed. HOW DO THEY KNOW WHEN I SLEEP?"

"Check your terms of service. They basically own your data."

The video went viral, garnering 2.3 million views in just 48 hours. #HOAWatching started trending. Suddenly, every grievance found an audience, every suspicion found confirmation.

Tommy watched the social media explosion with growing panic. "We're losing narrative control. The story's out there now."

John remained calm, studying the viral spread like a disease vector. "Who started this?"

"Brittany Weil. Sixteen. Sister of—"

"Timothy Weil. Ellen Marquez's student. The tablet." John smiled coldly. "Full circle. The system works even when it's exposed. Tommy, prepare the deepfake protocols."

"Sir?"

"Miss Trent is about to have a very public breakdown."

Digital Assassination

The video appeared on the same platforms where Maya Trent's growing investigation was gaining traction. It showed her—or someone who looked and sounded exactly like her—in what appeared to be a drunken rant about "conspiracy theories" and "paranoid delusions." The deepfake was perfect, down to her slight Brooklyn accent and the nervous gesture she made with her left hand.

Within hours, her credibility was shattered. The school board received "concerned parent" emails. Her substitute teaching assignments dried up. Even the garage group began to doubt—was she unstable? Had they been following a fantasist?

Maya knew it was fake. She'd been home that night, working on her investigation. But proving a negative in the digital age was nearly impossible. The video existed; therefore, it was real. Truth was consensus, and consensus was manufactured.

She sat in her apartment, laptop closed, feeling the walls close in. Every app on her phone was potentially compromised. Every camera a potential spy. Every interaction possibly recorded and weaponized.

But Maya Trent hadn't survived fifteen years of investigative journalism by folding under pressure. She pulled out an old burner phone, one she'd kept from her reporting days, and made a call.

"Eunice? It's Maya. That story you've been pitching about the HOA empire? I think it's time we talked."

Tommy's Crisis

Tommy Rodriguez stared at the deepfake rendering, watching Maya Trent's digital doppelganger destroy her own reputation in high definition. He'd built the system, trained the AI, perfected the process. But seeing it deployed against a substitute teacher whose only crime was curiosity... Something turned in his stomach.

"It's done," he told John. "The video's achieved full saturation. Her reputation is destroyed."

"Excellent work," John said, not looking up from his screens. "Begin monitoring for sympathy responses. Anyone defending her gets flagged for score adjustment."

Tommy hesitated. "Sir, she has a daughter. Thirteen. This will destroy her, too."

Now John looked up, his eyes cold. "Collateral damage is still damage, Tommy. The system requires examples. Ms. Trent chose to be one."

That night, Tommy sat in his apartment, surrounded by the servers and screens that were his life. He'd thought he was building something revolutionary—smart cities, efficient communities, the future of governance. But Maya's tears on the security footage looked very real. Her daughter's harassment at school was documented in cruel detail on social media.

He opened an encrypted partition on his personal server and began copying files. Not to leak—he wasn't brave enough for that. But to preserve. Because someday, someone would need to explain how the digital paradise became a digital prison.

And maybe, just maybe, that someone would be him.

Veronica's Temptation

The offer came through LinkedIn, professional and pristine. GovTech Solutions, a DC-based firm specializing in "community management innovation," wanted to hire her as Senior Vice President. The salary was three times what John paid her. The benefits were federal-grade. The opportunity was national.

Veronica read it in her office, door locked, knowing John was probably monitoring her screen but not caring. She was tired. Not physically—the work energized her. But morally. Each innovation made control easier and resistance harder. Each success felt like another bar in a cage she'd helped build.

"Interesting offer," John said, entering without knocking—he never knocked anymore.

"You were watching."

"I watch everything. It's an impressive package. GovTech is CIA-adjacent, you know. They want to replicate our model for federal housing, military bases, maybe even smart cities."

"And?"

John sat on the edge of her desk, a gesture both casual and possessive. "Take it."

Veronica blinked. "What?"

"Take the job. Learn their systems. Build their trust. Then bring it all back to us. Why conquer when we can infiltrate?"

She studied him, this man who'd turned her from a frustrated property manager into...what? His partner? His tool? His creation?

"What if I take it and don't come back?"

John smiled, the expression not reaching his eyes. "You will. Because out there, you're just another executive. Here, you're a queen. And queens don't abandon their kingdoms."

He was right, and they both knew it. The power was addictive. The control intoxicating. She could no more leave than an addict could quit cold turkey.

"I'll need guarantees," she said. "Maintained access to our systems. Consulting fees. Protection."

"Done." John stood, straightening his tie. "Oh, and Veronica? The Weil family is having issues. The daughter's TikTok has caused...complications. Handle it."

She nodded, already calculating responses. The girl would be fine—a few strategic interventions, some reputation rehabilitation. But it was another reminder: in John's world, everyone was either an asset or an obstacle.

And obstacles got optimized out of existence.

The Prediction Engine

PRISM had evolved. Version 3.0 didn't just watch—it predicted. Every data point fed into neural networks that modeled future behavior with terrifying accuracy. Tommy called it the Minority Report protocol, and he wasn't entirely joking.

"Look at this," he showed John, pulling up a heat map of Cypress Woods. "Based on communication patterns, financial stress indicators, and social network analysis, we can predict with 87% accuracy who will become a problem in the next 90 days."

Red dots appeared across the map. Future dissidents are identified before they realize they are dissidents themselves.

"What do you recommend?" John asked.

"Preemptive intervention. Positive reinforcement for those on the edge—surprise maintenance fixes, small financial breaks, community recognition. Make them grateful before they become resentful."

"Bread and circuses for the digital age," Veronica observed.

"It works," John said. "Implement it. But I want a secondary protocol. For those too far gone to save."

Tommy's fingers hesitated. "Secondary protocol?"

"Isolation. If someone's going to become a problem, separate them from potential allies. Digital obstacles to communication. Social engineering to create conflicts. Turn revolutionaries into hermits."

It was social murder, executed through algorithms. Tommy coded it with the same precision he'd once used for hacktivist causes, back when he thought technology would free people rather than cage them.

The Whisper Grows Louder

Despite everything—the surveillance, the manipulation, the digital assassination—the whisper network grew. Ellen Marquez's fall had backfired. Instead of cowering, she became a martyr. Her cookies now came with subversive messages. Her book club read 1984 and discussed it in terms everyone recognized.

Maya Trent, destroyed professionally but not spiritually, went underground. Her investigation continued through encrypted channels, building a case that would eventually surface. She knew John Masters wasn't who he claimed to be. The hole in his past was too perfect, too clean. It screamed witness protection.

And in the garage meetings that now rotated locations, used signal jammers, and required increasingly sophisticated operational security, the resistance learned. They couldn't beat the system digitally—John owned that battlefield. But analog resistance, human connections, whispered truths...those were harder to algorithm away.

"We need allies," Martin Glück said during one meeting. "People with power who haven't been compromised."

"There's a sheriff's election coming up," someone suggested. "The challenger, Rodriguez, he's been asking questions about United Community Foundation's influence."

"Then we help him," Maya said from her laptop screen—she attended virtually now, too hot to appear in person. "Every vote matters, but informed votes matter more."

They didn't know that John was already three moves ahead, that their systems saw he would have a close race, and, using the UCM app, it was going to be a lot closer than anyone had anticipated. Plus, Rodriguez's campaign was infiltrated, all in the name of optimizing democracy, complete with predetermined outcomes.

But they kept whispering. Because that's what humans do when pressed too hard—they find ways to push back. Even in perfect systems. Especially in perfect systems.

The Philosophy of Control

Late at night, after Veronica had left for her DC interview (wearing a wire, though she didn't know it), John stood in his command center, watching his empire function. Thousands of data streams painted a picture of perfect order. Crime: minimal. Property values: climbing. Resident satisfaction: 94% (the 6% were being processed).

But something nagged at him. A calculation that didn't balance.

He thought of Rose, his adoptive mother, and her persistent faith as he stroked her rosary beads that he still carried in his pocket. She'd believed in redemption through free will, through choice. He'd built a system that removed choice, that made the right decision the only decision.

"Too much order creates its own chaos," he murmured, remembering something from his Cleveland days. The Torrisi family had fallen not from external pressure but from internal rigidity. When systems became too perfect, they became brittle.

Was he making the same mistake?

The thought passed. No—his system was adaptive, learning, evolving. Every challenge made it stronger. Every resistance taught it new suppression techniques.

But still, the whispers grew louder.

On his screens, a notification: Ellen Marquez had just hosted another "book club." Attendance: twelve. Books discussed: Animal Farm, The Handmaid's Tale, Fahrenheit 451.

John smiled. Let them read their dystopias. They didn't realize they were living in a utopia—clean, safe, efficient. That it required surrendering privacy and autonomy was a small price. Everyone paid prices. The only choice was whether you knew what you were buying.

In John Masters' empire, at least the price tags were honest, even if they were written in invisible ink.

Seeds of Revolution

The battle lines had been drawn, tense but uncrossed. The whisper network grew louder, though still cloaked in shadows. John's system kept evolving, but subtle fractures began to show. And somewhere between the watchers and the watched, humanity's oldest conflict stirred: The need for order versus the desire for freedom.

John Masters had refined order to its final form—an optimized, airtight machine. But now, he was about to learn what Rose had always understood: The human spirit, messy and inefficient, followed its own ancient code. Older than any algorithm. And immune to control.

Chapter 10: The New Order

Queens Point's transformation was complete. What had been a sleepy retirement community with a part-time security guard was now a fortress of modern efficiency.

The guard shack looked like a forward operating base. Bullet-resistant glass. Multiple monitors showing feeds from dozens of cameras. Communications equipment that could coordinate with local law enforcement or operate independently.

And standing watch was Marcus Thompson—350 pounds of former Marine, hired after a "rigorous selection process" that had really been John and David identifying the perfect enforcer. Marcus wore tactical pants and a polo shirt that strained against his bulk. The Glock 19 on his hip was legal—he had all the permits. The body armor was practical—Florida had dangerous people.

"We don't call the cops anymore," residents would say with pride. "We handle things internally."

And they did. Minor disputes were mediated by community liaisons. Safety issues were addressed by Marcus and his team of similarly imposing "security specialists." Problems that once would have involved law enforcement were solved with quiet efficiency.

The police appreciated it. Calls from John's communities had dropped 67%. When they did respond, everything was documented, the video was archived, and witnesses were coached on their statements. It made their jobs easier.

"You're running your own police force," the sheriff told John at a fundraiser.

"We're being good neighbors," John replied. "Taking care of our own problems so you can focus on real crime."

The sheriff, who was facing a tough reelection, nodded appreciatively. Especially after John mentioned that his communities' Veterans' Voter Integrity Council was very interested in law enforcement issues.

Everything was connected. The saved residents became votes. The votes became political influence. The influence became power. The power became more saved residents, more votes, more influence, in an endless spiral of control.

At the entrance to Queens Point, a new sign had been erected. Elegant bronze letters on marble backing:

"A United Community Where Neighbors Help Neighbors, Where Tomorrow Begins Today"

Below it, in smaller text: "John Masters, Board President and Community Director"

But everyone knew the truth. John wasn't the director. He was the emperor. And his empire was just beginning to reveal its true ambitions.

As night fell over the manicured lawns and monitored streets, residents settled into their beds, secure in the knowledge that someone competent was in charge. Someone who cared. Someone who got things done. The fact that they'd traded their democratic freedoms for this security wasn't something they thought about. Why would they? They were happy. They were safe. They were valued.

And come election day, they would vote exactly as they should. Not because they were forced to, but because John Masters had made their lives so much better that any other choice would be unthinkable. The Chicago ward bosses of old would have wept with envy. They'd controlled through patronage and fear. John controlled through gratitude and algorithms. The political machine wasn't coming to Palm Beach County; it had already arrived.

Chapter 11: The Security Matrix

The Architecture of Authority

John Masters stood in the Queens Point security office, studying incident reports that would have made most HOA presidents weep. Noise complaints dismissed by police. Vandalism cases closed without investigation. Drug deals in parking lots that everyone knew about, but no one could prove. The traditional enforcement system—call cops, file reports, hope for justice—was broken beyond repair. John was fed up with it all. He'd gone all out fixing his communities' broken systems only to find out that the external systems of maintaining order and keeping citizens safe were all but useless. The threat of punishment was all but gone. No wonder when he visited CVS or Walgreens, he found his razor blades under lock and key. And things like baby formula and diapers were literally kept in a vault. That might be acceptable to others, but not to him.

"The problem with external enforcement," John told Marcus Thompson and David Krauss during a strategy session, "is that it's designed to fail. Police show up after the crime. Courts process cases months later. By then, the damage to community cohesion is permanent. So, we are setting up our own security system called CCU (Community Compliance Unit) to solve problems before they become major problems."

Marcus nodded slowly. The former Marine had done three tours in Afghanistan, two years with Blackwater, and most recently, private security for Miami nightclubs, where he'd learned that prevention beat prosecution every time. And it sure cut down on the PTSD.

"So, we become our own enforcement," Marcus said, his voice a low rumble that seemed to vibrate through the floor.

"No," John corrected. "We become something better. Police enforce laws written by distant politicians for theoretical citizens. We enforce standards created by this community for actual residents. Personal. Immediate. Effective."

John pulled up architectural plans on his tablet—not for buildings, but for a human system. "Every great civilization had internal enforcement. Roman Vigiles. Japanese machi-bugyō. Even American frontier towns had their own marshals before federal law arrived. We're not innovating—we're remembering."

Marcus studied the plans with the same intensity he'd once reserved for combat operations. Organizational charts, response protocols, escalation matrices. It wasn't just security—it was a parallel justice system.

"This is ambitious," Marcus said finally. "You're talking about replacing police, courts, even social services."

"I'm talking about making them irrelevant," John replied. "When problems are solved internally, external systems become unnecessary. And when we control problem resolution..."

"We control behavior."

"We optimize outcomes." John's smile was cold, calculated. "Are you interested?"

Marcus Thompson had left the Marines with commendations and nightmares. Left private military contracting with money and more nightmares. Left Miami security with the realization that he was wasting his tactical genius on drunk tourists. What John offered wasn't just a job—it was a mission. Purpose. The chance to build something that actually worked.

"When do I start?"

"You already have, talk to Krauss. He's already got the blueprint, and we'll be launching very soon."

Building the Legion

David Krauss left recruitment to Marcus Thompson. The recruitment strategy was surgical. They didn't advertise on job boards or hire from security companies. Instead, they hunted specific profiles through military networks, police forums, and private contractor databases.

"We need warriors who've become sheepdogs," David explained to John during their weekly briefing. "Trained killers who've learned to protect instead of destroy. Disciplined. Mature. Tired of seeing systems fail."

The first recruit was James Realto, a former LAPD SWAT officer who'd quit after watching the department abandon his neighborhood to gang violence. The second was Maria Santos, ex-Air Force Security Forces, who'd spent four years protecting nuclear weapons and now wanted to protect something that mattered more—community.

Each interview happened in Marcus's spartan office, walls decorated with tactical community maps. No HR pleasantries. Just direct questions.

"Why aren't you a cop anymore?" Marcus asked Realto.

"Because cops react. I want to prevent."

"What's your view on proportional force?"

"It's like cooking—too little and nothing changes. Too much and you ruin everything. The art is knowing exactly how much heat to apply."

"Can you follow orders from civilians?"

She smiled. "I've been following orders from civilians my whole career. At least here, the civilians actually live with the consequences of their decisions."

By month's end, Marcus had assembled twenty-four operators divided into five Community Compliance Units. Each CCU had a team leader, two patrol officers, a digital surveillance specialist, and a community liaison. They wore subdued tactical uniforms—black polos with discrete HOA logos, tactical pants, duty belts with non-lethal tools. Professional but not militaristic. Authoritative but not threatening.

"We're not playing soldier," Marcus told them during orientation. "We're not cops either. We're something new—community guardians. Think of yourselves as the immune system of a living organism. We identify threats, neutralize infections, maintain homeostasis."

The training was intensive. Legal boundaries—what they could and couldn't do under Florida law. De-escalation techniques adapted from hostage negotiation. Community psychology. Digital surveillance systems. Report writing that would stand up in court if needed.

But the real training was philosophical.

"Force is failure," Marcus drilled into them. "Every time we have to physically intervene, we've already lost. Our job is to make problems solve themselves. Through presence. Through prediction. Through making the right choice easier than the wrong one."

The Digital Nervous System

Tommy Rodriguez had further refined the already extensive surveillance network. Now he was building something more ambitious—a predictive enforcement system that would identify problems before they became incidents.

"Watch this," Tommy said, pulling up the Harbor Gardens interface. The screen showed a 3D map of the community with colored overlays. "Every camera feed, motion sensor, and access log feeds into our AI. But we're not just recording—we're learning."

He clicked on a yellow zone near the tennis courts. "Tuesday nights, 11 PM to 1 AM, we see unusual foot traffic here. Pattern analysis suggests drug deals. But instead of sending security to bust them..."

"We make the area inhospitable," Marcus finished. "Increase lighting. Schedule maintenance. Have security do highly visible patrols at 10:45."

"Exactly. The deals stop happening because the environment no longer supports them. No confrontation. No arrests. Just environmental pressure."

The system tracked everything. Who visited whom. Which cars didn't belong. When residents deviated from routine. It built behavioral baselines for every person in the community, flagging anomalies for human review.

"Privacy concerns?" Veronica asked during one demonstration.

"Privacy is maintained," Tommy insisted. "We're not watching inside homes. We're monitoring public spaces and common areas, which HOAs have always had the right to do. We're just doing it more efficiently."

But efficiency was a euphemism. The system created detailed profiles that would make social media companies envious. John knew who was having affairs (unusual visit patterns), who was struggling financially (late-night moving of belongings), and who was planning to cause trouble (increased communications with known agitators).

Monthly behavioral reports appeared on Marcus's desk like clockwork. Not just incidents, but predictions. Risk assessments. Intervention recommendations.

"Resident Harold Snyder, Building C," Marcus read from one report. "Alcohol purchases up 40%. Domestic disturbance probability rising. Recommend wellness check."

"Do it," John approved. "Frame it as community care. Have the liaison bring some food, check if he needs help. If there's a problem brewing, we solve it before it explodes."

The wellness check revealed Harold had lost his job and was spiraling. Instead of waiting for a crisis, the community liaison connected him with John's job placement network. Two weeks later, Harold was working again, grateful to the HOA that had noticed his struggle and helped.

He never knew the system had been watching his every purchase, every movement, every deviation from baseline. He only knew that when he needed help, it appeared.

The Enforcement Pyramid

Veronica had designed the response matrix with the same precision she brought to financial systems. Five levels, each calibrated to produce maximum compliance with minimum visibility.

"Level One is pure software," she explained to new CCU members. "Friendly notification through our app. 'Hey neighbor! We noticed your trash cans are still out. Just a friendly reminder to bring them in. Thanks for keeping Queens Point beautiful!'"

The message included a photo of the violation, a link to relevant rules, and a cheerful emoji. Ninety percent of issues resolved here.

Level Two brought human contact. A CCU member would knock on the door, introduce themselves, have a friendly chat. "Hi, I'm Officer Jones from Community Compliance. Just wanted to make sure you got our message about the trash cans. Anything we can help with?"

The conversation was documented, recorded, and analyzed. Were they defiant? Apologetic? Confused? The system learned, adapted, and predicted future behavior.

Level Three formalized things. Official HOA violation notice. Fines beginning at \$50, escalating to \$500. Legal language. Paper trail. The kind of documentation that made lawyers happy and residents miserable.

Level Four was theater. Security escort to the HOA office. Formal hearing. Marcus Thompson looming in the corner, saying nothing but radiating consequence. Most residents broke before reaching this level. Those who didn't were either very principled or very stupid.

Level Five was exile. Legal eviction for owners, lease termination for renters. But more often, strategic isolation. Parking privileges revoked. Amenity access restricted. Social events closed to them. Death by a thousand small cuts until leaving seemed like their idea.

"We've only had to use Level Five twice," Veronica reported. "Both times, the residents sold within sixty days."

"What about legal challenges?" a new recruit asked.

"Hard to challenge a system that follows every law, documents every interaction, and offers multiple opportunities for compliance," Veronica replied. "We're not arbitrary. We're methodical. Courts love methodical."

The Doctrine of Control

Marcus had distilled his enforcement philosophy into three words that appeared on every CCU vehicle, every uniform patch, every training manual: "Firm, Fair, Final."

"Firm means we don't negotiate core standards," he explained during a team meeting. "Noise ordinances aren't suggestions. Pet policies aren't optional. We enforce consistently, regardless of who violates them."

"Fair means proportional response. Kid's birthday party runs fifteen minutes late? Verbal reminder. Same family throwing ragers every weekend? We escalate. Context matters, but patterns matter more."

"Final means when we make a decision, it sticks. No appeals to friendship. No, just this once.' No exceptions unless John personally approves them. Predictability is power."

The doctrine worked because it removed human discretion from most decisions. CCU members didn't have to decide if they liked someone enough to let violations slide. The system decided. The matrix responded. The enforcement was algorithmic.

But there were always exceptions. And those exceptions revealed the true nature of John's system.

Selective Justice

Margaret Maxwell had been a problem since falling from Gold Tier. Her community criticism had evolved from blog posts to organized meetings. According to the strict enforcement matrix, her violations—unauthorized gatherings, distribution of unapproved flyers, noise complaints from her organizing sessions—should have escalated her to Level Four.

Instead, John intervened personally.

"Different approach," he told Marcus during their morning briefing. "Margaret isn't a criminal. She's a misguided idealist. Heavy enforcement makes her a martyr. We need surgical precision."

The plan was subtle. Margaret's meetings were never directly confronted. Instead, they experienced mysterious technical difficulties. Power outages during crucial moments. Plumbing emergencies that forced venue changes. Key supporters receiving unexpected opportunities—job offers, family emergencies, sudden windfalls that required immediate attention elsewhere.

"We're not suppressing dissent," John explained to Veronica. "We're creating friction. Every revolution requires momentum. We're just adding weight to the wheel."

Meanwhile, residents who supported John's vision found enforcement remarkably lenient. Dorothy Anderson's frequent violations of pet policies (her care aide's emotional support animal) were overlooked. Bruce Gordon's Uber pickups in fire lanes drew friendly reminders rather than fines. Jose's dog, Max Jr., somehow never triggered complaints despite barking during walks.

"The system has to be fair," Veronica noted during one strategy session, "or people will notice the favoritism."

"The system is fair," John corrected. "It fairly rewards those who contribute to community harmony and fairly sanctions those who disrupt it. Justice isn't blind—it's precisely targeted."

The selectivity extended beyond individual enforcement. Entire buildings received different treatment based on their collective compliance scores. Building A, filled with John's early supporters, enjoyed rapid maintenance response and lenient enforcement. Building F, home to several whisper network members, faced strict adherence to every regulation and mysteriously slow repair schedules.

Residents noticed, of course. But what could they say? The rules were being followed. The enforcement was documented. The favoritism was algorithmic, hidden in data patterns that suggested Building F simply had more violations, more complaints, more problems.

Which became self-fulfilling. Under constant scrutiny, Building F residents made more mistakes. Under constant pressure, they filed more complaints. The system created the reality it claimed to merely observe.

Veronica's Soft Power

While Marcus commanded the hard enforcement, Veronica orchestrated the social dynamics that made enforcement rarely necessary. Her Community Harmony Initiative was a masterclass in behavioral modification through social pressure.

"People fear isolation more than fines," she explained to her team of community liaisons. "We don't need to threaten eviction. We just need to threaten irrelevance."

Take the case of William Foster, a retired attorney who'd been questioning the legality of John's management and profit extraction systems. Traditional enforcement would have targeted his numerous technical violations—unauthorized modifications to his unit, improper parking, noise complaints from his late-night research sessions.

Instead, Veronica deployed social isolation. William found himself mysteriously dropped from the golf league roster (membership full). His dinner invitations dried up (hosts worried about their own community standing). The book club he'd founded and hosted for twenty years suddenly voted to change their meeting location—to a member's unit where William wasn't welcome.

"We're not ostracizing him," Veronica insisted when challenged. "Other residents are making independent choices about their associations. We simply ensure they have full information about the consequences of those associations."

The information came through community updates that never mentioned William by name but made clear that "certain residents' disruptive activities" were affecting everyone's quality of life. Property values were at risk. Assessments might increase. All because some people couldn't appreciate what they had.

Within three months, William Foster sold his unit and moved to a non-Masters community. He told people it was for health reasons. The real reason was that he couldn't bear another community event where people looked through him like glass.

"No enforcement action taken," Veronica reported to John. "Voluntary compliance achieved."

But her true genius lay in making enforcement feel like care. When CCU members conducted wellness checks, community liaisons followed up with resources. When violations were issued, mediators offered to help resolve underlying issues. When residents faced Level Four hearings, counselors provided support to help them "reintegrate into community standards."

"We're not punishing," Veronica would say at community meetings. "We're healing. Every enforcement action is an opportunity to strengthen our community bonds."

Residents nodded, applauded, and internalized the message. Getting caught wasn't failure—it was a chance for growth. The CCU wasn't oppressive—they were protective. The system wasn't authoritarian—it was therapeutic.

Even those being crushed by it often thanked their crushers.

Operation Clean Sweep

The true test of John's enforcement system came on a humid Thursday night in Harbor Gardens. The drug problem that had festered under previous management hadn't disappeared—it had simply moved deeper underground. But the digital surveillance system had been mapping it for months.

"We've identified the network," Marcus briefed John and Veronica in the secure conference room. "Twelve dealers, approximately forty regular buyers, three stash locations. All residents or regular visitors."

"Police?" Veronica asked.

"Already coordinated. Detective Riley is grateful for the intel. They've been trying to crack this for years." Marcus pulled up tactical plans. "But here's the beauty—we do the identification and isolation. They make the arrests. We look like heroes. They get stats. Everyone wins."

"Except the dealers," John noted.

"They made their choice," Marcus replied. "They turned our community into a marketplace. Now they face market correction."

Operation Clean Sweep launched at 3 AM. CCU teams, accompanied by sheriff's deputies, executed simultaneous actions across Harbor Gardens. Doors knocked. Warrants served. Suspects detained. All based on months of digital surveillance, behavioral analysis, and human intelligence gathering.

By sunrise, twelve arrests had been made. Three hundred thousand dollars in drugs seized. Zero injuries. Zero escapes. The operation was so smooth that most residents slept through it.

The morning communication was carefully crafted. Email, text, and paper notices all carried the same message: "Harbor Gardens is now DRUG FREE thanks to vigilant residents and proactive security. Your safety is our priority."

The community meeting that evening was electric. Residents who'd lived in fear for years suddenly felt empowered. The HOA had done what police couldn't—or wouldn't. John stood at the podium, accepting grateful applause with practiced humility.

"This is what happens when communities take responsibility for their own safety," he said. "We don't wait for outside help. We help ourselves."

The surveillance footage of the operation—carefully edited to protect ongoing investigations—played on screens behind him. CCU members in their tactical uniforms. Police officers shaking Marcus Thompson's hand. Drugs being wheeled away in evidence bags.

"Some people said our security measures were too much," John continued. "That our surveillance was invasive. That our enforcement was heavy-handed. Tonight proves them wrong. Tonight proves that systematic, professional, community-based enforcement works."

The applause was deafening. Even former critics stood and clapped. Margaret Maxwell remained seated, but she was one of only a few. The video would play on the community channel for weeks; a reminder of what John's system could accomplish.

What residents didn't see were the three families evicted for "lease violations" who'd refused to cooperate with the investigation. The two teenagers sent to "rehabilitation programs" that happened to be in different states. The maintenance worker who'd been providing inside information to dealers, now unemployed and facing conspiracy charges based on CCU intelligence.

Clean Sweep wasn't just about removing drugs. It was about demonstrating power. Showing that John's system could coordinate with law enforcement as equals. That his intelligence was better than theirs. That his enforcement was more effective.

The sheriff himself attended the next HOA board meeting to present John with a commendation. "Communities like Harbor Gardens are the future of law enforcement," he said. "Public-private partnerships that leverage technology and community knowledge to prevent crime, not just respond to it."

John accepted the award with grace, knowing it was more than recognition. It was validation. Legal authority acknowledging his parallel system. Police admitting they needed him as much, if not more than he needed them.

The Media Massage

The interview request from Channel 7 came two days after Clean Sweep. Sarah Walsh, investigative reporter known for hard-hitting exposés, wanted to discuss "concerns about private security overreach in HOA communities."

"It's a hit piece," Veronica warned. "She's gunning for us."

"She's giving us a platform," John corrected. "We just need to control the narrative."

The interview was scheduled for the Queens Point clubhouse, with its wall of community awards and pictures of smiling residents. John wore a conservative blue suit—authoritative but not intimidating. David Krauss and Marcus Thompson stood in the background—visible but not looming.

"Mr. Masters," Sarah began, her tone professionally neutral, "critics say you've created a private police force that operates outside traditional oversight. How do you respond?"

John smiled warmly. "I'd say those critics haven't had their homes burglarized while waiting forty-five minutes for police response. Our Community Compliance Units aren't police—they're neighbors helping neighbors. They can't arrest anyone. They can't use deadly force. They simply observe, report, and assist."

"But the surveillance systems, the behavioral monitoring— doesn't that cross into privacy violations?"

"Every camera we operate is in public spaces where no one has an expectation of privacy. Every piece of data we collect is either publicly available or voluntarily provided by residents who've agreed to our terms of service. We're not doing anything Amazon isn't doing—we're just doing it for community safety instead of profit."

Sarah leaned forward. "What about reports of selective enforcement? Residents who criticize your policies facing stricter scrutiny?"

John's expression grew serious. "Let me be absolutely clear: our enforcement is based on documented violations, not personal opinions. Every action is recorded, reviewed, and available for audit. If someone feels they've been unfairly targeted, we have a robust appeals process. The fact that some of our most vocal critics continue to live peacefully in our communities proves that dissent is not just tolerated but protected."

"Then why have so many critics moved away?"

"Perhaps because they discovered that complaining is easier than contributing. We've created communities where crime is down to almost nothing, property values are up 50–100% and more, and resident satisfaction is at historic highs. If someone is happier elsewhere, we wish them well. But for the thousands who've chosen to stay, we'll continue providing the safety and security they expect and deserve."

The interview continued for twenty minutes, John deflecting every attack with statistics, anecdotes, and perfectly rehearsed empathy. When Sarah tried to corner him about the quasi-military nature of CCU training, he pivoted to veterans' employment. When she questioned the surveillance network, he shared stories of missing pets found and medical emergencies detected.

"Let me ask you something," John said as the interview wound down. "If government can't keep us safe—and clearly they can't, given the latest crime statistics—don't communities have, not just the right, but the obligation to protect themselves? Isn't that the most American thing imaginable? Neighbors taking responsibility for their own security and that of their neighbors?"

Sarah had no ready answer for that. The interview aired that night, edited to seem balanced but clearly showing John as reasonable, prepared, and dedicated to community service. The B-roll footage of happy residents, clean streets, and professional security officers made his communities look like paradise.

"You turned a hit piece into a recruitment video," Veronica marveled afterward.

"I told the truth," John replied. "As much as was useful."

The whole truth was that John had built something unprecedented: a private enforcement system that was legal, effective, and expanding. Each successful operation brought more communities asking for United Community's management. Each media appearance brought more residents grateful for safety.

The enforcement wing wasn't just muscle. It was the visible expression of John's philosophy: that freedom was inefficient, that choice was overrated, that most people would gladly trade liberty for security if the security was professionally packaged and came with rising property values.

The New Normal

Six months after Operation Clean Sweep, John's enforcement model was becoming the new standard across United's communities. CCU vehicles were as common as mail trucks. Residents waved at tactical-uniformed officers like they were crossing guards. The surveillance systems were upgraded monthly, their predictive algorithms becoming eerily accurate.

David Krauss and Marcus Thompson had grown their force to sixty operators across eight communities and were rapidly implementing the process at the remaining United HOAs. Their morning briefings looked like military planning sessions, with threat assessments, patrol routes, and intervention strategies mapped with mathematical precision.

"We prevented fourteen domestic violence incidents last month," Krauss reported to John. "Intervened before violence occurred based on pattern recognition. Saved three lives from overdoses by detecting medical emergencies through behavioral anomalies. Stopped approximately $40,000 in burglary/theft through predictive patrol routing."

"And violations?" John asked.

"Down 30%. Not because people are behaving better, but because they're self-correcting before we need to intervene. The system is training them."

It was true. Residents had internalized the surveillance, monitoring themselves and each other. They brought their trash cans in immediately. They kept noise levels down. They reported suspicious activity—which increasingly meant anyone who didn't conform to community standards.

"We've created the safest communities in Florida," John told Veronica one evening as they reviewed expansion plans. "Crime is nearly zero. Property values are soaring. Residents are happier than ever."

"And freedom?" Veronica asked, though her tone suggested she already knew the answer.

"Freedom for what? To be victimized? To live in fear? To watch their property values decline?" John gestured at the monitors showing peaceful streets and content residents. "They have the freedom that matters—freedom from chaos. Freedom from uncertainty. Freedom from having to make hard decisions about their own security."

"And those who want different freedoms?"

"Can freely live elsewhere."

But elsewhere was shrinking. More communities were adopting John's model. Other management companies were licensing his enforcement protocols. The CCU uniform was becoming as familiar as any corporate logo.

In the command center, Tommy Rodriguez watched the updated security feeds from eight communities, soon to be twelve, eventually to be dozens. Each camera a neuron in an expanding nervous system. Each resident a cell in a growing organism. Each enforcement action an antibody maintaining health.

"We're not just managing communities anymore," Tommy observed. "We're engineering society."

John nodded, watching Margaret Maxwell's heat signature as she walked her carefully prescribed route, no longer organizing resistance but simply existing within acceptable parameters. "Society was always engineered. We're just being honest about it."

The enforcement wing had succeeded beyond all projections. Not through brutality but through bureaucracy. Not through oppression but through optimization. Not through fear but through the most powerful force in human society: the desire to belong.

And those who didn't belong? Well, the system had protocols for that, too.

As night fell over the monitored paradise of John's empire, sixty CCU operators began their shifts, with more being trained. Watching. Recording. Predicting. Preventing. Enforcing a peace that felt like freedom to those who stayed within its boundaries.

For everyone else, they were always free to find freedom elsewhere, which was getting smaller every day.

Chapter 12: The Empire Consolidates

John the Fixer Becomes John the Kingmaker

The transition happened so gradually that even John Masters didn't notice at first. He'd stopped fixing broken HOAs—now he was manufacturing their leadership from scratch. The Sunday afternoon gatherings at Queens Point had evolved from casual meetings into auditions for power, where potential board members competed for his blessing without realizing they were being evaluated.

"You have to understand," John explained to a rapt audience of six carefully selected residents, wine glasses in hand, the Atlantic Ocean glittering beyond, "board service isn't about Robert's Rules or budget reviews. It's about vision. It's about building something that lasts longer than we do."

Madeline Holsten nodded eagerly from her position on the Italian leather sofa. Six months ago, she'd been a nobody—a retired bookkeeper whose main achievement was perfect attendance at water aerobics. Now, after John's mentorship, she was the frontrunner for treasurer at Seaside Towers, a 400-unit complex ripe for United Community integration.

"But how do we handle the resistance?" asked David Park, an aerospace engineer who John was grooming for the Cypress Woods board. "The old guard doesn't want change."

John smiled, refilling David's glass with a 2018 Caymus that cost more than most people's car payments. "You don't handle resistance. You redirect it. Every opponent wants something—recognition, respect, relevance. Give them a role that feels important but keeps them away from real decisions."

It was Psychology 101 wrapped in Machiavelli, served with premium wine and ocean breezes. John had perfected the formula: identify ambitions, create obligations, establish loyalty before power. By the time his proteges won their elections—and they always won— they weren't just board members. They were disciples.

The real work happened after these gatherings. John would meet individually with his candidates, always in settings that reinforced his authority. A lunch at the Capital Grille, where he'd casually cover a $300 tab. A golf round at Trump International, where he'd introduce them to county commissioners. A yacht cruise where problems got solved between champagne toasts.

"This isn't bribery," he'd explained to Veronica when she questioned the expense reports. "It's investment. Every dollar spent on cultivation returns thousands in compliance."

The unmarked envelopes came later, once loyalty was established. Never cash—John wasn't that crude. Instead, they contained solutions to personal problems. Medical bills that disappeared. Grandchildren who suddenly received scholarship offers. Home repairs handled by contractors who insisted the HOA had already paid.

Karen Lasky had been his first real transformation. Three years ago, she'd been the nightmare resident of Harbor Gardens—filing complaints about everything, showing up to board meetings with binders of grievances, the woman everyone avoided at the pool. She'd been bitter, lonely, and desperate for relevance. A true "Karen" through and through.

John had seen potential where others saw pestilence.

"Karen," he'd said, approaching her after a particularly contentious meeting where she'd accused the board of embezzlement (she was right, but for the wrong reasons). "You have incredible attention to detail. Have you ever considered channeling that into leadership?"

The transformation took six months. John introduced her to power gradually—first as volunteer coordinator, then committee chair, finally as his hand-picked candidate for board president. He taught her to weaponize her negativity into "reform energy." Her bitterness became "passion for accountability." Her loneliness transformed into "dedication to community."

Now Karen Lasky ruled Harbor Gardens with an iron fist wrapped in procedural velvet. She'd cleaned out the old board, implemented United's systems, and delivered the highest satisfaction ratings in the community's history. She also reported every significant decision to John, though she'd never admit she wasn't really in charge.

"I gave her what she really wanted," John told Marcus Thompson during their weekly security briefing. "Not power—purpose. The power was just the delivery mechanism."

"And she'll do anything to keep it," Marcus observed.

"She'll do anything because she believes she's doing good. The best servants think they're leaders."

The Rise of The Triad

By year three of his empire, John had identified a truth about HOA governance: direct control was inefficient. Better to rule through proxies who thought they were partners. His three most successful converts had become known (though never to their faces) as The Triad—a triumvirate of true believers who spread United's gospel with religious fervor.

Karen Lasky was the enforcer. Her transformation from bitter complainer to community queen pin was so complete that new residents couldn't imagine her any other way. She ruled Harbor Gardens through a combination of maternal concern and bureaucratic brutality. Violations were handled swiftly but with explanations about "maintaining standards for everyone's benefit." Opposition was smothered with committee appointments and procedural quicksand.

"She's terrifying," one resident had whispered to another during a board meeting. "But effective."

That was the point. Karen's regime was authoritarian but delivered results. Property values up 35%. Crime down to zero. Maintenance issues were resolved before residents noticed them. She'd helped create a surveillance state that residents begged to live in.

Reggie Delacruz brought different skills to John's empire. The retired airline pilot and Air Force veteran ran Palmetto Estates like a military operation—precise, hierarchical, and unforgiving of incompetence. Where Karen ruled through bureaucracy, Reggie commanded through respect and barely veiled threat.

"I flew combat missions in Iraq," he'd tell anyone who questioned his methods. "I know what chaos looks like. You want chaos, move somewhere else. You want order, fall in line."

His monthly "Commander's Calls"—mandatory community meetings styled after military briefings—achieved 95% attendance. Residents received "mission objectives" (community goals), "threat assessments" (crime statistics), and "commendations" (public praise for compliance). The military terminology should have been ridiculous. Instead, it created unity.

"People want to belong to something bigger," Reggie explained to John during one of their strategy sessions. "The military taught me that. You give them a mission, a uniform—even if it's just a community T-shirt—and clear objectives, they'll march in formation."

Under Reggie's command, Palmetto Estates had become a fortress. His security protocols—developed with Marcus Thompson—included resident patrols, strategic camera placement, and intelligence gathering that would make the NSA jealous. The Venezuelan gang that had been eyeing the community took one look at Reggie's operation and decided to hunt elsewhere.

Angela Wu completed the triad with financial sophistication that turned HOA management into high finance. The widow of a hedge fund manager, she'd inherited money but not purpose until John recruited her. Her forensic accounting skills had uncovered decades of embezzlement at Coral Heights, leading to criminal charges against three former board members.

"They stole $1.8 million over twelve years," she'd reported to a shocked community meeting. "But that's not the real crime. The real crime is they stole it stupidly. No interest, no investment strategy, just cash sitting in personal accounts, easily clawed back and with what the insurance company paid, the HOA was made more than whole."

Under Angela's management, Coral Heights' reserves didn't just sit in banks—they worked. Strategic investments in treasury bills, careful timing of maintenance projects to capitalize on contractor desperation, bulk purchasing agreements that generated kickbacks disguised as "volume incentives." She'd turned the HOA into a financial engine that generated returns while maintaining perfect legal compliance.

"It's not about making money," she'd explain with the precise diction of someone who'd attended Swiss finishing schools. "It's about maximizing value for our residents. If that happens to generate surplus revenue, we're simply being efficient."

The Triad met monthly at rotating locations, ostensibly to share best practices. In reality, they coordinated strategies across their communities, creating a unified front that could mobilize thousands of voters, millions in purchasing power, and enough influence to sway county politics.

"We're not conspiring," Karen would insist if anyone questioned their meetings. "We're collaborating. There's a difference."

The difference, as John knew, was mostly semantic. But semantics mattered when avoiding RICO charges.

Playing Chess Across the County

The map in John's private office looked innocuous enough—colored pins marking various communities across Palm Beach and Broward Counties, with a few even stretching down into Miami-Dade. Red for direct United management. Blue for affiliated boards. Green for targeted acquisitions. To a casual observer, it might have been a real estate investment chart. To John, it was a battlefield where every pin represented a conquered territory.

"We now manage fifty-two HOA boards directly," Tommy Rodriguez reported during their Thursday intelligence briefing. "Another sixty-seven through secondary connections. Total units under some form of influence: 89,000. Total residents: approximately 240,000."

"Voting power?" John asked.

"In the last county election, our communities delivered 67,000 votes. Enough to swing any local race, most state legislative contests."

"And economically?"

Veronica pulled up the financial dashboard. "Annual HOA fees under management: $847 million. Maintenance and capital budgets: $1.2 billion. When you factor in our preferred vendor network, we're directing close to $2 billion in annual economic activity."

It was an empire built not through conquest but through service agreements. Every vendor who wanted HOA contracts had to meet United's standards—which meant using United systems, sharing data with United analytics, and often, giving United an equity stake.

"It's not a kickback if it's an investment," John had explained to his lawyer during one of their privilege-protected strategy sessions. "We're not taking money for contracts. We're investing in vendors we believe in, who happen to win contracts through superior service."

The web was intricate. Sunshine Maintenance LLC did landscaping for fifteen communities—a United entity owned 30%. Secure Home Systems provided security infrastructure for twenty-three—United had 25%. Aqua-Clear handled pool maintenance for thirty-one—United controlled 40% through another untraceable subsidiary.

Each company operated independently, competed "fairly" for contracts, and delivered high-quality service. All of their contracts with United were won through competitive bidding, their bids always coming in around 2% below the nearest competitor. They also shared data, coordinated pricing, and ensured that non-United communities paid premium rates that subsidized discounts for the faithful.

"Vertical integration," Angela Wu had called it admiringly. "You're not just managing communities. You're managing the entire ecosystem."

"Managing suggests control," John had corrected. "We're optimizing. Every efficiency we create benefits residents through lower costs and better service."

The fact that it also created an impenetrable network of financial interdependence was just good business. The fact that this network could be activated for political purposes was just strategic planning. The fact that it looked suspiciously like racketeering was why John kept very good lawyers on retainer.

Meanwhile, Back at the Guard Shack...

The transformation of Queens Point's security infrastructure had been so gradual that residents forgot it had once been a sleepy retiree with a clipboard. Now, the main entrance looked like an embassy checkpoint—reinforced structure, bulletproof glass, multiple monitors showing feeds from dozens of cameras.

Marcus Thompson stood in the command center—they didn't call it a guard shack anymore—reviewing staffing reports with his lieutenant, James Realto. The walls were covered with tactical maps of all United properties, response time charts, and threat assessment matrices.

"New hire orientation tomorrow," Realto reported. "Six more ex-military, two retired cops, one former federal marshal. All clean backgrounds, all hungry for structure."

"Good. Deploy them to the key properties first. Let them learn our methods before they develop bad habits." Marcus pulled up incident reports. "What's the threat picture?"

"Quiet on the domestic front. Two attempted break-ins at non-United communities last week. Both within three miles of our properties. We've increased perimeter patrols accordingly."

Marcus nodded. The strategy was working—create security so visible, so professional, that criminals chose easier targets. It wasn't about catching bad guys; it was about making them hunt elsewhere.

"International concerns?" Marcus asked, his tone suggesting this wasn't hypothetical.

Realto lowered his voice. "Chatter about the Venezuelans regrouping. They're looking at Bayshore Estates—it's failing, lots of vacancies, waterfront access. Perfect for their operations."

Bayshore Estates wasn't a United property—yet. But it bordered two that were, making it a potential infection that could spread.

"Recommendation?"

"Preemptive acquisition. Make them an offer before the Venezuelans get established."

Marcus considered this. "Run it by Mr. Masters. If he approves, we move fast. Better to overpay than to have a cancer on our border."

The security apparatus John had built went far beyond normal HOA protection. Each guard was trained in intelligence gathering, behavioral analysis, and predictive threat assessment. They didn't just respond to crime—they prevented it through environmental design, social pressure, and when necessary, direct intervention.

"We're not police," Marcus reminded every new hire. "We're sheepdogs. Our job is to make the wolves look elsewhere for their meals."

The Ghost of the Mob Returns

The intelligence came through old channels—a Brooklyn number John hadn't seen in years, appearing on a burner phone he'd almost forgotten he owned. The message was simple: "The Venezuelans are moving on Bayshore. They've got backing. You need friends."

John met his contact at a Cuban restaurant in Hialeah, far from his manicured kingdom. Joey Sorrento looked older, grayer, but his eyes still had the flat affect of a man who'd solved many problems with permanent solutions.

"MV," Joey said, using the name no one had called him since Cleveland. "Looking prosperous. Florida suits you."

"I'm retired, Joey. Different life now."

Joey laughed, a sound like gravel in a disposal. "Nobody retires from what we were. We just change industries." He leaned forward. "The Venezuelans aren't just looking for real estate. They're looking for infrastructure. Cleaning money through HOA contracts, using maintenance companies for distribution. Your kingdom's in their way."

"I can handle some South American street gang."

"Not a gang anymore. They've got Colombian backing, Mexican connections. This is cartel-adjacent shit, Johnny. They see your operation as either competition to eliminate or infrastructure to absorb."

John processed this, calculating angles. "What's your interest?"

"Same as always. Business. My people have interests in South Florida, too. Legitimate ones, mostly. We don't need a war fucking up property values." Joey slid a card across the table. "You need help, you call. Old times' sake."

"And the price?"

"No price. Consider it professional courtesy. You kept your mouth shut about me when it mattered. That bought you lifetime credit." Joey stood. "But MV? This ain't Cleveland. These Venezuelans don't follow the old rules. They see civilians as leverage, not boundaries. Protect your people."

After Joey left, John sat in the restaurant, drinking Cuban coffee and thinking. He'd built his empire to escape the violence of his past. Now that past was circling back, drawn by his success.

He called Marcus from the car. "Staff up Bayshore's neighboring properties. Full tactical teams, 24/7 coverage. And reach out to our federal contacts. If the Venezuelans are cartel-connected, DEA needs to know."

"Going legitimate?" Marcus asked.

"Going strategic. Let the feds handle the violence. We handle the aftermath." John smiled coldly. "Besides, nothing drops property values like a DEA raid. We'll pick up Bayshore for pennies once they're done."

Chapter 13: The Pickleball Payoff

The First Annual Palm Beach County Pickleball Championships

The courts gleamed under the mid-morning sun, newly painted and bordered with sponsor banners that fluttered like prayer flags in the humid breeze. Each court bore fresh lines in tournament-regulation white, the surfaces so pristine they seemed to glow against the manicured landscaping that surrounded them. A massive overhead sign stretched between two palm trees, its vinyl letters crisp and bold: "1st Annual Palm Beach County Pickleball Championships— Benefiting the United Community Foundation." Below it, smaller banners proclaimed the day's noble purpose: "Building Tomorrow's Communities Today" and "Where Sport Meets Service."

John Masters stood front and center in his signature cerulean polo—the same shade he'd worn to every major HOA event since taking office—next to Veronica Santiago, the magnetic and ever-poised CEO of United Community Foundation. Her cream-colored sundress moved like liquid silk in the morning air, and her smile held that perfect balance of warmth and authority that had made her the darling of Palm Beach philanthropy. Together, they looked every bit the visionary duo: he, the reform-minded HOA strategic advisor who'd transformed Sunset Palms from a sleepy retirement community into a model of progressive governance; she, the charismatic nonprofit leader who'd brought in grants and donations to Palm Beach County's most vulnerable populations.

The sponsorships had rolled in like a high tide. Doran & Doran: For the People had purchased the primary court naming rights, their bold red banner promising justice for injury victims displayed prominently above Court One. Sunrise Medical Center sponsored the medical tent, complete with a registered nurse and a defibrillator that everyone hoped would remain unused. Intracoastal Orthopedic Associates had funded the player registration area, their booth staffed by physical therapists offering free movement assessments to anyone over sixty.

Local real estate groups had set up elaborate displays around the courts' perimeter. Caldwell Banker showcased luxury condos with LED screens displaying virtual tours. Re/Max had brought a scaled model of a new 55+ community, complete with its own pickleball facility. Century 21 offered "Championship Home Buying" packages with promises of expedited closings for tournament participants.

The injury law firms had been more subtle but no less present. Martinez & Associates sponsored the scorekeeping tablets, each one displaying their firm's logo between sets. The Goldstein Law Group had funded the tournament brackets, printed on high-quality cardstock with their contact information discreetly placed at the bottom. Even the water stations bore small placards: "Staying Hydrated, Staying Safe – Brought to you by Personal Injury Partners PLLC."

An upscale CBD wellness brand called Zen Coast had perhaps the most popular booth, offering samples of their "Athletic Recovery Gummies" and "Joint Comfort Topicals" to players between matches. Their representative, a former yoga instructor named Moonbeam, dispensed advice about pain management and stress reduction with the enthusiasm of a true believer.

The silent auction table groaned under the weight of donated items. The centerpiece was a two-night stay at The Breakers, Palm Beach's legendary oceanfront resort, complete with spa treatments and dinner at their flagship restaurant. A full set of monogrammed pickleball paddles crafted from Brazilian cherry wood sat beside a wine collection valued at over $3000. Local restaurants had contributed dinner certificates, while boutiques offered shopping sprees and jewelry stores displayed gleaming tennis bracelets "perfect for the active lifestyle."

The tournament drew a who's who of suburban high society. Former college athletes in their sixties moved with the careful precision of bodies that remembered greatness. Minor TV personalities from local morning shows signed autographs and posed for selfies. Neighborhood socialites competed in color-coordinated team shirts—the Sunset Palms squad wore matching turquoise with "SP Champions" embroidered in gold thread. Even Moe and Sallie, along with Curtis from 105.5 of the Palm Beaches, appeared, with Curtis warming up the crowd with irreverent humor and jokes about pickleball injuries.

Professional videographers moved between courts with expensive equipment, capturing highlight reels for social media promotion. Overhead, a drone pilot named Kevin operated a high-end quadcopter, livestreaming aerial footage to the tournament's Facebook page, where viewers from around the county and world watched the action unfold. The production value was worthy of a professional sporting event.

Kids from the local high school worked the event for community service credit, selling branded water bottles for $5 each and tournament T-shirts for twenty. Their energy was infectious as they called out scores and cheered for dramatic shots. A DJ named Carlos spun tropical house music from a booth beside Smoothie Paradise, a food truck that had driven up from Fort Lauderdale specifically for the event. The bass line thumped softly under the morning air, adding an unexpectedly sophisticated soundtrack to the suburban competition.

By 10:30 AM, the first casualty occurred. Janel Rolston, a lovely sixty-nine-year-old widow who'd mistaken her enthusiasm for pickleball as talent, went down hard during her first-round match. She'd been playing aggressively, diving for a shot that any sensible person would have let go, when her right knee buckled with an audible pop that silenced Court Three. The crowd winced collectively as Janel's Achilles tendon snapped like a rubber band, her cry of pain cutting through the morning air.

"Oh my God, Janel!" shrieked her doubles partner, Margaret Maxwell, dropping her paddle and rushing to where Janel lay clutching her ankle.

Dr. Patricia Weinstein from Sunrise Medical Associates was on the scene within seconds, her medical training kicking in as she knelt beside Janel. "Don't move, sweetie. We need to keep that leg immobilized." She looked up at John, who had appeared courtside with remarkable speed. "We need an ambulance."

But before John could respond, Dr. Marcus Feldman of Intracoastal, the orthopedic surgeon who'd been watching from the sidelines, was already approaching with his business card extended. "Mrs. Rolston, I'm Dr. Feldman. I specialize in exactly this type of injury. My office can have you in for surgery tomorrow morning."

"Doctor," Dr. Weinstein said sharply, "she needs emergency care first."

"Of course, of course. But I'll ride with her to the hospital. Professional courtesy." His smile was practiced, professional, and predatory.

The second injury happened just before noon. Harold Brennan, a spry seventy-two-year-old retired engineer, had been dominating his bracket until he attempted an overhead smash that his body simply couldn't execute. His ACL snapped mid-leap, sending him sprawling across the court in a tangle of limbs and profanity that would have made his deceased wife blush.

"Son of a bitch!" Harold bellowed, clutching his knee as concerned players surrounded him. "Forty years of tennis and this damn paddle sport takes me down!"

The Goldstein Law Group representative, a sharp-eyed paralegal named Sandra Menendez, was taking notes before Dr. Weinstein had even reached Harold's side. She'd been positioned strategically near Court Two, clipboard in hand, ostensibly keeping score but actually conducting what amounted to field research.

"Mr. Brennan," Sandra said gently, "I'm Sandra from Goldstein Law Group. We're sponsoring today's event. Can you tell me exactly what happened?"

"Sandra," Veronica appeared beside them with the smooth efficiency of a diplomat, "I think Mr. Brennan needs medical attention before interviews."

But Sandra was persistent. "Of course, but it's important to document the circumstances while they're fresh in his memory. Mr.

Brennan, did anyone explain the risks of the sport? Were you given any safety materials?"

Harold looked confused through his pain. "Safety materials? Lady, it's paddle tennis with a wiffle ball. How dangerous could it be?"

The third injury struck at 1:15 PM, just as the semifinals were beginning. Doris Kovak, a seventy-year-old retired librarian with arms like pipe cleaners, caught her paddle on the net during an enthusiastic volley. The momentum sent her tumbling forward onto her outstretched wrist, which snapped with a sound like breaking kindling.

"Oh dear," she said with remarkable composure, staring down at her wrist, which was now bent at an anatomically impossible angle. "I don't think that's supposed to look like that."

This time, both Dr. Feldman and a new arrival—Dr. Steven Carlisle from Sunrise Medical Center's orthopedic department— rushed to assist. Dr. Carlisle had somehow materialized in the time since Harold's injury, despite not being on the original list of medical volunteers.

"Mrs. Kovak, I'm Dr. Carlisle," he said, gently examining her wrist. "This definitely needs surgical repair. I can schedule you first thing Monday morning."

"Actually," Dr. Feldman interrupted, "my practice specializes in exactly this type of fracture. Mrs. Kovak, I've been doing wrist reconstructions for thirty years."

"Gentlemen," Dr. Weinstein said with barely concealed irritation, "she needs an emergency room, not a consultation."

While the doctors argued professional precedence, the lawyers were having their own field day. Martinez & Associates had deployed a second paralegal, and Personal Injury Partners LLC had sent their top investigator, a former insurance adjuster named Rick Morano, who was photographing court conditions and interviewing witnesses.

"Ma'am," Rick approached Margaret Maxwell, who was still shaken from watching her partner Janel's injury, "I'm Rick Morano, and I'm just gathering information about today's events. Can you tell me what kind of safety briefing you received before play began?"

Margaret looked flustered. "Safety briefing? We just signed in and got our tournament brackets."

"Signed in where? What exactly did you sign?"

"Just the registration sheet, I think. And maybe something else? I didn't really read it."

Rick's eyes lit up like slot machine cherries. "Would you say the organizers made the risks clear to participants?"

"What risks? It's pickleball!"

"What we're doing today," John said into the wireless microphone, his hand resting lightly on Veronica's back, "is more than just sport. It's about community. It's about giving back to the place that gives us so much." His voice carried easily across the courts, trained from years of HOA meetings, community talks, and mob sit-downs. "When we invest in recreation, we invest in wellness. When we invest in wellness, we invest in our future."

He was pointedly ignoring the three ambulances that had arrived in the past two hours and the small crowd of personal injury lawyers who were circulating like sharks scenting blood in the water.

Thunderous applause erupted from the crowd of nearly two hundred spectators, though some clapped more cautiously now, having witnessed three separate medical emergencies. Someone in the back shouted, "We love you, Veronica!" and she acknowledged them with a graceful wave, her smile never wavering despite the chaos.

She leaned in to whisper to John, her breath warm against his ear: "They have no idea how good we are at this."

John's own smile remained perfectly in place, though internally he was calculating liability exposure and wondering why nobody had thought to mention that elderly people plus competitive sports minus liability waivers equaled a potential legal nightmare. "That's the point," he murmured back. "Though I'm starting to think we should have invested in better insurance."

"Relax," Veronica whispered. "Dr. Feldman already called his malpractice carrier. Apparently, he's seeing dollar signs, not liability."

The Grift Goes Pro

Three hours later, back in John's office, the air smelled faintly of eucalyptus from the aromatherapy diffuser Veronica had given him for his birthday—and faintly of the legal trouble that was brewing faster than a summer thunderstorm. The device hummed quietly on his credenza, next to framed photos of him cutting ribbons and shaking hands with county officials. The tournament was still in progress, though play had been suspended on two courts while maintenance crews cleaned up bloodstains and the remaining participants competed with the nervous energy of people who'd suddenly realized that recreational sports could be genuinely dangerous.

On his monitor, the spreadsheet was neatly arranged in color-coded columns that would have impressed any CPA. Total funds raised: $112,850. Registration fees: $28,400. Corporate sponsorships: $67,200. Silent auction proceeds: $17,250. Minor tournament expenses (permits, equipment rental, insurance): $15,450. Medical emergency response costs (not budgeted): $3,200. Net available for "community investment": $94,200.

What the spreadsheet didn't reflect was the feared legal exposure from three serious injuries and what appeared to be a complete absence of proper liability waivers. John was beginning to suspect that his assistant's "registration forms" had been nothing more than sign-in sheets with participant names and emergency contact information.

Veronica sat on the corner of his mahogany desk, one heel bouncing with slightly more agitation than usual as she fielded calls from reporters who'd gotten wind of the injuries. Her presence in his office had become so routine that his secretary no longer announced her arrivals. However, today, he might have appreciated the warning given the parade of lawyers who kept appearing in the parking lot.

"Channel 7 wants a statement about tournament safety protocols," she said, hanging up her phone with barely controlled frustration. "And apparently Rick Morano from Personal Injury Partners has been interviewing participants for the past two hours."

"What kind of interviews?"

"The kind where he asks leading questions about inadequate safety warnings and whether we properly explained the risks to elderly participants." Veronica's smile had developed a sharp edge. "He's particularly interested in Janel Rolston's case, since she's apparently the poster child for 'enthusiastic widow discovers that optimism doesn't replace physical reality.'"

John rubbed his temples, feeling the beginning of a headache that had nothing to do with the eucalyptus aromatherapy. "Tell me we have proper waivers."

"Define 'proper.'"

"Legal documents that transfer liability away from the HOA and the Foundation in case of participant injury."

Veronica's pause was telling. "We have registration forms."

"What do the registration forms say?"

"They collect contact information and ask about medical conditions."

"That's it?"

"And there's a line about participating at your own risk."

John stared at her. "A line? Not a full waiver with legal language and witnessed signatures?"

"I may have assumed that a casual community tournament wouldn't require the same documentation as a professional sporting event."

The phone rang, interrupting what was shaping up to be their first serious operational disagreement. John's assistant's voice came through the intercom: "Mr. Masters, there's a Dr. Feldman here to see you. He says it's about the tournament participants he's treating."

"Send him in," John said, though he suspected this conversation was going to make his headache considerably worse.

Dr. Andrew Feldman entered the office with the confident stride of a man who'd found a gold mine in his own backyard. He was tall, silver-haired, and wore the kind of expensive watch that suggested orthopedic surgery was very good business indeed. His handshake was firm, his smile was professional, and his eyes held the gleam of someone who'd just discovered an untapped revenue stream.

"Mr. Masters, Ms. Santiago, thank you for seeing me on such short notice." He settled into the leather chair across from John's desk without being invited to sit. "I wanted to discuss the three cases from today's tournament, and more importantly, the opportunities they represent."

"Opportunities?" John asked carefully.

"Well, yes. Mrs. Rolston's Achilles repair, Mr. Brennan's ACL reconstruction, Mrs. Kovak's wrist surgery—we're looking at approximately $180,000 in procedures, and that's just the initial surgeries. Physical therapy, follow-up care, potential complications...we could easily be talking about $300,000 in total medical revenue."

Veronica leaned forward slightly. "And you're telling us this because...?"

"Because I'd like to propose a partnership. Your community events are clearly generating significant demand for orthopedic services. I think we could work together to ensure that demand is met efficiently and profitably."

John felt like he was watching a slow-motion car crash. "Dr. Feldman, are you suggesting that we deliberately organize events that injure elderly people?"

"Oh, heavens no! Nothing deliberate. But let's be realistic— you're running athletic competitions for people in their sixties and seventies. Injuries are inevitable. The question is whether those injuries get treated by random emergency room doctors or by specialists who appreciate the value of ongoing relationships."

Dr. Feldman opened his briefcase and withdrew a folder thick with documentation. "I've prepared a proposal for a comprehensive sports medicine partnership. Intracoastal Orthopedic Associates would provide on-site medical support for all your future events. In exchange, injured participants would be referred to our practice for treatment. We'd also be happy to sponsor additional tournaments throughout the year."

"What kind of sponsorship are we talking about?" Veronica asked, her business instincts overriding her ethical concerns.

"Fifty thousand dollars per quarter for exclusive medical provider status. Plus, coverage of all emergency response costs for tournament-related injuries. And," he paused for effect, "we'd like to discuss expanding the program to your other communities in Palm Beach County."

John's headache was intensifying. "You want us to franchise injuring elderly people?"

"I want us to create a sustainable model for providing quality medical care to an underserved population while supporting community recreational programming." Dr. Feldman's tone suggested he'd practiced this pitch. "Mr. Masters, you've already demonstrated remarkable success at organizing events that engage seniors in physical activity. The fact that some participants get injured simply reflects the reality of an aging population pursuing active lifestyles."

Veronica was studying the proposal with the focused intensity of someone calculating profit margins. "What about liability? Our tournament today has already attracted attention from several personal injury firms."

"Already handled. As part of our partnership, Intracoastal would provide legal support for all event-related liability issues. Our lawyers are very experienced in sports medicine litigation."

"Because you get sued frequently?"

"Because we understand the legal landscape better than anyone. Mr. Masters, with proper waivers and medical supervision, your liability exposure is minimal. Without them..." He gestured toward the monitor where Rick Morano could be seen interviewing another tournament participant in the parking lot.

The conversation continued for another twenty minutes, with Dr. Feldman outlining a partnership that was simultaneously brilliant and morally questionable. He proposed a series of monthly tournaments designed to "promote active aging" while generating a steady stream of orthopedic patients. Each event would be staffed with medical professionals who could provide immediate care and seamless referrals to specialized treatment.

"Think of it as preventive medicine," Dr. Feldman explained. "We're not creating injuries—we're ensuring that inevitable injuries receive optimal treatment."

After he left, John and Veronica sat in contemplative silence for several minutes.

"It's not exactly what we planned," Veronica finally said.

"No kidding. We went from financial fraud to accidentally creating a medical-industrial complex."

"Accidentally?"

John looked at her sharply. "You're not seriously considering this."

"I'm considering that we have three injured people, no proper liability waivers, and a parking lot full of personal injury lawyers. Dr. Feldman is offering to solve all of those problems while paying us $200,000 a year for the privilege."

"He's offering to turn us into injury farmers."

"He's offering to turn a liability into an asset. John, we've already proven we can organize successful community events. If those events happen to require medical support, and if that medical support happens to be profitable, is that really our fault?"

John stared at the monitor showing the tournament courts, where the afternoon matches were concluding with considerably more caution than the morning rounds had begun. Players were stretching extensively, moving more carefully, and keeping a watchful eye on the medical tent that had been significantly reinforced since Janel Rolston's departure in the first ambulance.

"We should give the Foundation a nice little piece this time," Veronica said, returning to their original financial planning with remarkable equanimity. "Say…fifteen grand? Enough for a ribbon-cutting photo op and a couple of press releases about youth programming." She paused to scroll through her phone, monitoring the developing situation. "Maybe throw in a safety initiative announcement. The optics are becoming important."

"Non"-Profits Flourish

And so it did flow, just as they'd perfected increasingly sophisticated operations. The donations were routed through Palm County Youth Futures, the nonprofit Veronica had established, ostensibly to provide recreational opportunities for at-risk children. The organization's board consisted of well-meaning retirees who met quarterly for continental breakfast and rubber-stamped whatever initiatives Veronica presented.

From Youth Futures, the money flowed to their carefully constructed network of front companies. Sportive Strategies LLC handled "equipment procurement and facility management." Community Athletics Solutions provided "youth engagement consulting and program development." Heritage Urban Planning offered "recreational space optimization and community wellness assessment." Each company was legally registered, properly incorporated, and completely controlled by John and Veronica through layers of shell ownership that would have required a forensic accountant months to unravel.

"I even added a clause last month," Veronica said, finally setting down her phone and giving John her full attention. "Any urgent fund reallocations approved by the CEO of the Foundation are considered automatically ratified by the board, provided they align with our core mission of community enhancement." She sipped her matcha latte, bought from the organic café that had opened in the strip mall adjacent to Sunset Palms. "The beauty is that everything we do technically aligns with community enhancement."

John smirked, admiring once again the elegant simplicity of their system. "You're diabolical. I trained you well."

She winked, the gesture somehow both playful and predatory. "Learned it from the best! And completely tax-deductible too."

The money that eventually found its way back to them was laundered through consulting fees, management contracts, and equipment purchases from companies they secretly owned. Their take typically ran between 30 and 40% of any given fundraising event. The remainder actually did fund community improvements—just enough to avoid suspicion, while generating positive press coverage that kept their operation expanding. And on the surface, the scam was fully compliant with all IRS and Florida laws and rules.

Securing the Future

Two weeks later, at the monthly HOA board meeting held in the community center's main conference room, John introduced Resolution 2023-61: "Expansion of Recreational Improvement Autonomy." The conference room was larger than usual, accommodating not just the seven board members but nearly thirty residents who'd come to hear about the pickleball tournament's success and future plans.

"The idea," John explained from the podium, using a PowerPoint presentation he'd spent hours perfecting, "is to allow us the agility to move funds where they're needed most—playgrounds, youth centers, or yes, even more pickleball courts. We shouldn't let bureaucratic red tape hold us back from innovation and rapid response to community needs."

The presentation included charts showing increased property values in communities with robust recreational facilities, testimonials from residents about improved quality of life, and before-and-after photos of the pickleball courts that had transformed an unused corner of the community into a hub of social activity.

Veronica sat in the third row of the audience, positioned where John could see her without appearing to seek her approval. Her presence lent credibility to the proceedings—everyone knew about her foundation's work, and many residents had seen the glowing coverage of the tournament in the Palm Beach Post. When she gave a subtle nod of support during John's explanation of streamlined funding procedures, several undecided board members seemed to shift in their chairs.

"What Mr. Masters is proposing," said board member Elena Rodriguez, a retired accountant who'd moved to Sunset Palms five years earlier, "essentially gives the HOA executive committee discretionary authority over community improvement funds up to…what amount?"

"Twenty-five thousand dollars per project," John replied smoothly. "With full transparency, of course. All expenditures would be reported at the following month's meeting, and any resident can request detailed documentation at any time."

Board member Patricia Marks raised her hand. "And larger projects would still require full board approval?"

"Absolutely. This is about efficiency, not circumventing oversight. If we want to repair playground equipment or resurface a tennis court, we shouldn't have to wait six weeks for the next board meeting while kids go without safe recreational options."

The logic was compelling, especially when presented alongside photos of smiling children and active seniors enjoying the facilities that rapid decision-making had already produced. The resolution passed 6-1, with only Tom Brennan—no relation to Harold, the injured pickleball player—dissenting.

Brennan, a retired police detective with sharp eyes and a perpetually skeptical expression, had been asking uncomfortable questions since joining the board eight months earlier. "I'm not opposed to recreational improvements," he said during the discussion period, "but I think we need more robust financial controls, not fewer. Maybe we should be talking about hiring an independent auditor instead of concentrating more authority in fewer hands."

His concerns were politely noted and thoroughly ignored by the majority.

Afterward, as residents filed out discussing vacation plans and weekend social events, Veronica caught up with John in the hallway outside the conference room. The building was quieter now, with only the soft hum of air conditioning and distant sounds of evening activities from the community center's other rooms.

"Tom's becoming a problem," she said softly, her voice barely above a whisper. "We should dig into his HOA dues. Maybe he's behind on something. Use it to keep him in line."

John had anticipated this conversation. Brennan's investigative instincts made him dangerous, but his rigid personality also made him predictable. "Already working on it. My assistant pulled his payment history this afternoon. He's current on everything, but I found something interesting in his background check from when he joined the board."

"What kind of interesting?"

"He was forced into early retirement from Miami-Dade PD. Internal affairs investigation that never quite went public. Something about evidence handling procedures." John kept his voice level, professional. "Nothing criminal, but definitely the kind of thing that might make someone… cautious about casting stones."

Veronica's smile was sharp as winter sunlight. "Perfect. Sometimes the best offense is knowing when not to play defense."

Managing Optics

The buzz from the pickleball event continued building throughout the following week. The *Palm Beach Post* ran a follow-up editorial praising the "innovative public-private partnerships that are transforming community development in South Florida." The editorial specifically highlighted the collaboration between "forward-thinking HOA leadership" and "established nonprofit organizations" as a model for other communities to emulate.

Palm Beach County Parks & Recreation reposted photos of Veronica and John holding up a giant ceremonial check on their Instagram account, adding their own caption about the importance of community partnerships in expanding recreational opportunities. The post generated over three hundred likes and dozens of comments from residents praising the initiative.

Even Channel 5 featured the tournament as their Friday feel-good story, with weekend anchor Andrea Adler interviewing participants about the impact of community sports on senior wellness. The three-minute segment included aerial footage from the drone coverage and interviews with players who spoke glowingly about the sense of community the tournament had fostered.

But then came the offer John had been dreading since the tournament's success became impossible to ignore: a regional feature segment from NBC6's investigative unit.

The email arrived on a Tuesday morning, sent from a producer named Sarah Hughes. "We're developing a feature story about innovative community development models in South Florida," the email read. "We want to showcase the model partnership between a dynamic HOA president and a visionary nonprofit leader. Your pickleball tournament has been mentioned by several sources as an example of how creative thinking can benefit entire communities."

The message went on to outline a proposed shooting schedule that would include interviews with both John and Veronica, footage of community facilities, and conversations with residents about the impact of their partnership. "We're particularly interested in how you've managed to attract corporate sponsorship for community events and how other neighborhoods might replicate your success."

Veronica laughed when John forwarded her the email, but her amusement carried an edge. "They have no idea how dynamic we really are."

John frowned as he read through the proposed questions the producer had attached. Most were softball inquiries about community engagement and nonprofit partnerships, but several probed deeper into funding mechanisms and oversight procedures. "The more attention we get, the more exposure we risk. Television producers have research teams. They dig."

"Relax," Veronica said, though her tone suggested she was taking the situation more seriously than her words indicated. "We control the narrative. Let them look. We've given them everything they want to see—successful community programs, happy residents, measurable improvements to quality of life. What are they going to find? That we're too good at our jobs?"

John appreciated her confidence, but his experience in Cleveland had taught him that success often bred its own dangers. "It's not about what they'll find. It's about what they might stumble across while they're looking."

Veronica moved to his window, gazing out at the pickleball courts where a group of residents were engaged in an enthusiastic morning match. "Then we give them such a good story that they never think to look for a different one. I'll arrange for them to interview some of our scholarship recipients. Maybe we can time it with the playground renovation announcement."

"You think we should do it?"

"I think we don't have a choice. Refusing would raise more questions than cooperating. Besides," she turned back to him with that predatory smile he'd come to know so well, "I've always wanted to be on television."

Quiet Threats

That night, after dinner with Veronica at the posh New York Prime Steakhouse, back home, they reviewed quarterly disbursements to their network of shell firms in the privacy of his home office, a message pinged his burner phone—a device he'd maintained out of habit more than necessity, though recent events were making him grateful for old-fashioned paranoia.

The message was brief and seemingly innocuous: "Your backswing's looking stiff. Better stretch before the next tournament. – A Friend"

The words hit him like ice water. In Cleveland, "backswing" had been Max Vecchio's signature term for the moment when a profitable scheme was about to fall apart—the critical point where everything could go wrong if you weren't prepared to pivot quickly. Very few people knew that particular piece of slang, and none of them should have been anywhere near Palm Beach County.

Veronica read the message over his shoulder. Her presence in his personal space had become as natural as her presence in his office, though infinitely more complicated.

"Someone from your past?" she asked, her voice carefully neutral.

"Maybe," John said, though his mind was already racing through possibilities. "Could be someone sniffing around from Cleveland. Or it could be somebody local who's done their homework."

The Cleveland possibility worried him most. When Max Vecchio had disappeared and turned state's evidence, he burned many bridges. Obviously, Vinny, his son, and numerous others would never forget. There were several people he deliberately withheld information on, people who were always on his side and often sent him unexpected funds, because they knew it was the right thing to do. If someone from that world had tracked him to Florida, the sophisticated financial schemes he and Veronica had constructed could be the least of his problems.

Veronica nodded slowly, her expression thoughtful. "If they push, we push back. I've handled worse than anonymous threats."

"This isn't just a threat. It's information. Someone knows enough about my background to reference things that happened many years ago. That's not amateur hour."

"Fine. So what do you want to do? Run? Start over somewhere else?" Her tone suggested she found the idea distasteful. "We've built something here, John. Something profitable and sustainable. I'm not walking away from it because of one cryptic text message."

John appreciated her resolve, but he also knew the difference between calculated risk and reckless exposure. "We may have to burn one of the LLCs. Create some distance between us and the money flow."

"Fine. Just make sure it's not one that got press coverage. And make sure the burn doesn't splash back on the Foundation. I've got board members from three different country clubs, and they don't like surprises."

The conversation continued for another hour as they worked through contingency plans that John hoped they'd never need to implement. They identified which shell companies could be dissolved with minimal impact, which bank accounts could be closed quickly, and which documentation needed to be secured or destroyed. In John's mind, he was insulating Veronica from any fallout that would enable her to carry on, should he find it necessary to disappear. It was the kind of planning that John had hoped was behind him when he'd reinvented himself as a respectable community leader.

A Perfect Partnership

Later that week, John stood in front of the full-length mirror in his bedroom, studying his reflection with the critical eye of a man who'd spent years crafting his image. His reflection looked sharp: clean lines, careful grooming, the polished effect of someone who'd never been anything other than John Masters, successful HOA president, business executive, and community advocate. The cerulean polo had been replaced by a charcoal business suit for his morning meeting with county planning officials about the affordable housing initiative Veronica had mentioned.

But behind the eyes, in the depths that the mirror couldn't quite reveal, he saw what he always had: Max Vecchio, the Cleveland numbers man/accountant/hustler who'd gotten out just in time. The man who'd learned that the key to a successful long-term hustle wasn't just knowing how to take money from people—it was knowing how to make them grateful for the privilege.

Veronica entered behind him, adjusting her earrings in preparation for her own morning appointment with the NBC6 producer who'd been calling twice a day since their initial inquiry.

She'd decided to meet with Melissa Johnson privately first, ostensibly to discuss the Foundation's broader mission before any formal interview. In reality, she wanted to assess the producer's knowledge and intentions before committing to anything more substantial.

"You're brooding again," she said, catching his eye in the mirror. "Don't. We built something better here. They get their playgrounds and their tournaments. We get our freedom and our financial security. And nobody gets hurt who doesn't deserve it."

John turned toward her, noting how the morning light caught the silver bracelet she wore—a gift from a grateful widow whose property tax appeal Veronica had helped navigate through their foundation's Senior Advocacy Program. "What if someone starts pulling at the threads? What if this anonymous messenger isn't the only one asking questions?"

Veronica stepped closer, close enough that he could smell her perfume—something expensive and subtle that probably cost more than most people's monthly rent. Their faces were inches apart, and he could see the calculation behind her smile.

"Then we spin a better story. We've got testimonials from dozens of residents, documentation of every community improvement we've funded, and support from every major civic organization in the county. If someone wants to question our methods, they have to explain why they're opposed to youth programs and senior wellness initiatives."

"And if spinning doesn't work?" he questioned.

Her smile never wavered, but something shifted in her eyes. "Then we cut them out. Quietly. Professionally. The same way we've handled every other obstacle."

John kissed her forehead, a gesture that had become both affectionate and strategic—a way of maintaining intimacy while keeping his thoughts hidden. "To next year's championship?"

"To the empire," she whispered, her breath warm against his ear.

The Long Game

Outside, the morning was already heating up, promising another day of the humid subtropical weather that drew retirees and tourists to South Florida year-round. The banners from the pickleball tournament had been taken down, but new signs had appeared around the Sunset Palms community: "Coming Soon: Youth Education Center," "Phase Two Recreational Improvements Beginning this Fall," and "Community Garden Project—Now Accepting Volunteers."

Each sign represented another layer in the expanding web of legitimate community improvements that provided cover for their more profitable activities. The youth education center would cost nearly $200,000 to build, but it would also justify the creation of Educational Futures LLC, another shell company that could process contracts and consulting fees. The recreational improvements would require ongoing maintenance contracts that could be fulfilled by Heritage Urban Planning at premium rates. The community garden would provide opportunities for equipment purchases, landscaping contracts, and educational programming—all revenue streams that could be carefully managed to benefit their network of front companies.

John's phone buzzed with a text from Tom Brennan: "Reviewed the quarterly financials last night. Would like to discuss some questions before next week's board meeting. Coffee sometime this week?"

The message was polite and professional, but John could read the subtext. Brennan's detective instincts were kicking in, and he was preparing to ask the kind of detailed questions that could unravel months of careful construction. The information about his early retirement from Miami-Dade PD might provide leverage, but John knew better than to underestimate a suspicious cop, even a retired one.

He forwarded the message to Veronica with a single word: "Accelerate."

Her response came back within minutes: "Already on it. NBC6 interview scheduled for next Tuesday. Youth center groundbreaking moved to Thursday. By the time Brennan starts asking serious questions, we'll have enough positive momentum to make him look like an obstructionist."

John smiled despite his concerns. Veronica's instinct for timing and public relations was one of the reasons their partnership worked so well. She understood that in the world of community development and nonprofit funding, perception was often more important than reality. If they could maintain the appearance of successful, innovative leadership, the financial details would be dismissed as the concerns of small-minded people who didn't understand the bigger picture.

His phone buzzed again, this time with a message from an unknown number: "Max always said the backswing was the most important part of any game. Looking forward to watching yours. - A Fan"

This message was different—more direct, more personal. Someone definitely knew about his past, and they were making it clear that they were watching his current activities. The question was whether they wanted money, revenge, or something else entirely.

John deleted the message and made a mental note to have the phone number traced through one of Krauss's contacts in county law enforcement. If someone from Cleveland had found him, he needed to know who and what they wanted before their operation expanded any further.

But first, he had a county planning meeting to attend, where he would discuss the affordable housing initiative that could provide federal matching funds for their community development projects. The irony wasn't lost on him that his skills as a financial schemer had made him extremely effective at navigating the bureaucratic maze of government funding and community development.

As he drove his new Tesla Model S Plaid toward the county building, John reflected on the strange trajectory that had brought him from Cleveland street corners to Palm Beach County boardrooms. The fundamental principles were the same—identify what people wanted, figure out how to give it to them while taking something for yourself, and always stay three steps ahead of anyone who might be asking uncomfortable questions.

The difference was that in Cleveland, he'd been taking money from people who couldn't afford to lose it. Here in Palm Beach County, he was redistributing wealth from corporations and retirees to community improvements while skimming more than enough to ensure his own comfortable lifestyle. The victims, if they could be called that, were previously poorly run HOAs, insurance companies, real estate developers, and federal agencies that would never miss the relatively small amounts he and Veronica diverted. It was, he had to admit, a more elegant approach than anything he'd attempted in his younger days. Communities that were deteriorating faster than a motorcycle in an I-95 truck crash were thriving like they never had in their bleak histories. Property values were booming, and so was their cash flow.

The county building came into view, its glass facade reflecting the morning sun like a promise of legitimacy and respectability. John straightened his tie, checked his appearance in the rearview mirror, and prepared to be the kind of community leader that Palm Beach County deserved—honest, dedicated, and completely committed to building a better future for everyone.

And if that future happened to include a comfortable retirement fund for John Masters and Veronica Santiago, well, that was simply the cost of effective leadership in the modern world.

Outside, the banners still fluttered in the wind, proclaiming a better community built on unity, health, and just a touch of perfectly legal, strategically necessary, and beautifully executed embezzlement.

Chapter 14: A Healthy Community Is a Happy—and Profitable—One

In the aftermath of a ruptured Achilles tendon, three torn ligaments, a shattered wrist, and one very public lawsuit threat, John Masters did what any visionary would do—he launched a wellness initiative.

Officially, it was called The United Communities Wellness Project, a holistic, community-wide effort to "support senior health through proactive, integrative care." Unofficially, it was a Medicare mill with better lighting.

The first step was repurposing the underused multipurpose rooms in the Sunset Palms Clubhouse. Within two weeks, Room A had become a chiropractic suite run by Dr. Illya Dovensky, DC, who previously worked on a Norwegian cruise line and referred to every spinal adjustment as a "miracle reset." Room B housed a Reiki healer known only as Sister Faith, whose credentials were printed on pastel cardstock and whose vibe could best be described as "sedated crystal healer/dealer."

Room C was allocated to Dr. Kapoor, a tele-psychiatrist based in Goa, who provided cognitive wellness consultations via iPad. He spoke softly, prescribed happy pills liberally, and never once turned on his camera. Room D was shared by a hypnotherapist, a breathwork coach, and a recently certified tai chi instructor named Linda, who ran fall prevention classes in socks.

Room E was given to Elsa Swerdlowe, licensed massage therapist. Elsa had once worked at a high-end spa at the Boca Raton Resort until an unfortunate misunderstanding involving a county commissioner's wife and a peppermint body wrap ended her career in luxury wellness. But at United Wellness, she found redemption—and willing bodies. With her leopard-print scrubs, orthopedic clogs, and a playlist of ambient whale sounds, Elsa offered a blend of lymphatic drainage, Swedish deep tissue, and unsolicited life advice. Her hands were strong, her gossip stronger, and her loyalty absolute—especially after John helped resolve her outstanding licensing issues with the state board using what he referred to as "administrative lubrication."

Each practitioner paid monthly rent to the United Community Foundation, which in turn billed Medicare for eligible services through a labyrinthine system of subcontracting and compliance documentation. Veronica oversaw the setup, naturally, and even hired a part-time grant writer to apply for government subsidies under the Senior Holistic Wellness Pilot Program.

John put their IT guru, Tommy Rodriguez, on the project immediately. The goal was to create a profit stream that effortlessly laundered Medicare money from each provider to hidden UCM subsidiaries and back again to the providers. It would be paperless, secure, and nearly invisible to outside auditors. All the residents had to do was click the appointment tab—and everything else, from scheduling to billing to documentation, happened automatically. Electronic medical records had never worked so seamlessly.

For his trouble, John greeted Tommy one morning with a large envelope. Inside was a cool $125,000 in cash for his efforts. Tommy's conscience started feeling much better.

The money flowed faster than anyone expected.

It started with modest returns—$300 for balance assessments, $600 for mobility screening—but once the full reimbursement codes kicked in, the operation hit its stride. By the end of the quarter, they were clearing nearly $40,000 a month in Medicare, Medicaid, and insurance revenue, with minimal overhead and near-total deniability.

John was initially skeptical. "This feels like we're just billing Medicare for social visits," he said one morning, sipping his third espresso.

Veronica didn't look up from her tablet. "My grandmother didn't need physical therapy. She needed someone to ask how she was feeling. Medicare paid for that then, and it pays for it now."

"She got a Valium prescription and a conversation, John replied."

"Exactly. We've simply streamlined the model."

To the residents of Willowbrook Estates, the newly expanded wellness program was a godsend. Appointments were short, affirming, and required no transportation. Most of them didn't care about the treatments—they just liked having someone to talk to and vent about how their no-good kids didn't care about them. And in exchange for a blood pressure check and a bowl of sugar-free mints, they were unknowingly participating in one of the most lucrative "wellness" experiments in South Florida.

Veronica drafted a press release: "Willowbrook Leads the Way in Preventive Senior Care." Local outlets picked it up. Palm Beach Health Magazine did a glossy feature. A regional news segment aired showing smiling retirees stretching in slow motion while soft jazz played underneath.

In the video, John stood next to Veronica beneath a new banner that read: "A Healthy Community Is a Happy Community." He gave a short speech about wellness, vitality, gratitude, and the importance of accessible wellness options for seniors. Behind him, a chiropractor high-fived a patient who had just "aligned his third lumbar into divine harmony."

The real genius, of course, was that every provider on-site was part of a shell company owned or controlled by John and Veronica. The chiropractors paid rent. The Foundation got a cut. The billing services were routed through a back-office firm registered in Nevada under an LLC called Holistic Harmony Consulting, which just happened to share a mailing address with John's numerous other shell companies in Las Vegas.

Veronica's monthly spreadsheets showed exactly what John had feared—and what he now couldn't stop smiling at: this wasn't just sustainable, it was scalable too. It was time to expand the wellness experiment to all of United's other communities.

By Q3, they'd added aromatherapy, vitamin infusion therapy, and a mental wellness booth where a former madam named Alana conducted "empathic listening sessions" with residents who just wanted to vent about their kids. Alana charged $90 for forty minutes and always had a waitlist.

UCM launched a mobile app called WellNet, which tracked appointments, issued reminders, and logged "wellness scores" based on a ten-question mood survey. The app didn't actually sync with any provider system, but it gave residents something to show their kids.

By the end of the year, John was giving interviews about "community-centered care" and consulting with two neighboring developments about how to implement similar programs.

And no one—not one auditor, not one inspector, not one journalist—asked a single hard question. Why would they? The seniors were happy and actually healthier. The services were available on demand. The outcomes were "improved." And everyone involved was making enough money to look the other way.

Except John. He wasn't looking away. He was staring straight at the numbers, the coverage, the potential. For the first time in his career, he understood why real hospitals build entire wings off of nothing but outpatient billables and hope.

"Veronica," he said one night, holding up the latest income projection, "if we add dental hygiene and grief counseling, we could break three million next year."

She didn't even blink. "Only if we make the grief counseling optional. You don't want them processing too much."

John smiled, knowing exactly what she meant. A healthy community is a happy community—and wildly profitable one at that.

Chapter 15: The Internal Revolt

The Investigator's Questions

Tom Brennan had been reviewing the financial statements for three hours, and the numbers weren't making sense. Seated at his kitchen table with ledgers spread across the surface like a puzzle missing crucial pieces, he traced expenditures through Citizens for Community Growth with the methodical precision of a man who'd spent forty years catching embezzlement schemes.

The nonprofit's monthly report lay open beside his laptop, professionally formatted and impressively detailed. Gourmet Intentions LLC had billed $12,500 for "premium event coordination and vendor management services." Heritage Pantry Co. had charged $8,200 for "specialty consultation and market analysis." Community First Contracting was requesting $15,600 for "preliminary site assessment and regulatory compliance consultation."

On paper, it all looked legitimate. But Tom had called each company's listed phone number that morning, and none of them answered with anything more than generic voicemails. No receptionist, no company-specific greetings, no sense that actual human beings worked at these addresses.

He opened his laptop and began searching for business registrations. Heritage Pantry Co. was incorporated in Delaware six weeks ago. Gourmet Intentions LLC had been filed in Nevada two months earlier. Community First Contracting was registered in Wyoming just last month.

All three companies shared the same registered agent service. All three had been incorporated within a narrow timeframe. And all three were billing Citizens for Community Growth for services that seemed designed to justify the exact amount of money the bake sale had raised.

Tom reached for his phone and dialed John Masters' direct line.

"Tom," John's voice was warm, professional. "What can I do for you?"

"I've been going through the nonprofit's vendor payments," Tom said without preamble. "I have some concerns about documentation."

There was a pause. Brief, but noticeable. "What kind of concerns?"

"I can't reach anyone at these companies. The phone numbers go to voicemail. The business registrations are all recent. And frankly, the invoicing patterns look suspicious."

"Tom, I appreciate your diligence, but I'm not sure what you're implying. These are legitimate vendors providing real services for our community improvement projects."

"Then I'd like to see contracts. References. Proof of insurance. The kind of documentation we should have on file before paying anyone $15,000."

John's tone shifted slightly, becoming more formal. "Of course. I'll have that information compiled and sent to you by the end of the week."

"I'd prefer to review it before the next board meeting. In fact, I think we should put any further nonprofit disbursements on hold until we can verify these vendors."

The silence on the other end of the line stretched long enough for Tom to wonder if the call had dropped.

"Tom," John said finally, "I have to ask—is there something specific that's prompted this level of...scrutiny? We've been working together for over a year, and I've never had my judgment questioned this thoroughly."

It was a subtle pivot, Tom realized. John was making this about trust and working relationships rather than financial oversight. But Tom had seen this tactic before, usually from executives who were hiding something.

"It's not about trust," Tom replied. "It's about fiduciary responsibility. We owe it to the community to ensure donations are being used appropriately."

"Absolutely. And they are. But I have to say, this level of suspicion feels unusual coming from you. Is everything okay at home? You seem more...on edge lately."

Tom felt his jaw tighten. Decades of detective work had taught him to recognize when someone was trying to gaslight him.

"Everything's fine, John. I'm just doing my job."

"Of course you are. And I respect that. I'll get you that documentation."

After John hung up, Tom sat staring at his phone. The conversation had felt wrong—not just the deflection about documentation, but the personal comments about his state of mind. It was exactly the kind of response he'd expect from someone who was trying to shift focus away from uncomfortable questions.

He pulled out a yellow legal pad and began making notes. Not just about the vendor payments, but about the conversation itself. The pauses, the deflections, the subtle attempts to make him question his own judgment.

Tom Brennan had been investigating fraud since before John Masters was born. And everything about this situation told him that the HOA consultant was running a con.

Research and Reconnaissance

The next morning, Tom drove to the address listed for Gourmet Intentions LLC. According to the business registration, the company operated out of a strip mall in Plantation, between a nail salon and a cell phone repair shop. The suite number led him to a narrow door with frosted glass and no signage.

He tried the handle. Locked. He peered through the glass but could see nothing except an empty reception area with a single desk and chair. No computer, no phone, no indication that anyone had ever worked there.

The nail salon next door was busy with the pre-lunch crowd. Tom walked in and approached the reception desk, where a young woman with elaborate fingernails was scheduling appointments.

"Excuse me," he said. "I'm looking for the catering company next door. Gourmet Intentions?"

She looked confused. "No catering company. That space has been empty for months. Owner says he's still looking for a tenant."

Tom thanked her and walked back to his car. He drove to the address listed for Heritage Pantry Co., which turned out to be a UPS Store in Coral Springs. The business address was a mailbox.

Community First Contracting was supposedly located in a Boca Raton office complex. The address led him to a building directory that showed no such company. The suite number belonged to a virtual office service that rented business addresses by the month.

By afternoon, Tom had confirmed what he'd suspected that morning. All three companies were shells—empty registrations designed to create the appearance of legitimate business activity while funneling money back to their creators.

He spent the evening compiling his findings into a detailed report. Phone records showing unanswered calls. Photos of empty offices and mailbox addresses. Business registration documents showing suspicious patterns in incorporation timing and registered agents.

The evidence was circumstantial but compelling. Someone was using Citizens for Community Growth to launder money through fake vendors. And the only person with access to approve those payments was John Masters.

Tom drafted an email to the other board members, outlining his concerns and requesting an emergency meeting to discuss financial oversight procedures. He attached his research, redacted the most inflammatory language, and focused on the need for better documentation and vendor verification.

He was about to hit send when his phone rang. John Masters' name appeared on the screen.

"Tom, I wanted to follow up on our conversation yesterday. I know you had some concerns about vendor documentation."

"I did. And I still do."

"Well, I've been thinking about our discussion, and I realize there might be some confusion about how the nonprofit procurement process works. Would you have time to meet tomorrow? I'd like to walk you through the vendor selection criteria and show you some of the documentation you requested."

Tom hesitated. Meeting with John alone felt risky, especially given what he'd discovered about the shell companies. But he also wanted to give the man a chance to provide legitimate explanations before he escalated his concerns to the full board.

"Okay," he said. "But I want to see everything. Contracts, insurance certificates, references. The complete vendor files."

"Absolutely. How about coffee at nine? There's a Starbucks on Federal Highway that's usually quiet in the morning."

After agreeing to the meeting, Tom saved his email draft without sending it. He wanted to hear John's explanations first. Maybe there was something he was missing, some legitimate reason for the suspicious patterns he'd identified.

But he also printed copies of all his research and put them in a sealed envelope, which he left on his wife's dresser with a note: "If anything happens to me, give this to the police."

It felt melodramatic, but Tom had been in on enough corporate fraud cases to know that people who asked inconvenient questions sometimes found themselves facing inconvenient consequences.

The Coffee Shop Confrontation

The Starbucks on Federal Highway was exactly as John had promised—quiet, anonymous, the kind of place where two businessmen could have a private conversation without being overheard. Tom arrived five minutes early and chose a corner table with his back to the wall, a habit left over from his days auditing mob-connected businesses in Chicago.

John walked in precisely on time, carrying a leather portfolio and wearing the kind of confident smile that Tom had learned to distrust in corporate executives. He ordered a complex coffee drink and sat down across from Tom with the easy familiarity of someone who was completely comfortable with the situation.

"Tom, thanks for meeting me. I know yesterday's conversation left some things unresolved, and I wanted to clear the air."

"I'd like to see the vendor documentation we discussed."

John opened his portfolio and removed a stack of papers. "Of course. Here are the contracts with all three companies, along with their insurance certificates and business references."

Tom accepted the documents and began reviewing them. The contracts looked professional—detailed scope of work, payment terms, performance milestones. The insurance certificates appeared legitimate, with policy numbers and carrier information. The references included phone numbers for previous clients.

But something felt off. The contracts were all dated within the past two weeks, well after the companies had submitted their invoices. The insurance certificates showed effective dates that were suspiciously recent. And the references were all from companies Tom had never heard of.

"These contracts are dated after the work was supposedly performed," Tom said.

"Right. We started with preliminary agreements and formalized the contracts once we determined the scope of work. Pretty standard practice in consulting relationships."

"And these references?"

"Previous clients. You're welcome to call them."

Tom studied the documents more carefully. They were professionally formatted, with consistent fonts and layouts. But they felt manufactured, like props in a stage production designed to fool casual observers.

"John, I need to ask you something directly. Are these companies real?"

John's expression didn't change, but Tom caught a flicker of something—irritation, maybe, or calculation.

"Of course they're real. Tom, I have to say, I'm concerned about the direction of this conversation. You're asking questions that suggest you think I'm stealing from the community."

"I'm asking questions about financial oversight. That's my job as treasurer."

"Your job is to review financial reports and ensure compliance with board policies. It's not to conduct shadow investigations of legitimately approved vendors."

The response was delivered calmly, but Tom heard the edge underneath. John was getting defensive, which in Tom's experience usually meant someone was hiding something important.

"I visited the addresses for these companies yesterday," Tom said. "Gourmet Intentions is an empty office space. Heritage Pantry is a mailbox. Community First Contracting doesn't exist at the address listed in their registration."

John was quiet for a long moment, his fingers drumming against his coffee cup.

"Tom," he said finally, "I think you might be suffering from some kind of stress-related paranoia. You're seeing patterns that don't exist, making accusations that don't have any basis in reality."

"I'm seeing shell companies with fake addresses billing our nonprofit for services they're not providing."

"You're seeing legitimate vendors who use virtual offices and mail forwarding services because they're small businesses that can't afford traditional office space. It's incredibly common in consulting work."

John leaned forward, his voice taking on a tone of concerned friendliness. "Look, I know you've been under a lot of pressure lately. The treasurer position is demanding, and you've been putting in long hours on financial reviews. Maybe it would be better if you took a step back from some of the more intensive oversight responsibilities."

Tom felt his blood pressure rising. "Are you suggesting I resign?"

"I'm suggesting you might benefit from focusing on the bigger picture rather than getting lost in administrative details. The community trusts us to manage their interests effectively, not to waste time chasing conspiracy theories."

The conversation was clearly over. John gathered his papers, stood up, and extended his hand for a shake that Tom didn't return.

"I hope you'll consider what we've discussed," John said. "I'd hate to see your valuable contributions to the community overshadowed by...misunderstandings."

After John left, Tom sat alone at the corner table, staring at his untouched coffee. The meeting had been a setup—not an attempt to provide documentation, but an opportunity to gauge how much Tom knew and to deliver a warning disguised as friendly concern.

Tom pulled out his phone and opened the draft email he'd prepared the night before. He added a new paragraph describing the coffee shop meeting, included photos of the empty office spaces he'd visited, and changed the subject line to "URGENT: Financial Irregularities Requiring Board Action."

Then he hit send to all six board members.

The Smear Campaign Begins

The first email arrived in board member Janet Kowalski's inbox at 6:23 AM, sent from an anonymous Gmail account with the subject line "Concerns About Tom Brennan's Recent Behavior."

Dear Board Members,

I'm writing as a concerned resident who has observed some troubling patterns in Mr. Brennan's conduct during recent community meetings. Several neighbors have mentioned that he seems agitated, confrontational, and suspicious of routine administrative procedures. There are rumors that he's been making unfounded accusations about financial irregularities, despite having no evidence to support these claims.

I understand that Mr. Brennan has been under significant personal stress lately, and I wonder if this might be affecting his judgment. Perhaps the board should consider whether he's still capable of fulfilling his treasurer responsibilities effectively.

I prefer to remain anonymous to avoid becoming involved in community politics, but I felt this information was too important not to share.

A Concerned Neighbor

Janet read the email twice, then checked the sender address. She'd never seen the account before, and the message felt oddly formal for a concerned neighbor. But the content was troubling, especially in light of Tom's recent email about vendor documentation.

Similar emails arrived in the inboxes of the other board members throughout the morning. Each was slightly different—different phrasing, different anonymous accounts, different specific claims about Tom's behavior. But the theme was consistent: Tom Brennan was acting strangely, making unreasonable demands, and possibly suffering from stress-related judgment problems.

By lunch, Dr. Martinez had received a call from a resident claiming that Tom had been "aggressively questioning" people about their political affiliations during the pickleball tournament. Susan Lee got a voicemail reporting that Tom had been seen taking photos of people's houses without permission. Board president Janet Kowalski was told that Tom had made inappropriate comments about John Masters' management style during a neighborhood barbecue.

None of the callers were willing to provide their names. All claimed to be acting out of concern for community harmony. And all suggested that Tom's recent behavior indicated serious personal or professional problems.

The cumulative effect was precisely what John had intended. By the time the board members gathered for their emergency meeting that evening, Tom Brennan's credibility had been systematically undermined by a coordinated whisper campaign that made his financial concerns seem like the paranoid delusions of a man under stress.

The Violation Notice

Tom found the HOA violation notice taped to his front door when he returned from grocery shopping on Thursday afternoon. The official letterhead and formal language made his stomach drop before he'd even read the specific charges.

NOTICE OF COVENANT VIOLATION Case #: WB-2023-0847 Property: 2847 Magnolia Circle Owner: Thomas & Patricia Brennan

Dear Mr. Brennan,

This notice is to inform you that your property has been found in violation of the following Willowbrook Estates Homeowners Association covenants and restrictions:

Section 4.2.1: Unauthorized modifications to approved landscaping design Section 6.1.3: Maintenance of exterior paint in non-approved color scheme Section 8.4.2: Storage of non-residential equipment in driveway.

Photographic evidence of these violations has been documented and is available for review. You have fourteen (14) days from the date of this notice to remedy all violations or face additional fines and potential legal action.

Initial fine: $500.00 Daily continuing violation fee: $50.00

To schedule a compliance inspection or discuss remediation options, please contact the HOA office at your earliest convenience.

Sincerely, United Community Management.

Tom read the notice three times, his confusion growing with each pass. The violations made no sense. He hadn't modified his landscaping—the plants were the same ones approved by the architectural review committee when he'd moved in two years ago. His house was painted in the standard beige that was required for his section of the development. And he'd never stored any equipment in his driveway.

He walked around his property, looking for anything that might have triggered the violation notice. Everything appeared exactly as it had for months. The landscaping was well-maintained, the paint was fresh, and his driveway was empty except for his and his wife's cars.

Tom pulled out his phone and called the HOA office.

"United Community, this is Veronica."

"Veronica, this is Tom Brennan. I just received a violation notice that doesn't make any sense. Can you help me understand what prompted these charges?"

There was a pause. "Oh, Tom. I heard about the notice. John mentioned there had been some compliance issues identified during a routine inspection."

"What compliance issues? I haven't changed anything about my property."

"Let me pull up the file." Tom could hear typing in the background. "Okay, it says here that the violations were documented with photographs taken on...Tuesday afternoon."

"Tuesday afternoon, I was playing poker at the casino. My wife was at her book club. Nobody was home to see any inspection."

"Well, the photos show clear violations of the approved standards. I can email them to you if you'd like to review them."

"Please do."

The photos arrived in Tom's inbox ten minutes later. The first showed his front garden, with a red circle drawn around a small section where the mulch appeared darker than the surrounding area. The second was a close-up of his house's exterior, with an arrow pointing to what looked like a slight color variation near the garage.

The third showed his driveway with what appeared to be a wheelbarrow partially visible at the edge of the frame.

Tom studied the images carefully. The dark mulch in his garden was from a recent repair where his sprinkler system had leaked—hardly an unauthorized landscaping modification. The color variation on his house was a shadow cast by the neighbor's tree. And the wheelbarrow in the driveway photo didn't belong to him.

He called the office again.

"Veronica, I've reviewed the photos. These violations are based on misunderstandings. The mulch is from a sprinkler repair, the color variation is a shadow, and that wheelbarrow isn't mine."

"Tom, I understand your frustration, but these determinations are made by qualified inspectors using established criteria. If you'd like to appeal the violations, you can request a hearing with the architectural review committee."

"How long does the appeal process take?"

"Usually about thirty days. But the fines continue to accrue while the appeal is pending."

Tom did the math. Thirty days at $50 per day would cost him $1,500, on top of the initial $500 fine. Even if he won the appeal, the process would be expensive and time-consuming.

"This is harassment," he said.

"Tom, I really don't think—"

"This is retaliation for asking questions about vendor documentation. John is using HOA enforcement to intimidate me."

Veronica's tone became carefully neutral. "I can't comment on the motivations behind compliance enforcement. If you have concerns about the process, you should discuss them with the board."

After hanging up, Tom sat in his kitchen and realized he was facing a calculated campaign designed to undermine his credibility and drain his resources. The anonymous emails about his behavior, the violation notice for non-existent problems, the expensive appeal process—it was all designed to force him into silence or resignation.

But Tom had spent forty years dealing with corporate bullies and financial criminals. He wasn't going to be intimidated by a small-time con artist running an HOA scam.

He opened his laptop and began drafting a new email to the board members, this time including copies of the violation notice and his analysis of the doctored photographs. If John Masters wanted a fight, Tom was prepared to give him one.

Board Meeting: The Fix Is In

The emergency board meeting was held in the community center's main conference room, around the oval table that had been donated by a resident who'd upgraded to a larger dining set. Six board members sat in their usual chairs, but the atmosphere was different—charged with tension and uncomfortable awareness that they were dealing with serious accusations.

John Masters sat at the head of the table, projecting the calm authority of someone who was completely confident in his position. He'd spent the past two days carefully orchestrating the evening's events, and everything was proceeding exactly as planned.

"Before we address Tom's concerns about vendor documentation," John began, "I think we need to discuss some troubling information that's come to my attention regarding Tom's recent behavior and judgment."

Tom felt his stomach clench. This wasn't how he'd expected the meeting to begin.

"Several residents have contacted me with concerns about Tom's conduct during community events," John continued. "There are reports of aggressive questioning, inappropriate photography of residents' properties, and what some have described as paranoid accusations about routine administrative procedures."

"That's completely false," Tom said. "I haven't—"

"Tom, I know this is difficult to hear, but I've also had to issue a violation notice for your property. The compliance issues were documented with photographs and represent clear violations of our community standards."

Janet Kowalski shifted uncomfortably in her chair. "John, I have to say, I've received some anonymous emails about Tom's behavior, but I don't feel comfortable making personnel decisions based on unverified complaints."

"I understand your reluctance," John replied. "But we also have a responsibility to ensure that board members are capable of fulfilling their duties effectively. When a treasurer begins making unfounded accusations about financial irregularities, it raises serious questions about judgment and competence."

Dr. Martinez leaned forward. "What financial irregularities? I reviewed Tom's email about vendor documentation, and his concerns seemed reasonable."

John opened his portfolio and removed a stack of papers. "I'm glad you asked. Here are the complete vendor files for all three companies Tom questioned. Contracts, insurance certificates, business references, and documentation of services performed."

He distributed copies to each board member. The documents looked exactly like the ones he'd shown Tom at Starbucks, but with additional pages of supporting materials—invoices, progress reports, even testimonials from satisfied clients.

"As you can see," John continued, "these are legitimate vendors providing real services for our community improvement projects. Tom's concerns are based on misunderstandings about how consulting relationships work and a failure to review available documentation before making accusations."

Tom stared at the papers in disbelief. The documents were even more elaborate than what he'd seen two days earlier, with additional layers of false evidence designed to make his concerns look baseless.

"These are fabricated," he said. "I visited the addresses for these companies. They don't exist."

"Tom," John's voice carried a note of gentle concern, "this is exactly the kind of statement that makes me worry about your current state of mind. You're making serious accusations without evidence."

"I have evidence. I took photos of the empty offices. I have documentation showing these are shell companies."

"Do you have those photos with you tonight?"

Tom reached for his briefcase, then realized he'd left his research materials at home. In his rush to prepare for the meeting, he'd forgotten to bring the evidence that would support his claims.

"I left them at home, but I can get them—"

"Tom, we can't evaluate claims based on evidence you don't have with you. And frankly, even if you produced photos of empty offices, that wouldn't prove these companies are fraudulent. Many small businesses operate with virtual addresses and minimal physical presence."

Susan Lee, who had been quietly reviewing the vendor files, looked up from the papers. "These documents look comprehensive to me. I'm not seeing the red flags Tom described."

The mood in the room was shifting. Tom could feel it happening—the carefully prepared narrative was taking hold, making his concerns seem increasingly unreasonable and paranoid. It was a masterclass in gaslighting done by a true professional.

"I move that we accept the vendor documentation as satisfactory and close this matter," Janet said. "We've spent enough time on administrative details that should have been resolved through normal channels."

"Seconded," said Dr. Martinez.

"All in favor?"

Five hands went up. Tom's remained in his lap.

"Motion carries. Now, let's move on to the budget proposal for next fiscal year."

John opened another section of his portfolio and began distributing budget documents. The numbers were staggering— nearly double the previous year's expenditures, with massive line items for community improvements, professional services, and administrative costs.

"Given the success of our recent fundraising efforts," John explained, "we're in a position to dramatically expand our community enhancement programs. This budget reflects our commitment to making Willowbrook Estates a premier residential community in South Florida."

Tom scanned the budget quickly, his accountant's eye immediately catching the irregularities. Consulting fees were budgeted at $200,000. Event coordination was allocated $150,000. Legal and professional services were projected at $180,000.

"These numbers are absurd," Tom said. "You're budgeting more for consulting fees than most corporations spend on their entire operations."

"Tom," John's voice carried a note of tired patience, "we've already established that your concerns about vendor relationships are based on misunderstandings. This budget reflects the level of investment necessary to maintain our community's standards."

Janet Kowalski raised her hand. "John, these are significant increases from last year. Can you walk us through the justification for the higher spending levels?"

"Absolutely. We're expanding our community improvement programs, upgrading our technology infrastructure, and investing in professional services that will ensure long-term financial stability. The increased costs reflect our commitment to excellence."

It was the same kind of vague, buzzword-heavy explanation that John had been using for months. But this time, it was attached to a budget that would give him access to hundreds of thousands of dollars in community funds.

"I vote against this budget," Tom said. "It's fiscally irresponsible and lacks sufficient detail to justify the expenditures."

"Noted," John replied. "Any other discussion?"

The room was quiet. Tom could see the other board members reviewing the numbers, but none of them seemed prepared to challenge John's recommendations.

"All in favor of approving the budget as presented?"

Five hands went up again. Tom's vote was the only dissent.

"Motion carries unanimously," John announced, despite Tom's opposing vote.

As the meeting ended and board members began gathering their papers, Tom realized he'd been outmaneuvered completely. The smear campaign had undermined his credibility, the violation notice had painted him as a hypocrite, and the manufactured vendor documentation had made his concerns look baseless.

John had won every battle, and Tom was left sitting alone at the conference table, wondering how a small-time HOA manager had managed to execute such a sophisticated campaign of manipulation and intimidation. Little did he know, he was dealing with Max Vecchio.

The Aftermath: Complete Victory

The next morning, John stood in his home office reviewing the previous evening's results with the satisfaction of someone who'd executed a flawless operation. The board had unanimously approved his budget—well, unanimously minus Tom Brennan's irrelevant dissent—giving him access to over half a million dollars in community funds for the coming fiscal year.

More importantly, Tom Brennan's credibility had been completely destroyed. The other board members now viewed him as a paranoid troublemaker whose concerns could be safely ignored. The violation notice would keep him busy with administrative appeals for the next month. And the anonymous complaint campaign had established a narrative that would undermine any future accusations he might make.

John's phone rang. Veronica's name appeared on the screen.

"Good morning," he answered.

"John, I wanted to follow up on last night's meeting. I know the Tom situation was difficult, but I think you handled it perfectly."

"Thank you. I hate to see anyone go through personal struggles, but we can't let individual problems compromise our community responsibilities."

"Absolutely. Although I have to ask—are you completely confident about those vendor files? Some of Tom's questions might come back to bite us."

John felt a familiar tightness in his chest. Veronica was his partner in crime, so if she had some misgivings, he had to take them seriously.

"The vendor files are completely legitimate," he said. "But I understand why Tom's concerns might have seemed reasonable on the surface. That's what makes his situation so unfortunate."

"Of course. We are in this thing together. I just want to make sure we have all our administrative details properly documented so there isn't any fallout that can come back to United."

His laptop chimed with a new email. The subject line made him smile: "Resignation from Board Position."

Dear Fellow Board Members,

After careful consideration, I have decided to resign from my position as treasurer of the Willowbrook Estates HOA, effective immediately. Recent events have made it clear that my approach to financial oversight is not compatible with the board's current direction.

I wish you all success in your future endeavors.

Thomas Brennan

John forwarded the email to the other board members with a brief note expressing regret about Tom's decision and suggesting that they begin the search for a replacement treasurer immediately.

He had several candidates in mind—residents who were competent enough to handle basic financial reporting but not sophisticated enough to recognize sophisticated fraud even when it was staring them right in their faces.

The phone rang again. This time, it was Joyce Henderson from the PR firm.

"John, I have fantastic news. The *Wall Street Journal* wants to do a feature story on your community management innovations. They're calling it 'The Suburban CEO,' and they want to put you on the cover."

John's blood ran cold. Media attention was precisely what he didn't need right now, especially with Tom Brennan's accusations still fresh, but hopefully fading quickly from the community's consciousness. "I'm flattered, but I prefer to keep the focus on the community rather than individual personalities."

"Are you serious? This is the *Wall Street Journal*. Cover story. This is exactly the kind of exposure that builds personal brands and opens doors to bigger opportunities."

John stared out his office window at the perfectly manicured community that had become another address in his kingdom. Everything was under control. Tom Brennan had been neutralized. The budget was approved. He had access to hundreds of thousands of additional dollars in community funds.

Maybe it was time to accept some recognition for what he'd accomplished.

"You know what?" he said. "Set up the interview."

As he hung up, John felt the familiar thrill of a successful operation reaching its conclusion. He'd defeated the internal revolt, eliminated the threat to his financial schemes, and positioned himself for even greater success in the coming year.

But in the back of his mind, Max Vecchio's voice whispered a warning that John Masters was too confident to hear: *Every growing criminal enterprise eventually reaches the point where success becomes the biggest risk of all.*

Outside, Willowbrook Estates sparkled in the morning sun, peaceful and prosperous and utterly unaware that their trusted leader had just stolen their future, one nearly unanimous vote at a time.

Chapter 16: Courts, Cameras, and Control

The Pitch: Safety Through Technology

The October community meeting drew the largest crowd in Willowbrook Estates' history. The clubhouse's main room was packed beyond capacity, with residents standing along the walls and streaming in from the adjacent hallway. John Masters stood at the front of the room beside a large presentation screen, wearing his most reassuring smile and the navy blazer that focus groups had determined conveyed both authority and approachability.

"Friends," he began, his voice carrying easily through the wireless microphone system he'd had installed the previous month, "tonight we're going to discuss the future of community safety. Not just here in Willowbrook Estates, but for suburban communities across America."

The presentation slides behind him showed a map of South Florida dotted with red crime statistics—break-ins, vandalism, package theft, the everyday violations that turned suburban paradise into suburban anxiety. John had spent hours selecting the most alarming numbers from police reports, carefully choosing incidents from neighboring communities to create the impression of escalating danger.

"These numbers represent more than statistics," John continued, gesturing toward the screen. "They represent our neighbors' violated sense of security. Children who can't play outside without supervision. Families who double-check their locks every night. Seniors who feel unsafe in their own driveways."

Mrs. Pinsky nodded emphatically from the front row. Behind her, the Maxwell family leaned forward with obvious concern. Even skeptical Mr. Patterson was paying attention, his usual scowl replaced by genuine worry.

"But what if I told you that we have an opportunity to change all of that? What if Willowbrook Estates could become the safest community in South Florida—not through luck or chance, but through technology and innovation?"

John clicked to the next slide, revealing a sleek promotional video from SecureSpace Technologies. The imagery was compelling—crystal-clear security cameras with facial recognition capabilities, motion sensors that could distinguish between residents and intruders, and smart doorbells that automatically recorded suspicious activity. The technology looked like something from a science fiction movie, but the presentation made it seem accessible and practical.

"SecureSpace Technologies has chosen Willowbrook Estates as the pilot site for their next-generation community security platform," John announced. "This isn't just about cameras and alarms. This is about creating an intelligent network that can predict and prevent security incidents before they happen."

The video showed a split-screen demonstration: on the left, a traditional security system that could only record incidents after they occurred; on the right, the SecureSpace platform identifying potential threats in real-time and alerting authorities before crimes could be committed.

"The system uses artificial intelligence to analyze behavioral patterns and identify anomalies," John explained. "Loitering near mailboxes during unusual hours. Vehicles circling the community repeatedly that don't belong to residents. Individuals whose movement patterns suggest criminal intent. The technology can spot these warning signs and notify both security personnel and law enforcement before anything happens."

Janet Kowalski raised her hand. "This sounds incredible, but what's the cost? And what about privacy concerns?"

John had anticipated both questions. "Excellent points, Janet. Normally, a system like this would cost each household several thousand dollars to implement. But because we're serving as the pilot community, SecureSpace is covering the entire installation and maintenance cost for the first two years. This is a hundred-thousand-dollar security upgrade that won't cost residents a single penny."

A murmur of impressed surprise rippled through the crowd. Free high-tech security was exactly the kind of offer that sounded too good to pass up.

"As for privacy," John continued, "the system is designed to protect residents, not spy on them. The cameras focus on common areas, entry points, and perimeter security. The AI analyzes behavior patterns but doesn't store personal information. And all data is encrypted and protected by the same security protocols used by Fortune 500 companies."

It was a carefully crafted response that sounded comprehensive while avoiding specific details about data collection, storage, or sharing. John had learned that most people stopped listening after hearing buzzwords like "encrypted" and "Fortune 500."

Dr. Julio Andres stood up in the middle section. "Who has access to the surveillance data? Can law enforcement view the footage without warrants?"

Another excellent question that John had prepared for. "The system is owned and operated by the Willowbrook Estates HOA, not by any government agency. Law enforcement can request access through normal legal channels, just like they would for any privately owned security system. But the primary purpose is community protection, not law enforcement surveillance."

The answer was technically true but deliberately misleading. The partnership agreement with SecureSpace included provisions for data sharing with law enforcement agencies, academic researchers, and "approved third parties" for purposes that were vaguely defined in the contract's fine print.

"I'd like to propose a motion," said Susan Lee from the back of the room. "That we authorize the HOA board to implement the SecureSpace pilot program, contingent on final review of the contract terms."

"Seconded," called out Mrs. Hendricks.

The vote was overwhelming—forty-seven in favor, three opposed, two abstentions. John had won another decisive victory, and this time he'd done it with the enthusiastic support of residents who genuinely believed they were making their community safer.

After the meeting, as residents filed out, discussing the exciting new security features they'd soon enjoy, John remained at the front of the room reviewing his notes. The presentation had gone perfectly, but the real work was just beginning.

His phone buzzed with a text from a number he didn't recognize: *Impressive presentation. Looking forward to seeing the beta test results. - DS*

DS. Daniel Stein, the SecureSpace Technologies executive who'd approached John six months earlier with a proposal that had nothing to do with community safety and everything to do with social control.

Behind the Scenes: The Real Product

The SecureSpace Technologies office occupied two floors of a glass tower in downtown Fort Lauderdale, with the kind of minimalist design that suggested both cutting-edge innovation and serious venture capital backing. John arrived for his meeting at precisely 2 PM, dressed in the business casual attire that marked him as a technology partner rather than a traditional client.

Daniel Stein met him in the lobby—mid-forties, Stanford MBA, the kind of executive who wore jeans with blazers and spoke in the optimistic jargon of Silicon Valley disruption. He led John through a workspace filled with young programmers hunched over in front of multiple monitors, their screens displaying code that looked more like mathematical equations than software development.

"Welcome to the future of behavioral analytics," Daniel said as they settled into his corner office. "What your residents voted for last night was just the consumer-facing application. The real product is much more interesting."

He turned his laptop toward John, revealing a dashboard filled with data visualizations that looked like something from a military command center. Heat maps showed movement patterns throughout a residential community. Behavioral profiles tracked individual residents' daily routines. Predictive algorithms calculated probability scores for various types of rule violations.

"This is our current deployment in a community outside Phoenix," he explained. "Three hundred households, eighteen months of data collection, behavioral prediction accuracy rates approaching 85%."

John studied the screen with growing fascination. The system wasn't just monitoring for security threats—it was analyzing every aspect of residents' daily lives. Time stamps showed when people left for work, returned home, walked their dogs, checked their mail. Pattern recognition algorithms identified deviations from normal routines and flagged them for review.

"You're tracking everything," John said.

"Everything visible in common areas," Daniel corrected. "But the real breakthrough is in behavioral prediction. Watch this."

He clicked through a series of case studies. Resident profiles showed individuals whose routine changes had preceded HOA violations by an average of six days. The system had identified people who were likely to violate parking restrictions, neglect landscaping requirements, or ignore architectural guidelines—all before the violations actually occurred.

"Imagine being able to prevent rule violations instead of just punishing them after the fact," Daniel continued. "Imagine sending friendly reminders to residents who are trending toward non-compliance. Imagine optimizing community rules based on actual behavioral data rather than guesswork."

"This is behavioral control disguised as security," John realized.

"This is community optimization through data-driven insights. We're not controlling anyone—we're providing tools that help communities run more efficiently."

The distinction felt meaningless to John. Whether they called it optimization or control, the result was the same: total surveillance of residents' daily activities, analyzed by algorithms designed to predict and modify behavior.

"What's the business model?" John asked.

"Multiple revenue streams. We license the software to HOA management companies and municipal governments. We sell anonymized behavioral data to academic researchers studying urban planning and social dynamics. And we partner with consumer brands who want to understand suburban lifestyle patterns."

John felt a familiar flutter of excitement—the same feeling he'd gotten when he first understood how nonprofit money laundering schemes work. This wasn't just about surveillance; it was about monetizing every aspect of suburban life.

"We sell data about residents without their knowledge?"

"We sell anonymized, aggregated data that complies with all privacy regulations. Individual residents can't be identified, but the behavioral patterns are incredibly valuable for market research and social science applications."

Daniel pulled up another screen showing potential revenue projections. A community the size of Willowbrook Estates could generate $50,000–$80,000 annually in data licensing fees, with additional revenue from consulting services and software upgrades.

"The HOA gets a percentage of the data revenue," Daniel added. "Usually 15 to 20%, depending on the size of the community and the quality of the behavioral data."

John did the quick calculation. Willowbrook Estates could earn a windfall just for letting SecureSpace monitor residents' daily activities. Combined with the federal grants available for pilot programs in "smart community" technology, the surveillance system would actually be profitable for the HOA.

"When can we start installation?" John asked.

"Our technical team can begin next week. Full deployment usually takes about a month, with another month for AI calibration and behavioral baseline establishment. You'll start seeing meaningful data analytics within sixty days."

They spent another hour reviewing the technical specifications, legal agreements, and implementation timeline. The contract was more complex than John had expected, with detailed provisions about data ownership, revenue sharing, and liability protection. But the core arrangement was straightforward: SecureSpace would provide free surveillance technology in exchange for the right to monetize resident behavioral data.

As John prepared to leave, Daniel handed him a tablet loaded with demonstration software. "This will let you see how the system works in real-time once we're operational. Administrative access, full analytics dashboard, the complete community oversight package."

Walking to his car, John felt the familiar sense of having discovered something valuable that nobody else understood. His neighbors thought they were getting free security cameras. SecureSpace thought they were getting behavioral research data. But John was getting something more powerful than either: total information awareness about every resident in his community.

In the right hands, that kind of information was the ultimate tool for prediction, "guidance, and assistance."

Installation and Initial Resistance

The SecureSpace installation team arrived on a Monday morning in unmarked white vans that could have belonged to any telecommunications contractor. John had deliberately scheduled the work to begin while most residents were at their jobs, minimizing the number of questions about the extensive equipment being installed throughout the community.

The cameras were more sophisticated than the promotional materials had suggested. In addition to the obvious security monitors at entry points and common areas, the team installed dozens of smaller sensors disguised as landscaping fixtures, mailbox components, and architectural details. Each sensor was equipped with facial recognition technology, motion tracking capabilities, and directional microphones that could isolate conversations from ambient noise.

John watched the installation from his office window, using the tablet Daniel had provided to monitor the system as it came online. The interface was remarkably intuitive—a bird's-eye view of the community with color-coded indicators showing sensor coverage, behavioral tracking zones, and data collection points.

By Wednesday, the system was operational enough to begin generating basic analytics. John spent his lunch break reviewing the initial data, fascinated by the level of detail the platform could extract from seemingly routine activities.

Mrs. Chang's morning routine was mapped with military precision: garage door opened at 7:23 AM, vehicle departed at 7:26 AM, returned at 6:47 PM every weekday except Thursday, when she stopped at the grocery store and arrived home at 7:15 PM. The system had already identified her Thursday deviation as a recurring pattern and labeled it as "routine variance—non-anomalous."

Mr. Patterson's behavior was more interesting. His movement patterns showed him taking photographs of various residents' properties—not unusual for someone documenting HOA violations, but the system had flagged the activity because he'd been focusing on recently installed surveillance equipment. His behavioral profile showed elevated stress indicators and non-routine patrol patterns that the AI classified as "potentially disruptive."

Surveillance Goes Live

By Saturday morning, the SecureSpace system was generating more data than John had imagined possible. The dashboard on his tablet displayed a real-time map of the community with colored dots representing every resident's location and activity status. Green dots indicated normal behavioral patterns, yellow dots showed minor deviations from routine, and red dots flagged activities that the AI classified as anomalous or potentially problematic.

John sat on his patio with coffee and the tablet, watching his neighbors' lives unfold in digital abstraction. Mrs. Pinsky's green dot moved from her kitchen to her garden to her mailbox in patterns so predictable that the system had already learned to anticipate her movements with 94% accuracy. The Martinez family's dots clustered around their pool area—a Saturday morning routine that the AI had catalogued as "weekend leisure activity, non-anomalous."

But it was the red dots that captured John's attention. Mr. Patterson had been flagged for photographing surveillance equipment, his behavioral profile updated with notes about "anti-surveillance sentiment" and "potential community disruption risk." A teenager from the Kowalski family was showing as yellow because his sleep patterns had shifted dramatically over the past week—the AI couldn't determine if this represented normal adolescent behavior or something that required attention.

John's phone buzzed with a call from Daniel Steinberg.

"How's the beta test proceeding?" he asked.

"The data quality is incredible. I'm seeing behavioral patterns I never would have noticed without the AI analysis."

"That's exactly what we hoped. The system learns exponentially—the more data it collects, the better it becomes at predicting and flagging unusual behavior. Are you seeing any residents who might be problematic for community management?"

John looked at the red dot on his screen. "There are a few individuals showing signs of oppositional behavior. Anti-surveillance sentiment, unusual communication patterns, potential organizing activities."

"Perfect. That's exactly the kind of intelligence that helps community leaders address problems before they escalate. The Phoenix pilot identified several residents who were planning to challenge HOA policies months before they actually took action."

"What happened to those residents?"

"Various outcomes. Some were persuaded to take a more collaborative approach through targeted communication strategies.

Others found that their concerns became less relevant as the community implemented data-driven policy improvements. A few decided that the community wasn't a good fit for their lifestyle preferences."

The euphemistic language was clear enough. The surveillance system had been used to identify, pressure, and ultimately drive out residents who opposed community policies.

"The key is intervention before opposition becomes organized," Daniel continued. "Individual concerns can be addressed through personal outreach and conflict resolution. But once resistance becomes a group effort, it becomes much more difficult to manage."

John understood the implication. Bella Anderson was currently operating as an individual critic, but her "oppositional networking behavior" suggested she was trying to build broader resistance to the surveillance system. The AI was recommending intervention before her opposition could gain momentum.

"What kind of intervention strategies do you recommend?"

"That depends on the specific behavioral profile and community dynamics. Sometimes direct confrontation works—challenging the individual's concerns and motivations in public forums. Sometimes indirect pressure is more effective—using community social dynamics to isolate problematic individuals. The system can provide detailed recommendations based on psychological profiling and social network analysis."

After the call ended, John spent another hour reviewing Bella's data profile. The AI had analyzed her communication patterns, social connections, and recent behavioral changes to create a comprehensive psychological assessment. The system classified her as "high-intelligence, high-influence, moderate paranoia tendency" with recommendations for "social isolation strategy" and "credibility undermining tactics."

It was like having a military intelligence operation focused on suburban HOA politics.

John's laptop chimed with a new email from Bella: "Board Meeting Request – Emergency Review of Surveillance Contract."

226

The email included a detailed legal analysis of the SecureSpace agreement, highlighting the sections that authorized comprehensive behavioral monitoring and commercial data sharing. She'd also attached academic articles about surveillance overreach in residential communities and legal precedents for privacy violations in HOA governance.

John forwarded the email to Daniel Stein with a brief note: "Need immediate consultation on resistance management strategies."

The response came back within an hour: "Recommend implementing social pressure protocols immediately. Detailed strategy document attached."

The strategy document was fifteen pages of subtle psychological pressure techniques disguised as community management best practices. Social isolation tactics designed to undermine problematic residents' credibility and influence. Communication strategies for reframing surveillance as safety and opposition as paranoia. Even specific language for questioning critics' mental stability and community loyalty.

It was exactly the kind of sophisticated operation that Max Vecchio would have admired—and precisely the kind of power that John Masters had never imagined he could wield.

Bella's Digital Footprint

The AI had been tracking Bella for six days when it discovered her research into surveillance law and privacy rights. The system flagged her Google searches for "HOA surveillance overreach," "resident privacy rights," and "community surveillance legal challenges" as indicators of escalating opposition to community policies.

John reviewed her digital behavior profile over his Monday morning coffee, fascinated by how thoroughly the system could reconstruct someone's activities and motivations. The AI had mapped her communication network, identified key relationships that could amplify her influence, and predicted her likely next steps based on similar behavioral patterns from other surveillance deployments.

Bella had made phone calls to three attorneys who specialized in privacy law. She'd downloaded academic papers about surveillance capitalism and residential monitoring. She'd even researched case studies of communities that had successfully challenged private surveillance programs.

Most troubling, she'd scheduled lunch meetings with four other board members over the past week—meetings that the system's location tracking confirmed had actually taken place. The AI classified this as "coalition-building behavior" and recommended immediate intervention to prevent organized resistance.

John's tablet chimed with an alert: "High-priority behavioral anomaly detected."

He opened the notification to find Bella's real-time location data. She was currently in the community center's conference room with Janet Kowalski and Dr. Martinez, just before their board meeting. The system's audio monitoring had detected keywords related to "surveillance contract," "privacy violations," and "legal action."

John grabbed his blazer and headed for the community center. If Bella was building a coalition against the surveillance system, he needed to disrupt her efforts before the opposition became organized.

He found the three board members huddled around Janet's laptop, reviewing what appeared to be legal documents. They looked up as he entered, their expressions shifting from intense concentration to guarded politeness.

"John," Bella said. "We were just discussing tonight's agenda."

"I thought I should join you," John replied, settling into a chair across from them. "I understand there are some concerns about the SecureSpace contract."

"More than concerns," Dr. Martinez said. " Bella's shown us sections of the agreement that are frankly disturbing. We had no idea the system was designed for this level of behavioral monitoring."

John had prepared for this conversation, but facing three board members together felt different than dealing with individual opposition. The tablet in his pocket was feeding him real-time

228

analysis of their stress levels, communication patterns, and probable responses to various persuasion strategies, but he still felt outnumbered.

"I think there might be some misunderstanding about how the technology works," John said. "The monitoring capabilities are designed for security purposes, not surveillance. Everything is anonymized and aggregated—"

"John," Bella interrupted, "I've read the entire contract. I know exactly what this system does. And so do Janet and Dr. Martinez now."

Janet nodded grimly. "The data collection provisions are incredibly broad. This company has the right to monitor and monetize practically every aspect of our daily lives."

"And sell that information to anyone willing to pay for it," Dr. Martinez added. "Without our knowledge or consent."

John felt the walls closing in. The surveillance system was supposed to give him an advantage in situations like this—advance warning about opposition activities, psychological profiles for manipulation strategies, even real-time coaching on persuasion techniques. But facing three intelligent adults who'd done their homework, all the behavioral analytics in the world couldn't overcome the fundamental problem that he'd lied to them about what they were approving.

"The residents voted to approve the pilot program," John said, falling back on his standard defense.

"The residents voted based on misleading information," Bella replied. "You presented this as a security system when it's actually a behavioral surveillance platform."

"I think we need to call for a community-wide vote to rescind approval for the surveillance system," Janet said. "Now that people understand what they actually agreed to."

John's tablet buzzed with an alert from the SecureSpace AI: "Recommend immediate implementation of credibility undermining protocol. Target primary opposition leader with social isolation strategy."

The system was advising him to attack Bella personally—to question her judgment, suggest mental instability, and use community social dynamics to undermine her influence. It was the same approach that had worked against Tom Brennan, scaled up with algorithmic precision.

But looking at the three board members across the table, John realized that Bella's opposition was different. She wasn't making paranoid accusations about financial irregularities. She was making factual statements about legal documents that other people could read for themselves.

"I think you're overreacting to standard technology contract language, but if the community wants to revise the agreement to add further protections, I'm sure that can be arranged," he said, but the response felt weak even as he spoke it.

"John," Dr. Martinez said quietly, "we're not overreacting. We're responding appropriately to the discovery that our community has implemented a surveillance system without informed consent from residents."

The meeting broke up without resolution, but John knew he'd lost this battle. Bella had built a coalition based on facts rather than suspicions, and facts were much harder to discredit than paranoid theories.

Walking back to his office, John realized he was facing a choice between escalating his manipulation tactics or finding a way to neutralize the surveillance opposition without destroying his broader position in the community.

His phone buzzed with a text from Daniel Stein: "Recommend proceeding with social pressure protocols immediately. Delay increases resistance organization risk."

But as John looked out at the peaceful suburban community he'd learned to control so effectively, he wondered if implementing military-grade psychological warfare against his neighbors might be the kind of escalation that even Max Vecchio would have considered too dangerous.

The Community Awakens

The special board meeting was scheduled for Thursday evening, but by Tuesday afternoon, word had spread throughout Willowbrook Estates about the surveillance controversy. John's tablet showed the results in real-time: increased communication activity between residents, unusual gathering patterns around the mailbox clusters, and elevated stress indicators across multiple households.

The SecureSpace AI was generating dozens of alerts as residents began researching surveillance law, privacy rights, and HOA governance procedures. The system flagged these activities as "coordinated oppositional behavior" and recommended immediate intervention to prevent community-wide resistance from organizing.

John's phone rang constantly with calls from concerned residents who'd heard rumors about hidden cameras and data collection. Each conversation followed a similar pattern—initial confusion about what the surveillance system actually did, growing alarm as John explained the behavioral monitoring capabilities, and final anger about being misled during the original community vote.

Mrs. Maxwell called at 2 PM with questions that John couldn't answer satisfactorily. "Mr. Masters, my daughter heard that the cameras are recording our private conversations. Is that true?"

"The system doesn't record private conversations, Mrs. Maxwell. The audio monitoring is designed to detect security threats in common areas."

"But what about the microphones in the mailbox area? Jennifer says they can hear people talking when they pick up their mail."

John checked his tablet. The surveillance data showed that Jennifer Maxwell, age sixteen, had been testing the audio pickup range of various sensors throughout the community. Her behavioral profile had been updated to reflect "anti-surveillance activism" and "potential systems disruption risk."

"The audio capabilities are very limited and focused on security applications," John said, though he knew it was a lie. The directional microphones could isolate individual conversations from fifty feet away.

By Wednesday evening, the community's digital communication patterns had shifted dramatically. The AI detected encrypted messaging apps being downloaded, private social media groups being created, and research activities focused on surveillance law and privacy rights. The system classified the community's behavioral status as "pre-revolutionary" and recommended immediate implementation of "maximum pressure protocols."

John found himself in the surreal position of using military-grade behavioral analytics to monitor a suburban uprising over HOA governance policies. The technology that was supposed to give him total control was instead providing detailed documentation of his authority collapsing in real-time.

The breakthrough came when Mrs. Pinsky called with a question that changed everything: "Mr. Masters, my granddaughter is studying computer science at FAU. She looked at the cameras around my house and says they're not just security monitors. She says they're behavioral tracking devices like the ones used in China for social credit monitoring. Is that true?"

John's blood ran cold. If residents were connecting the surveillance system to international examples of authoritarian social control, the political implications would be catastrophic. The China comparison would turn a community management issue into an ideological crisis about freedom and democracy.

"Mrs. Pinsky, that's not an accurate comparison. Our system is designed for community safety, not social control."

"But they do track our behavior patterns and create profiles about how we live our daily lives?"

John realized there was no good answer to that question. "The system monitors activity in common areas for security purposes."

"So yes, they track our behavior."

"In a very limited and security-focused way."

But Mrs. Pinsky had already hung up.

That evening, Tommy, with John by his side, had hacked into a private Facebook group called "Willowbrook Privacy Concerns" that had attracted over forty members in just six hours. The discussion threads showed residents sharing research about surveillance overreach, comparing notes about suspicious equipment installations, and organizing opposition to the Thursday board meeting.

The SecureSpace AI classified the Facebook group as a "digital insurgency platform" and recommended immediate action to "disrupt communications infrastructure" and "neutralize key organizing nodes." The system was essentially advising John to engage in cyber warfare against his own community.

John's laptop chimed with a video call from Daniel Stein.

"I'm monitoring the situation in real-time," he said without preamble. "The resistance is organizing faster than our models predicted. We need to implement aggressive countermeasures immediately."

"What kind of countermeasures?"

"Social media manipulation to discredit opposition leaders. Anonymous complaints about property violations to distract troublemakers. Targeted communication campaigns to fragment the resistance coalition."

Daniel's screen showed a dashboard filled with psychological profiles and manipulation strategies. The AI had identified Bella as the primary target for "credibility destruction," Mrs. Pinsky as a "high-influence vulnerable node" for "isolation protocols," and Jennifer Maxwell as a "youth agitator" requiring "parental pressure intervention."

"This is psychological warfare," John realized.

"This is community management using data-driven insights. The alternative is losing control of the pilot program and potentially facing legal challenges that could destroy the entire business model."

John stared at the manipulation strategies displayed on his screen. The technology was offering him tools to psychologically manipulate, isolate, and discredit anyone who opposed his policies. It was power that Max Vecchio could never have imagined—and power that John Masters was sure wouldn't be effective.

"What happens if I don't implement the countermeasures?"

"The resistance organizes, the surveillance system gets terminated, and you lose control of community governance. Plus, SecureSpace faces potential legal liability for privacy violations, which means we'll need to hold someone responsible for misrepresenting the contract terms to residents."

The threat was clear. If John didn't help SecureSpace weather the surveillance controversy, the company would make him the scapegoat for the entire operation.

John closed his laptop and walked to his window. Outside, Willowbrook Estates looked exactly as it had for months—peaceful, prosperous, orderly. But his tablet showed a different reality: a community in digital revolt, organizing resistance to surveillance technology that most residents hadn't known they were agreeing to install.

For the first time since leaving Cleveland, John felt like he was losing control of his own operation. The technology that was supposed to give him unprecedented power over his community was instead documenting his authority collapsing in high-definition detail.

The Vote: Democracy vs. Data

The Thursday evening board meeting drew a crowd that exceeded even the original surveillance presentation. Every seat in the community center was filled, with dozens of residents standing along the walls and overflowing into the adjacent hallway. John arrived to find camera crews from two local news stations setting up equipment in the parking lot—someone had contacted the media about the surveillance controversy.

The surveillance system's real-time analytics showed stress levels throughout the room that were off the charts. Red dots clustered around key opposition figures, yellow indicators highlighted residents who were still undecided, and the AI's behavioral prediction algorithms suggested a 73% probability that the community vote would terminate the SecureSpace contract.

John took his position at the head of the conference table, but for the first time since becoming United's director, he felt like he was facing a hostile audience rather than supportive residents. The tablet in his portfolio was feeding him real-time coaching on crowd psychology and persuasion strategies, but the sheer number of angry residents made the situation feel unmanageable.

Bella stood up before John could call the meeting to order. "Before we begin, I want everyone to understand exactly what we're voting on tonight. This isn't about security cameras or community safety. This is about whether we're going to allow a private company to monitor and monetize every aspect of our daily lives."

She distributed printed copies of the surveillance contract sections that authorized behavioral tracking, data collection, and commercial sharing. John watched his neighbors' expressions change from confusion to alarm as they read the legal language that he'd buried in forty-seven pages of technical documentation.

"The system that was sold to us as crime prevention is actually designed for behavioral control," she continued. "It tracks when we leave our houses, maps our daily routines, analyzes our social interactions, and creates psychological profiles that can be sold to marketers, researchers, and law enforcement agencies."

Mrs. Pinsky stood up from the front row. "Mr. Masters, is this true? Are they really monitoring our daily activities like Mrs. Martinez says?"

John felt every eye in the room focused on him. The AI was feeding him response strategies designed to minimize the surveillance concerns while maintaining credibility, but every recommended talking point felt increasingly desperate.

"The system monitors activity in common areas for security purposes," John said. "The behavioral analytics are designed to identify potential security threats, not to spy on residents."

"But they do create profiles about our daily routines?" Mrs. Maxwell asked.

"The system learns normal activity patterns so it can identify anomalies that might represent security risks."

"And this company sells information about our behavior to other businesses?"

John's tablet was flashing warnings about "truth-telling protocols" and "credibility preservation strategies," but he realized that any honest answer would destroy his position entirely.

"The data sharing provisions are standard for technology contracts—"

"That's not an answer," Dr. Martinez interrupted. "Do they sell information about our behavior or not?"

The room was silent except for the clicking of news cameras and the soft hum of air conditioning. John could feel his carefully constructed authority dissolving under the weight of questions he couldn't answer honestly.

"Some anonymized data may be shared for research purposes," he said finally.

The reaction was immediate and overwhelming. Residents began talking over each other, voices rising with anger and disbelief. Someone called out, "We never agreed to be research subjects!" Another voice demanded, "How much money are they making from spying on us?"

Janet Kowalski stood up and raised her hand for attention. "I move that we immediately terminate the SecureSpace contract and remove all surveillance equipment from the community."

"Seconded!" came from multiple voices.

John realized he was watching his most ambitious operation collapse in real-time. The surveillance system that was supposed to give him unprecedented control over his community was instead providing detailed documentation of his complete loss of authority.

"All in favor of terminating the surveillance contract?"

John didn't bother counting the raised hands. The vote was overwhelmingly in favor of removing the surveillance system, with only a handful of residents abstaining and no visible opposition.

As the meeting broke up and residents filed out, discussing their anger about being deceived, John remained seated at the conference table, staring at his tablet's real-time analysis of the community's psychological state. The AI classified the evening's events as "authority collapse scenario" and recommended "immediate evacuation protocols" for community leadership.

His phone buzzed with a text from Daniel: *Unfortunate outcome. Recommend discussion about contractual obligations and liability issues.*

John had done his best to insulate Veronica from this controversy. He realized that losing the surveillance battle might be the least of his problems, and his emergency exit plan called for leaving her as the last "man" standing. If SecureSpace decided to hold him responsible for the contract termination, he could face legal and financial consequences that would threaten everything he'd built in Willowbrook Estates.

Walking to his car through the parking lot filled with news vans and angry residents, John felt like Max Vecchio again for the first time in months—not because he was successfully running a con, but because he was trying to figure out how to escape one before it destroyed him completely.

Chapter 17: The Great Expansion

Scouting New Territory

The surveillance defeat at Willowbrook Estates had taught John Masters a valuable lesson: never put all your operations in one community basket. Sitting in his car outside the Paradise Creek Country Club on a crisp February morning, he studied his target with the practiced eye of someone who'd learned to identify vulnerable systems from a distance.

Paradise Creek was everything Willowbrook Estates wasn't— old money instead of new wealth, established prestige instead of manufactured exclusivity, and most importantly, governance structures that had been allowed to atrophy through decades of complacent neglect. The community newsletter he'd picked up from their unmanned information kiosk told the story in bureaucratic detail: board meetings with quorum issues, maintenance projects delayed for months due to "procedural considerations," and resident complaints that disappeared into administrative limbo.

It was precisely the kind of institutional weakness that Max Vecchio had learned to exploit, now dressed in the legitimate business attire of John Masters' suburban expansion strategy.

His phone buzzed with a call from Marcus, his security consultant, who'd helped him survive the Cleveland revelations.

"You sure about this Paradise Creek move?" Marcus asked without preamble. "Seems like you've got enough challenges with Willowbrook for now."

"That's exactly why we're going to diversify," John replied, watching a grounds crew half-heartedly trim hedges around the country club entrance. "Willowbrook is compromised—too many people asking questions, too much scrutiny on every decision. Paradise Creek gives me a fresh start with better demographics."

"Better demographics, meaning what?"

"Older residents, established wealth, lower engagement with community governance. The kind of people who write checks and trust other people to handle the details."

John had spent three weeks researching Paradise Creek's resident profile through public records, social media analysis, and careful observation. The community skewed heavily toward retirees with substantial assets but minimal interest in hands-on community management. Perfect marks for the kind of sophisticated operation he was already running in United's lower-scale communities.

"How do you even get access to their governance system?" Marcus asked.

"Same way I got into Willowbrook and all the others— demonstrate value, build relationships, identify needs they didn't know they had. Except this time, I'm coming in as an established expert with a track record of successful community management."

John pulled up the consulting proposal he'd been refining for weeks. UCM would offer Paradise Creek a comprehensive community management assessment, identifying inefficiencies in their current systems and proposing modern solutions that would enhance both property values and resident satisfaction. The initial consultation would be free, funded by John's demonstrated commitment to suburban community excellence.

It was the same basic scheme he'd been running for years, just scaled up with better credentials and more sophisticated target selection.

"What about the Willowbrook situation?" Marcus pressed. "Another resident named Henrietta Dicarlos is asking questions about your financial management. Tom Brennan might be gone, but the surveillance controversy made a lot of residents suspicious about your other projects."

"That's why I need to close the deal here before the Willowbrook issues reach critical mass. If I can demonstrate success at Paradise Creek, it validates my expertise and gives me leverage to handle any problems back home."

John had learned this strategy from watching corporate executives manage multiple crises simultaneously. When you're facing scrutiny in one market, you expand into new markets to prove your competence and create additional revenue streams to fund damage control.

His laptop chimed with an email notification. Joyce Henderson from the PR firm had sent him a draft press release: "United Expands Community Management Services to Historic Paradise Creek Development."

The press release positioned John's expansion as a natural evolution of his successful HOA innovations, with quotes from satisfied Willowbrook residents and testimonials about improved property values and community satisfaction. It was exactly the kind of legitimacy-building content that would help him gain credibility with Paradise Creek's board of directors.

"Send me the final version," John texted back to Angela. "And start reaching out to local media about the suburban community management trend story."

Hanging up with Marcus, John drove slowly through Paradise Creek's winding streets, cataloguing opportunities and vulnerabilities with the systematic attention of someone planning a long-term operation. The tennis courts were underutilized—maybe six people playing on a Tuesday morning when the facilities could accommodate sixty. The community center looked like it hadn't been updated since the 1990s. Most telling, the HOA office appeared to be staffed by one part-time secretary working out of a cramped room behind the clubhouse pro shop.

It was an organization begging for professional management and modern systems, which John was more than happy to provide both.

The Charm Offensive

The Paradise Creek board of directors met monthly in the country club's private dining room, around a mahogany table that had hosted business discussions since the 1960s. John arrived for the March meeting fifteen minutes early, dressed in his most conservative suit and carrying a leather portfolio that projected exactly the right combination of professionalism and respect for traditional institutions.

Board president Charlotte Vandenberg was seventy-two years old and had been managing Paradise Creek's affairs for the past eight years with the kind of genteel inefficiency that comes from having more good intentions than actual expertise. She greeted John with the gracious hospitality of someone who'd been raised to treat all visitors as potential assets to the community.

"Mr. Masters, we're so pleased you could join us. I've heard wonderful things about your work at Willowbrook Estates and all your other HOA clients."

"Thank you, Mrs. Vandenberg. I'm honored to have the opportunity to learn about Paradise Creek's unique character and discuss how UCM might be able to support your community's goals."

The other board members filtered in over the next few minutes—retired executives, successful professionals, the kind of accomplished individuals who'd spent their careers managing complex organizations but had never focused those skills on homeowners' association governance. John recognized the type immediately: competent people operating outside their areas of expertise, vulnerable to anyone who could demonstrate relevant knowledge and practical solutions.

"Before we begin," Charlotte announced, "I should mention that we're facing some budgetary pressures this year. Maintenance costs are rising faster than our revenue, and we're going to need to either raise assessments or reduce services."

John smiled sympathetically. It was just the opening he'd been hoping for.

"Mrs. Vandenberg, that's precisely the kind of challenge that modern community management techniques can address. Would you mind if I shared some examples of how we've helped other communities optimize their operations?"

He opened his laptop, set up his portable project and screen, thus beginning a highly sophisticated presentation that he'd built specifically for Paradise Creek's demographic profile. Instead of the high-tech marketing materials he'd used at Willowbrook, John focused on tradition, stability, and proven results. The slides showed elegant community improvements, satisfied residents, and financial performance metrics that emphasized long-term value preservation over rapid growth.

"At Willowbrook Estates, we implemented operational efficiencies that reduced administrative costs by 30% while substantially improving service quality," John explained, clicking through before-and-after photos of community amenities. "We negotiated better vendor contracts, streamlined maintenance scheduling, and introduced revenue diversification strategies that eliminated the need for assessment increases."

Board member Robert Chiarelli leaned forward with obvious interest. "What kind of revenue diversification?"

"Corporate partnerships, facility rental programs, and strategic marketing initiatives that leverage the community's prestige to generate additional income streams. For example, we partnered with a luxury catering company to offer exclusive events for residents while generating revenue from non-resident bookings during off-peak hours."

It was a complete fabrication, but it sounded exactly like the kind of innovative solution that successful business executives would appreciate. John had learned that the best lies contained enough truth to seem plausible while promising benefits that the audience wanted to believe were possible.

"The key," John continued, "is treating community management as a business operation rather than a volunteer hobby. No disrespect to the excellent work you've been doing, but professional management techniques can unlock efficiencies that aren't visible to people who are managing communities as a side responsibility."

Charlotte nodded thoughtfully. "We've certainly struggled with the increasing complexity of HOA administration. The legal requirements alone have become overwhelming."

"That's exactly why communities like Paradise Creek will greatly benefit from professional management services. UCM handles all the regulatory compliance, vendor management, and financial administration, while the board maintains oversight and policy control. You get professional results without losing local autonomy."

John spent the next hour walking through specific examples of operational improvements, cost savings, and resident satisfaction enhancements that he claimed to have delivered at other communities. Many of the examples were fictional, but they were based on real management challenges that every HOA faced, making them sound credible to people who'd been struggling with those same issues. And no one could argue with the rapidly increasing property values achieved by John in all 52 HOAs United currently manages.

By the end of the presentation, the Paradise Creek board was sold on both the need for professional management and John's ability to provide it. Charlotte called for a motion to approve a six-month consulting contract with United, with options for expanded services based on initial results.

The vote was unanimous.

Driving home from the country club, John felt the familiar rush of a successful acquisition. Paradise Creek represented everything he'd learned about community management over his past years of experience, applied to a target that was perfectly positioned for the kind of sophisticated operation he was planning.

Unlike other communities, where he'd had to build credibility from scratch due to United's prior incompetent management style, Paradise Creek was giving him immediate access to their governance systems based on his established reputation. And unlike his previous targets, Paradise Creek had the kind of financial resources and institutional prestige that could support much larger operations.

John called Tommy Rodriguez with an update on his expansion plans.

"Sounds like you're getting greedy," Tommy said. "Running a scheme on a high-end community like Paradise could be asking for trouble. The residents there are a completely different breed than Queens Point or Millennial Village. You've got former CEO's, lawyers, accountants, and ever former members of the Council on Foreign Relations. Deep staters who wrote the book on gaslighting and control."

"It's not greed, it's risk management. If one operation gets compromised, I need alternatives. Plus, Paradise Creek has ten times the assets of our average community. The revenue potential is enormous."

"And the risk?"

"Minimal. These people want to be managed. They're paying me to take responsibility for problems they're tired of dealing with. It's the perfect setup for long-term operations."

John was already planning his next moves: assessment increases disguised as facility improvements, vendor contracts that would funnel money through his shell companies, and prestige projects that would enhance the community's reputation while generating substantial profits for UCM.

Paradise Creek wasn't just his next target—it was his graduation to the major leagues of suburban fraud. From there, he was already targeting General's Cove and Whitfield Country Estates. Hundreds of millions more in cash flow and potential profit extraction.

Modernizing Paradise

Within thirty days of signing the consulting contract, John had transformed Paradise Creek's administrative operations from genteel chaos into sleek efficiency. The part-time secretary was replaced with a full-time office manager trained in UCM's standardized procedures. The handwritten meeting minutes were digitized and automated. Most importantly, the financial reporting was centralized through UCM's accounting systems, giving John direct oversight of all community expenditures.

The changes were universally welcomed by residents who'd grown frustrated with the previous administration's slow response times and bureaucratic confusion. John's morning office hours at the country club drew steady streams of residents seeking assistance with maintenance requests, architectural approvals, and community policy questions—all of which were now handled through professional systems that consistently produced timely results.

"Mr. Masters," Charlotte Vandenberg said during their weekly check-in meeting, "I have to say, the improvement in our administrative efficiency has been remarkable. Residents are commenting on how much more responsive we've become."

"Thank you, Mrs. Vandenberg. The key is treating community management as a professional service rather than a volunteer obligation. When you apply business principles to HOA operations, the results speak for themselves."

John opened his laptop to review the month's operational metrics. Response times for resident requests had improved by 78%. Vendor payment processing had accelerated from an average of six weeks to five business days. Even the community newsletter had been upgraded from a photocopied bulletin to a professionally designed digital publication that residents looked forward to reading.

But the real transformation was happening behind the scenes, where John was systematically restructuring Paradise Creek's vendor relationships and financial procedures to create massive opportunities for revenue extraction.

"I'd like to discuss some additional operational improvements," John continued, pulling up a presentation he'd prepared for this conversation. "Specifically, I think we can optimize our facility utilization and vendor management in ways that will actually reduce costs while improving services."

The first slide showed usage statistics for Paradise Creek's tennis courts—beautifully maintained facilities that were underutilized by residents whose interest in tennis had declined as they aged. John had documented daily usage patterns that showed the courts sitting empty for 70% of daylight hours.

"Tennis participation has been declining in your demographic for years," John explained. "Meanwhile, pickleball has exploded in popularity among active adults. Converting three of our four tennis courts to dedicated pickleball facilities would dramatically increase usage while positioning Paradise Creek as a forward-thinking community."

Charlotte looked skeptical. "The tennis courts are one of our signature amenities. Many residents moved here specifically for the tennis facilities."

"I understand the concern, but the data tells a different story. Our current tennis usage averages six players per day across four courts. Pickleball courts can accommodate twelve players simultaneously in the same space, with much higher participation rates among our community."

John clicked to the next slide, showing vibrant photos of pickleball tournaments at upscale retirement communities. The imagery was carefully selected to suggest energy, social interaction, and modern amenities that enhanced property values.

"More importantly, pickleball facilities can generate significant revenue through tournament hosting, equipment sales, and corporate sponsorship opportunities. I've identified partners who would pay for naming rights and advertising placement in exchange for facility access during off-peak hours."

The financial projections were impressive—$50,000 annually in naming rights, $30,000 in tournament fees, and $20,000 in equipment and concession sales. John had created the numbers from scratch, but they were based on real market data that made them seem achievable to people who weren't familiar with recreational facility economics.

"Corporate sponsorship for our recreational facilities?" Charlotte asked.

"Tasteful, high-end partnerships that enhance rather than detract from the community's prestige. Think luxury automotive brands, premium financial services, upscale healthcare providers— companies that want to associate with Paradise Creek's demographic profile."

John showed mockups of the proposed signage and branding integration. Instead of garish commercial advertisements, the designs featured elegant plaques and discrete logos that suggested sophisticated partnerships rather than crass commercialization.

"The Bentley Pickleball Pavilion," he said, pointing to a rendering of the renovated facility. "The Raymond James Financial Fitness Center. The Mayo Clinic Wellness Courts. These partnerships position Paradise Creek as a premium community while generating revenue that reduces assessment pressures on residents."

By the end of the presentation, Charlotte was nodding enthusiastically. The combination of increased facility usage, revenue generation, and enhanced community prestige was exactly what Paradise Creek needed to address their budgetary pressures while maintaining their elite status.

"What would implementation look like?" she asked.

"I can have the court conversion completed within sixty days, with corporate partnerships finalized by the end of the quarter. The initial renovation costs would be covered by sponsor commitments, so there's no financial risk to the community."

It was another complete fabrication—John had no sponsor commitments and no realistic timeline for court conversion. But he'd learned that people would agree to almost anything if you eliminated their financial risk while promising the benefits they wanted to believe were possible.

"I move that we authorize Mr. Masters to proceed with the pickleball conversion and corporate partnership program," Charlotte announced to the board.

The motion was seconded and approved unanimously, giving John authorization to begin his most ambitious revenue extraction scheme yet.

The Rebranding Campaign

The Paradise Creek newsletter had been a four-page photocopied bulletin for as long as anyone could remember—community announcements, board meeting minutes, and the occasional recipe from residents who'd volunteered to fill space. John's first issue as editor transformed it into a hybrid digital and glossy sixteen-page magazine that looked like it belonged in an upscale hotel lobby.

"Paradise Creek Reports" featured professional photography of the community's amenities, lifestyle articles about active retirement living, and resident spotlights that made the community feel like an exclusive club rather than a housing development. Most importantly, it included advertisement pages and digital banner ads from "community partners" who were paying substantial fees for access to Paradise Creek's affluent demographic.

John sat in his temporary office at the country club, reviewing the advertising revenue from the first issue. Bentley of Fort Lauderdale to pay $5,000 monthly for a full-page spread featuring their latest luxury SUV parked in front of the country club. Raymond James Financial had purchased the back cover for $3,500 per month to promote their wealth management services. Even the local Mayo Clinic affiliate had bought a half-page ad promoting their executive health programs. And, of course, Dr. Feldman's Intracoastal Orthopedic was in on the act, paying $10,000 per month.

The total advertising revenue for the first issue was $23,500—more than Paradise Creek's entire annual newsletter budget had been under the previous administration. And John was keeping 60% of the revenue as UCM's management fee, with the remaining 40% going to offset community administrative costs. And, of course, there was a digital ad agency that jumped at the opportunity for access to Paradise Creek's average residential net worth that hovered in the mid-eight-figure range.

Charlotte Vandenberg was thrilled by the professional quality and positive resident response. "The feedback has been overwhelmingly positive," Charlotte told John during their weekly meeting. "Residents love the new format, and several people have commented on how sophisticated it makes our community appear."

"Thank you, Mrs. Vandenberg. The key is treating the newsletter as a status symbol rather than an information bulletin. When you present the community professionally, it enhances property values and attracts the kind of residents who appreciate quality."

John opened his laptop to show Charlotte the preliminary results from their digital marketing campaign. Paradise Creek now had a professional website, participation in UCM's comprehensive app, active social media presence, and online reputation management that positioned the community as a premier destination for discerning retirees.

"We're also seeing interest from real estate agents who want to feature Paradise Creek in their luxury property marketing," John continued. "I've negotiated partnerships that give us referral fees while enhancing the community's market profile."

The referral fee arrangement was another revenue stream that John had created by positioning himself as Paradise Creek's exclusive marketing representative. Real estate agents paid UCM a portion of their commission in the community, supposedly to fund marketing and promotional activities that benefited all residents.

In reality, most of the referral fees went directly into John's shell company accounts, with just enough money actually spent on marketing to maintain the appearance of legitimate business activity.

"What about the pickleball courts?" Charlotte asked. "How is the conversion progressing?"

John clicked to a presentation slide showing architectural renderings of the renovated facility. The designs were impressive— modern courts with professional-grade surfaces, elegant pavilion structures, and discrete sponsor branding that enhanced rather than detracted from the aesthetic appeal.

"Construction begins next month, with completion scheduled for early summer. I've finalized partnerships with three major sponsors who are covering the full renovation cost in exchange for naming rights and promotional opportunities."

The sponsor partnerships were fictional, but John had learned to present future commitments as established facts when dealing with clients who trusted his expertise. By the time the construction timeline arrived, he'd either find real sponsors or finance the project through other revenue streams he was developing.

"The Lexus Pickleball Pavilion sounds very prestigious," Charlotte said.

"Exactly. We're positioning Paradise Creek as the premier active retirement community in South Florida. The corporate partnerships enhance that brand while generating revenue that keeps assessments stable."

John's phone buzzed with a text from Daniel Stein at SecureSpace Technologies: *Heard about your Paradise Creek expansion. Interested in discussing surveillance opportunities for established communities.*

John deleted the message immediately. The surveillance debacle at Willowbrook had taught him to avoid high-profile surveillance tech projects that could generate resident opposition. The United App still served its purpose well. Paradise Creek's operation was focusing on financial extraction through legitimate-seeming business partnerships rather than invasive monitoring systems. Even after United's "cut," Paradise was still benefiting. While its prior security system had been adequate, Marcus's upgrades made sure that potential intruders knew they weren't welcome and would be dealt with harshly. In addition, they had found that the few crimes that did occur were mostly the result of landscapers, rideshare drivers, delivery, and service personnel. Marcus had a few intense conversations with these outsiders and soon, Paradise's crime problem all but disappeared.

"I'd like to discuss expanding our corporate partnership program," John said, pulling up another presentation. "I've identified opportunities in luxury automotive, premium healthcare, financial services, and lifestyle brands that could generate significant additional revenue."

The slides showed potential partnerships with BMW, Mercedes-Benz, Audi, and Tesla for automotive marketing campaigns targeted at Paradise Creek residents. Healthcare partnerships with Mayo Clinic, Cleveland Clinic, and Johns Hopkins for executive wellness programs. Financial services relationships with Morgan Stanley, J.P. Morgan Chase—Private Banking, and Goldman Sachs for wealth management seminars.

"Each partnership would generate between $25,000 and $50,000 annually," John explained, "while providing residents with exclusive access to premium services and products."

Charlotte was taking notes enthusiastically. "This could completely transform our budget situation. Instead of raising assessments, we'd be generating revenue." And property values would continue to escalate.

"That's exactly the goal. Professional community management should pay for itself through operational efficiencies and revenue enhancement."

By the end of the meeting, John had authorization to pursue corporate partnerships worth more than $200,000 in annual revenue, some of which would reduce residents' financial burden, while creating major profit extraction opportunities for United.

Walking to his car through Paradise Creek's meticulously maintained grounds, John felt like he'd finally achieved the kind of sophisticated operation that Max Vecchio had always dreamed of running. While the less affluent HOA extraction schemes were still United's highly profitable bread and butter, he and Veronica were now in the big leagues. They were now operating with clients who paid them substantial fees to solve problems they didn't have the expertise to handle themselves.

It was the perfect criminal enterprise—apparently legal, economically and socially beneficial, and enormously profitable for someone who understood how to structure contracts in his favor.

Revenue Streams and Shell Games

John had transformed Paradise Creek into a corporate partnership showcase that generated more revenue than most small and medium-sized businesses. The pickleball courts were under construction with funding from "sponsors" who existed only in John's carefully crafted financial documents. The monthly print and web-based newsletter was selling advertising space faster than he could create content. And the real estate referral program was producing steady income from agents who appreciated access to Paradise Creek's affluent client base.

John sat in his expanded office space—he'd convinced Charlotte to let him convert an unused storage room into a proper UCM administrative center—reviewing the monthly financial reports that showed just how profitable community management could be when structured properly.

The corporate partnership revenue was flowing through a network of shell companies that made the Willowbrook bake and fleece sales operation look like amateur hour. Heritage Marketing Solutions collected advertising fees from the newsletter sponsors. Community Relations Inc. managed the real estate referral program. Prestige Facility Management handled the pickleball court naming rights and corporate event coordination.

Each shell company took its percentage of the revenue before passing the remainder to Paradise Creek's accounts, creating multiple opportunities for profit extraction while maintaining the appearance of legitimate business operations. The Paradise Creek board saw monthly reports showing substantial revenue from corporate partnerships, reduced operating expenses, and improved community security and amenities—what they'd been promised when they hired UCM's services.

John's laptop chimed with a video call from Tommy Rodriguez.

"How's the expansion going?" Tommy asked.

"Better than I projected. Paradise Creek is generating about $40,000 a month in extractable revenue, compared to maybe $10,000 from Willowbrook at its peak."

"Jesus. What's the difference?"

"Demographics and scale. Paradise Creek residents have serious money, and they're used to paying for premium services. Plus, the community has prestige value that I can monetize through corporate partnerships."

John shared his screen to show Tommy the revenue dashboard he'd created to track his various operations. The numbers were impressive—$180,000 in gross revenue from Paradise Creek operations over the past four months, with approximately 70% flowing through to John and Veronica's shell companies after legitimate expenses and management fees.

"That's a hell of a lot of money to be skimming from one community," Tommy said. "You sure this is sustainable?"

"It's not skimming, it's management consulting. Every dollar I'm taking comes from revenue streams that didn't exist before I got involved. The residents are getting enhanced safety, services, and amenities, the community is generating positive cash flow, and we're getting paid for creating value."

It was true, technically. They had created legitimate revenue through corporate partnerships, advertising sales, and marketing programs that benefited Paradise Creek residents. The fact that they were extracting most of the profits through shell companies was simply efficient business organization.

"What about oversight? Who's reviewing your financial arrangements?"

"Charlotte Vandenberg reviews monthly reports that show revenue, expenses, and net community benefit. She's thrilled with the results because assessments are stable, amenities are improving, and residents are happy."

John clicked through the financial reports he provided to the Paradise Creek board. The documents were professionally formatted, clearly presented, and completely accurate—they just didn't include detailed breakdowns of his management fee structures or shell company arrangements.

"The beauty of this operation is that everyone wins," John continued. "Residents get better services, stable costs, and rapidly increasing property values. Corporate sponsors get access to an affluent demographic. And we get paid for creating value that didn't exist before."

"And if someone starts asking detailed questions about UCM fee arrangements?"

"Then I provide detailed explanations of standard consulting practices in community management. Everything I'm doing is legal and documented. The contracts are clear about management fees and revenue sharing."

John had learned from the Tom Brennan situation to ensure that all his financial arrangements were technically legitimate, even if they weren't entirely transparent. The shell company structures were complex enough to discourage casual scrutiny, but straightforward enough to withstand professional accounting review if necessary.

His phone buzzed with a call from Joyce at the PR firm.

"John, I have some interesting news. *Southern Living* wants to do a feature story on Paradise Creek as an example of innovative community management. They're calling it 'The Future of Retirement Living' and they want to interview you about your corporate partnership model."

John felt his stomach tighten. Media attention had caused nothing but problems at Willowbrook, and national magazine coverage would bring the kind of scrutiny that could threaten his entire operation.

"I appreciate the interest, but I prefer to keep the focus on the community rather than the management company."

"Are you kidding? This is *Southern Living*. It's the perfect platform to establish you as a thought leader in community management innovation."

"Let me think about it and get back to you."

After hanging up, John realized they were facing the same dilemma that had plagued their Willowbrook operations: success brought attention, and attention brought scrutiny. The more effective their operations became, the more likely they were to attract investigation from people who might recognize what he was actually doing.

But Paradise Creek represented a level of financial opportunity that was too significant to abandon because of media concerns. If he and Veronica could maintain their corporate partnership revenue streams for another year, they'd have a path to expand operations in the numerous other wealthy communities throughout South Florida.

John opened his secure browser and began researching *Southern Living's* editorial process, circulation demographics, and typical story development timeline. If he was going to accept national media coverage, he needed to understand what kind of exposure he was risking and how to manage the narrative to his advantage.

The Corporate Sponsors

The Lexus Pickleball Pavilion was everything John had promised it would be—elegant, modern, and busy with residents who'd discovered that pickleball was more engaging than tennis for their age demographic. The ribbon-cutting ceremony in June drew over a hundred residents, local dignitaries, and representatives from the corporate sponsors who'd made the facility possible.

John and Veronica stood at the podium beside Charlotte Vandenberg, wearing their most confident smiles as he addressed the crowd gathered around the newly renovated courts. Behind him, discrete plaques and signage identified the corporate partners who'd "invested in Paradise Creek's commitment to active, healthy retirement living."

"Today represents more than just new recreational facilities," John announced. "It represents a new model for community development that benefits residents, corporate partners, and the broader South Florida region."

The crowd applauded appreciatively. The pickleball courts were genuinely impressive—professional-grade surfaces, elegant pavilion structures, and amenities that rivaled private athletic clubs. Most residents had no idea that the "corporate sponsors" funding the project were actually shell companies that John had created to justify the construction expenses.

Lexus of Fort Lauderdale had indeed contributed $25,000 toward the project—a legitimate corporate partnership that John had negotiated by promising them the right to place new vehicles around the community and to allow purchase directly through United's app. But the additional $75,000 in construction costs had been funded through John's network of shell companies, using revenue extracted from the community's other corporate partnership programs.

"Paradise Creek has become a model for innovative public-private partnerships," Charlotte said, taking the microphone. "Veronica and John have shown us how communities can enhance amenities while reducing costs through strategic corporate relationships."

The local media coverage was extensive and positive—exactly the kind of legitimacy-building publicity that would help them expand operations to other wealthy communities. The newspaper photos showed happy residents enjoying state-of-the-art facilities, satisfied corporate sponsors promoting their community involvement, and professional management that delivered results.

But John's attention was focused on the man standing at the back of the crowd, taking notes and occasionally photographing the corporate signage. He'd noticed the observer during setup but hadn't been able to identify him—middle-aged, professionally dressed, the kind of careful attention to detail that suggested either journalism or law enforcement.

After the ceremony, John approached the man directly.

"I don't think we've met," John said, extending his hand. "John Masters, United Community."

"David Mand," the man replied, accepting the handshake. "I'm a reporter with the *South Florida Business Journal*. I'm working on a story about innovative community management practices."

John felt his blood pressure spike, but he maintained his professional composure. "That's wonderful. Paradise Creek has been a great example of what's possible when you apply modern business principles to HOA administration."

"I'd love to schedule an interview with you about your corporate partnership model. It seems like you've created some unique revenue arrangements that other communities might want to emulate."

"I'd be happy to discuss our approach. Why don't you contact my office to schedule something next week?"

John handed the reporter his business card while mentally calculating how much investigation he could withstand before his shell company arrangements became problematic. The corporate partnerships were legitimate, but the financial structures he'd used to extract profits were complex enough to raise questions from someone who understood business reporting.

His phone buzzed with a text from Marcus: *Saw the news coverage. You're getting a lot of attention for someone who's supposed to be keeping a low profile.*

John typed back: *Calculated risk. Credibility building for expansion opportunities.*

But walking back to his car after the ceremony, John wondered if he was making the same mistake that had nearly threatened his Willowbrook operations. Success bred attention, attention bred scrutiny, and scrutiny was the enemy of anyone running sophisticated fraud operations from behind the curtain of witness protection.

Back in his office, his laptop chimed with an email from the *Southern Living* editor: *John – After seeing the Paradise Creek coverage, we're even more interested in the community management feature story. Can we schedule the interview for next month?*

John shared the email with Veronica while discreetly rubbing the small of her back. National magazine coverage would establish them as legitimate experts in luxury community management innovation, opening doors to consulting opportunities throughout the Southeast. But it would also expand his public profile, which could be dangerous if anyone from his Cleveland past was paying attention to rising suburban business success stories.

He was standing at the crossroads between Max Vecchio's paranoid caution and John Masters' ambitious expansion plans. And for the first time in years, he wasn't sure which identity was making better decisions.

Empire Building

By September, their operation had expanded beyond Paradise Creek to include consulting contracts for numerous luxury HOAs in South Florida. The corporate partnership model had proven so successful that he had a queue of HOA boards waiting to hire UCM to replicate the revenue generation strategies they'd pioneered together.

John sat in United's Boca Raton office—reviewing financial reports that showed just how profitable suburban community management could be when scaled properly.

Coral Bay Estates had implemented a corporate partnership program that was generating $300,000 annually in advertising revenue. Sunrise Hills had converted its underutilized clubhouse into a premium event venue that was booked solid with corporate functions. Even smaller communities like Bayshore Gardens were finding that targeted marketing partnerships could offset traditional assessment increases while improving amenities.

Hundreds of thousands in additional revenue were flowing through UCM's various shell operations. John and Veronica's shells were extracting as much as 60% for management fees, consulting services, and administrative overhead. It was more money than Max Vecchio had ever dreamed of stealing without the inherent risks of mob life. They were generated through technically legitimate operations that were socially and economically beneficial to the communities they managed.

"This is getting big enough to attract serious attention," Tommy warned during their monthly security check-in. "You're running what amounts to a regional business empire built on financial alchemy."

"It's not magic, it's innovation," John replied. "I'm creating value for communities, enhancing security, providing services they require, and getting paid for expertise that produces measurable results."

But even John had to admit that the scale of their operations was becoming challenging to manage discreetly. UCM now employed over 250 people, maintained management control of fifty-five communities, and consulting arrangements with several dozen more, as well as indirect control over numerous others. It generated so much revenue that its sophisticated accounting and laundering systems were reaching their capacity, and it was getting more difficult to avoid attracting legal attention. He hoped that Earl Morrison was enjoying his enforced retirement in his island estate in Belize. At times like these, he gave serious thought to joining him there. And then he would remember the hot, wet mess that United had been when he and Veronica deposed Earl, and the thoughts would go away.

His phone rang with a call from Charlotte Vandenberg.

"John, I have some concerning news. A reporter from the *Miami Herald* called, asking questions about our corporate partnership arrangements. Specifically, he wanted information about the management fees and revenue sharing with UCM."

John's stomach dropped. Media scrutiny of his financial arrangements was exactly what he'd been trying to avoid by maintaining low-profile operations.

"What kind of questions?"

"He was asking whether residents are aware of how much revenue you're realizing from the corporate partnerships, and whether the board has oversight of your fee arrangements. I told him that all our financial arrangements are properly documented and approved, but he seemed to think there might be transparency issues."

"Did he mention what prompted his investigation?"

"He said someone had contacted the newspaper with concerns about HOA management companies that use corporate partnerships to generate excessive profits at residents' expense."

John realized that his expansion success had finally attracted the kind of investigative attention that could threaten his entire operation. Someone—possibly Tom Brennan, possibly Eunice Garland, possibly a disgruntled resident from one of his other communities— had tipped off reporters about his financial arrangements.

"Charlotte, I think the best approach is complete transparency. I'll prepare detailed financial reports showing exactly how our partnership revenue is structured and how it benefits the community. When people see the actual numbers, they'll understand that everyone wins from these arrangements."

"I hope you're right. But I have to say, some board members are asking whether we should review our consulting contract to ensure we're getting appropriate value for our management fees."

After hanging up, John realized he was facing the inevitable consequence of successful operations: scrutiny from people who understood business well enough to recognize when profit extraction was disproportionate to value creation.

He could handle individual critics like Tom Brennan through intimidation and manipulation. However, a media investigation backed by financial expertise would require a different approach— either complete transparency about his arrangements or a strategic retreat from operations that couldn't withstand scrutiny.

John opened his laptop and began drafting a comprehensive financial disclosure document that would explain his management fee structures, shell company arrangements, and profit distribution methods. If he was going to face an investigation, he needed documentation that demonstrated everything he was doing was legal, ethical, and beneficial to the communities he served.

But as he worked through the numbers, John realized that complete transparency would reveal just how much money he was extracting from community operations—amounts that would shock residents and board members who thought they were paying for basic management services.

For the first time since arriving in Florida, John wondered if his suburban empire had grown too large to manage, and whether Max Vecchio's instinct for simpler, smaller-scale operations might have been smarter than John Masters' ambition for regional dominance.

His phone buzzed with a text from an unknown number: *Impressive business model. We should discuss expansion opportunities. —V*

V for Victorio. The Cleveland enforcer who'd been tracking his operations was now taking an interest in his legitimate business success.

John deleted the message and stared out his office window at the Boca Raton skyline. He'd built an empire by transforming suburban, corrupt, declining HOAs into showcase communities, yielding massive profits for himself and Veronica. But empires attracted attention from enemies who could destroy everything he'd worked to create.

The question was whether John Masters was smart enough to manage the threats that Max Vecchio's success had generated.

Chapter 18: The Final Move

The Empire Falls

Max Vecchio—John Masters to those who thought they knew him—had built an empire out of rotting concrete and HOA consulting contracts. Fifty-seven homeowners' associations stretched across South Florida like a suburban kingdom, each one generating huge amounts of assessments, wellness operations, pickleball profits, and capital funds that flowed through his carefully constructed network of shell companies and vendor "relationships."

From his balcony at Queens Point, he could see the crown jewel of his operation glistening like a five-star resort in the morning sun. What had once been a tired retirement community with cracked tennis courts and faded amenities was now a showcase of modern middle-class luxury that drew admiring coverage from lifestyle magazines and real estate publications. The transformation was magnificent—and entirely paid for by residents who had no idea how much of their money was disappearing into Max's pockets.

Repair contracts that went to companies he secretly owned. Property flips that generated massive profits through insider knowledge of development plans. The pickleball expansion schemes that had spread across three counties and eventually the state, each one more profitable than the last. Especially monthly community pickleball events that led to burgeoning medical and wellness revenue splits, which had been systematically skimmed for profit.

It was glorious. But the more he built, the taller the mountain of enemies became beneath him.

The FBI had been circling for months, led by Agent Dale Harrison's white-collar crime unit. It had finally connected the dots between all the different communities and one sophisticated criminal mastermind. Federal investigators now understood that John Masters (f/k/a Max Vecchio) wasn't just another corrupt HOA manager—he was running the largest suburban HOA fraud operation in American history.

The mob had been slower to catch on, long assuming Max Vecchio was dead or buried deep in witness protection after his Cleveland disappearance over a decade ago. Besides, they had massive legal problems, and they were trying to stay out of jail or to get out of jail. But his controlled public profile was now out of control, and the Cleveland enforcers were making inquiries about the HOA kingpin down in Palm Beach County who bore a suspicious resemblance to their old financial fixer/manager. Vinny Torrisi had been asking uncomfortable questions from inside his prison cell, and uncomfortable questions from Cleveland enforcers usually preceded untimely deaths. Finally, convinced that John Masters was in fact Max Vecchio, they put out a $250,000 contract on him—for termination with extreme prejudice.

Even the residents—those formerly docile retirees who had once thanked him for replacing moldy pool chairs and organizing community events—had started asking questions about why their fees had doubled while their contractors all drove Bentleys. Tom Brennan's financial concerns had spread to other communities.

They all wanted the truth, and they wanted blood, his blood.

The Supreme Court Intervention

Inside the US Supreme Court's main courtroom, a clerk's voice echoed through chambers that had seen decades of constitutional drama: "Conviction overturned."

The Supreme Court reversed Vincent "Vinny" Torrisi's RICO verdict and life sentence; the old Cleveland boss whose prosecution had been built on testimony by Max Vecchio and numerous witnesses, hit the judicial lottery. The Court noted gross due process violations, tainted testimony, and prosecutorial misconduct had undermined the entire case that federal investigators had spent years constructing.

Everything Max had helped orchestrate during his cooperation with federal authorities was now in legal jeopardy. The extensive mob financial records he'd provided, the testimony about money laundering operations. The insider knowledge of organized crime activities that had seemed so valuable when Agent Garcia was negotiating his cooperation agreement was all now in jeopardy.

He was the linchpin, the star witness, the trusted turncoat whose credibility could make or break a dozen reconstituted federal prosecutions. Without his testimony, cases worth hundreds of millions of dollars in criminal forfeiture would collapse. High-ranking mobsters who'd been awaiting appellate court decisions while in federal custody would walk free. Operations that had taken thousands of man-hours to execute would be lost forever.

The clerk's announcement triggered a cascade of phone calls from the Supreme Court to the Justice Department to the FBI field offices that were coordinating Max's upcoming arrest. Federal prosecutors who had been planning to charge him with RICO, fraud, and money laundering suddenly realized they now needed him alive and more cooperative than ever. They justified their decision to let him skate on the HOA fraud network because, regardless of what he had stolen, he had drastically improved the lives of thousands of South Florida residents. They may not have approved of his methods, but they couldn't deny his results. Finally, the AG's office called the FBI and the US Attorney for Florida's Southern District. The orders were given: pick him up immediately, put him in a safe place, and keep him there until he was needed.

John Masters' "Death"

Deputy Clint Moore, the grizzled DOJ handler who'd babysat Max since the beginning, got the call just after dinner. Surveillance had picked up chatter. The hit was real. Imminent. They had hours, not days. They had to act now.

At 10:30 PM, they rolled up on John's Queens Point residence in a black Suburban and two nondescript sedans. No sirens. No lights. Just quiet men with serious faces and weapons drawn. He was awake—he'd felt it coming, like a drop in barometric pressure before a storm. He was packed and Max Senior was on his leash, sensing something was about to happen.

"WE have to go now," Clint said, tossing him a burner phone. "Get in. You've got just minutes to die."

Two blocks away, John's Tesla was remotely driven along the infamous Brightline tracks, with a body in the driver's seat that resembled John/Max enough to pass for him after the fire did its work. At 11:43 PM, it drove through the flashing gates and directly into the path of the oncoming high-speed Miami-bound Brightline train, where it was promptly obliterated, like so many vehicles before it. Between the highly explosive lithium-ion batteries and the three full propane tanks in the trunk, the Tesla became a massive fireball that rattled windows as far away as Delray Beach. The remains were unrecognizable. Freshly minted dental records and a wallet with the forged, burned ID of John Masters completed the illusion and established that Masters had ceased living.

Upon learning of Master's death, Veronica Santiago said, shaking her head, "I always told John that damn Tesla autopilot was going to get him killed. He'd just wave me off and say, 'Driving myself is inefficient. My time has better uses, like optimizing profits.'"

But James Lawless was just getting started.

By sunrise, he was halfway across the country, riding shotgun in a federal Gulfstream GS 650 with Clint sitting silently beside him. The files had been scrubbed. The DMV, passport office, credit bureaus—every trace of his old life deleted or reissued under a new name.

They dropped him in Nevada three days later. Diamond Point Falls. It was a forgotten, crumbling retirement community with cracked sidewalks, overgrown hedges looking more like a scene from the zombie apocalypse, complete with retired bikers and burned-out meth cookers. And just like that, the rebirth began.

Diamond Point Falls

The Nevada sun beat down on Diamond Point Falls with the kind of merciless intensity that made everything look bleached and desperate.

The Hawthorne Army Depot, located in Hawthorne, Nevada, whose claim to fame was that it was the largest ammo dump in the world. Rumor had it that Diamond Point Falls was built on reclaimed depot land and that it was sitting on large amounts of unexploded ordnance. The community was so depressing it made Queens Point's original condition look like the Four Seasons—disintegrating roads almost beyond repair, rusting tennis court fences that were more hole than wire, golf carts sitting on cinder blocks like automotive graveyards.

Here, dreams weren't deferred—they were dead and tax-defaulted. Residents lived on fixed incomes that barely covered basic expenses, let alone the kind of amenities that other retirement communities took for granted. The HOA office operated out of a converted garage. Board meetings were held in someone's living room because the community center had been condemned for structural problems.

It was the kind of place where a man could completely disappear, assuming he could stand the isolation and institutional neglect.

A new resident had just arrived, moving into the corner villa that had been empty for eight months, because nobody wanted to pay the back assessments that came with the property. James Lawless, they called him—a quiet, bearded gentleman who claimed to be a retired commercial real estate developer from the Midwest. Said he was here for the peace and quiet. Said he just wanted to keep to himself.

The management board welcomed him enthusiastically, especially after he paid cash for the villa and offered to help with some of the community's more pressing maintenance issues. Having someone with construction experience was exactly what Diamond Point Falls needed, even if he seemed a little too knowledgeable about HOA financial management for a retiree who claimed to want simplicity.

But Clint Moore wasn't fooled.

The deputy from the US Marshall's Special Witness Re-Relocation Unit had been personally managing Max's case again since the Supreme Court reversal that had again transformed him from federal target to protected witness. He'd overseen the identity creation, the financial arrangements, and the careful selection of

Diamond Point Falls as a location remote enough and depressing enough to discourage the kind of ambition that had gotten Max in trouble before.

Clint paid James Lawless a visit two days after his arrival, standing in the middle of the bleak living room that came with furniture that looked like it had been salvaged from indigent estate sales and low-end garage clearances.

"Keep it clean, Max," he said, dispensing with the false identity now that they were alone. "Keep it boring. One more slip, and there won't be anyone left to swoop in and save your ass. You're important, but you're not Sammy 'the Bull' Gravano."

The warning was delivered with the tired authority of someone who'd relocated dozens of witnesses over the years and understood exactly how quickly boredom could lead to the kind of risk-taking that got John Masters "killed."

"The Cleveland prosecutions you aided are moving towards retrials based on your expected cooperation and testimony," Clint continued. "You're valuable enough to protect, but not valuable enough to protect indefinitely."

Max nodded politely, hands behind his back, projecting the kind of humble gratitude that federal handlers expected from witnesses who understood how precarious their situations really were.

But he was smiling.

The Envelope

After Clint left, Lawless sat down with a lukewarm coffee and turned on the television to catch up on the outside world he'd been separated from during his federal debriefing, constant verbal abuse, warnings to keep his nose clean, and identity reconstruction. *Fox News* was running a special report on pickleball's meteoric rise across American retirement communities, complete with statistics about court construction and equipment sales that had grown by 300% over the past few years.

Max nodded and started thinking about pickleball's many potential revenue streams. Even in witness protection, his mind immediately jumped to the opportunities that most people couldn't see in what appeared to be a simple, if misguided, fitness and recreational trend.

Just as he was beginning to relax into the kind of mindless television consumption that was supposed to characterize his new quiet life, an envelope slid under his front door. Max Senior growled and jumped towards the door. Max held Rose's rosary beads in his hand as he reached for the envelope.

No return address. No postal markings. Just plain white paper that someone had hand-delivered while he was still distracted by federal agents and news programming.

Lawless opened it with the caution of someone who'd learned that unexpected communications usually brought unwelcome complications.

Inside was a single sheet of paper with a brief printed message:

The Diamond Point Falls Board has approved your proposal for expanded pickleball courts. Final vote: 4-3. Some yelling and minor property damage occurred. Construction to begin immediately.

James grinned.

He hadn't submitted any proposal for pickleball courts. He'd been in Diamond Point Falls for less than a week and had spent most of that time meeting with his federal handlers, unpacking his minimal belongings, and getting settled in.

But someone had been paying attention to his background, understood his expertise, and recognized an opportunity when they saw one. They had done their research and decided that James Lawless' supposed commercial real estate experience might be exactly what their struggling community needed.

They never learn.

The Message

Max picked up one of his burner phones and typed a message to the one person who would appreciate the irony of his situation. Veronica Santiago had avoided all charges and came out smelling like a rose, just as she and John had planned. She retained control of UCM and had hired a special consultant by the name of James Lawless. His purpose, she explained to UCM's board, was to help fill John's vacancy and assist with planning and strategy. Additionally, he was part of a new generation that helped coach HOA boards and executives. She knew his advice would prove invaluable, which is why he was being paid $50,000 per month. His future value would be well in excess of that lofty number.

Guess what just got approved at my new place? Some things never change. – J

The response came back within minutes: *Please tell me you're not serious. You literally just got there. – V*

They approached me. I think it's destiny. – J

It's stupidity. Clint will kill you if you start another operation. – V

Not an operation. Community service. These people need help. – J

You need help. Professional psychological help. – V

He laughed and set down the phone. Veronica's concern was touching, but she didn't understand that witness protection was just another kind of prison unless you found ways to make it interesting. Diamond Point Falls might be depressed and depressing, and volatile in a way that even he never imagined, but it was also full of untapped potential for someone who understood community development and revenue optimization.

He walked to his window and looked out at the community that would be his home for the foreseeable future. Crumbling pavement that could be repaired through special assessments. Empty lots that could be redeveloped through strategic partnerships. Residents who were probably so desperate for improved amenities that they'd approve almost any reasonable proposal.

He thought of Rose for the first time in a long time. It was time to build again.

After all, the federal government needed him alive and cooperative for ongoing prosecutions and the inevitable appeals that could take years to complete. The Cleveland crime family was too busy dealing with a fresh round of superseding indictments and even more asset seizures to worry about revenge against a witness who was apparently dead again. And Diamond Point Falls was so far off the radar that nobody would think to look for sophisticated criminal operations in a nearly defunct Nevada retirement community, where the most significant controversy was usually about pool maintenance schedules or the lack thereof.

James/Max opened his laptop and began researching pickleball court construction costs, local municipal permitting requirements, and potential corporate sponsors who might be interested in marketing opportunities in underserved retirement communities.

James Lawless was about to show the world what Diamond Point Falls could become with the right kind of professional management.

And Max Vecchio was again about to prove that witness protection was just another system that could be optimized for profit.

END OF BOOK ONE

Appendix

5 Insider Techniques for Realtors:

How to Keep Dysfunctional HOA & Condo Boards from Killing Your Deal

Get the HOA Docs Early—and Read the Red Flags

Most real estate deals hit turbulence when surprises emerge late in the process. One of the most overlooked yet crucial steps is obtaining the HOA documents upfront. These documents are more than just fine print—they are the DNA of the community. Reserves that are underfunded mean looming special assessments. Pending lawsuits suggest conflict, uncertainty, and possible financial liabilities. Restrictive rules, such as bans on pets over a certain size or arbitrary leasing restrictions, can derail a deal if a buyer learns about them late. By proactively obtaining and reviewing these documents, you can anticipate and neutralize objections before they become deal-breakers. Share a quick summary with your buyer that translates the key risks into everyday language. This single step shows your professionalism and can turn you into the trusted guide.

Make Friends with the Gatekeeper

Every HOA has a gatekeeper—the person who, intentionally or not, controls access to information. This might be the board president, the management company, or even the community's secretary. Establishing rapport with this person is essential. A simple courtesy call, respectful tone, and prompt follow-ups can pay dividends. If they see you as cooperative, they're more likely to respond quickly, provide complete documents, or give your buyer the benefit of the doubt. On the other hand, a combative relationship can lead to "lost paperwork," unexplained delays, or the rigid enforcement of discretionary rules. Approach these relationships strategically: a little kindness can shorten timelines and keep your deal intact.

Translate HOA-Speak for Your Buyer

HOA documents are notorious for vague, open-ended language. Words like "subject to review" or "community standards" may sound harmless, but to buyers, they can create fear of arbitrary enforcement. Your role is to decode this jargon into clear, practical meaning. For example, explain that "subject to review" might mean the board has final approval on exterior paint colors, not that they can ban the buyer's furniture. When buyers feel they understand the rules, they're less likely to panic. This builds trust and confidence, ensuring they remain committed to the deal rather than backing out over uncertainty.

Watch the Transfer & Application Fees

One of the fastest ways to kill a deal at the finish line is an unexpected financial surprise. HOAs often impose transfer fees, move-in fees, or so-called "capital contributions" that buyers don't learn about until closing. These can range from a few hundred dollars to several thousand. A buyer who's already stretched to afford the property may balk at the last minute. Protect yourself by identifying these fees early, presenting them clearly to your buyer, and building them into the financial conversation. Transparency turns a potential landmine into a manageable detail, and it demonstrates your thoroughness as a realtor.

Have the "Nightmare Story" Ready—Then the Solution

HOA nightmares are legendary, and buyers often expect them. Instead of avoiding the subject, embrace it. Share a real-world "nightmare story" that illustrates the pitfalls of a dysfunctional board—such as a board that tried to enforce arbitrary fines, delayed approvals for months, or mishandled reserves. But here's the key: always pair the story with how you resolved the problem. This shows resilience and competence. Buyers will think: "If my agent could handle that, they can handle anything." By controlling the narrative, you not only manage expectations but also highlight your value as the professional who can navigate even the messiest HOA drama.

Final Thoughts

HOA and condo boards don't have to be deal-killers. With the right preparation, communication, and perspective, you can turn these potential obstacles into opportunities to prove your value as a realtor. The techniques in this guide are designed to give you an edge: anticipate problems before they occur, reassure your buyers, and position yourself as the calm professional who gets deals across the finish line. Mastering these approaches won't just save individual transactions—it will build your reputation, win referrals, and strengthen your business over time.

www.ingramcontent.com/pod-product-compliance
Lightning Source LLC
Chambersburg PA
CBHW071501110726
47908CB00003B/683